THE THEORY
OF CROWS

THE
THEORY
OF
CROWS

A NOVEL

DAVID A. ROBERTSON

HARPER **PERENNIAL**

Published by Harper Perennial, an imprint of HarperCollins Publishers Ltd

First edition

HarperCollins books may be purchased for educational, business
or sales promotional use through our Special Markets Department.

HarperCollins Publishers Ltd
Bay Adelaide Centre, East Tower
22 Adelaide Street West, 41st Floor
Toronto, Ontario, Canada
M5H 4E3

www.harpercollins.ca

Library and Archives Canada Cataloguing in Publication

Title: The theory of crows : a novel / David A. Robertson.
Names: Robertson, David, 1977- author.
Identifiers: Canadiana (print) 20220257426 | Canadiana (ebook) 20220257450
ISBN 9781443465168 (softcover) | ISBN 9781443465175 (ebook)
Classification: LCC PS8585.O32115 T54 2022 | DDC C813/.6—dc23

Printed and bound in the United States of America
LSC/H 10 9 8 7 6 5 4 3 2 1

For Emily

And now it frightens me, the dreams that I possess
To think I was acting like a believer
When I was just angry and depressed
—Sufjan Stevens, "The Ascension"

PART
ONE

I was eight when my grandmother died. She'd gone to residential school when she was five, until she was about as old as you are now. If you think about the worst things kids went through in those schools, then you can imagine what happened to my grandmother. She went through hell, came out the other side, but the flames never really went out. Survivors talk about their experiences now, and I think it helps them, but nobody was listening back then, and so there was nobody to talk to. My grandmother died from a lung issue. I'm not sure what kind, just that eventually she couldn't breathe anymore. Maybe keeping in all that truth took the breath from her body. Sucked it clean out.

Or maybe she just died.

"Now what?" I asked my mother, lying in bed one night after the funeral.

"Now nothing," she said. (Your grandfather believes in Creator, your grandmother not so much.)

"What do you mean nothing?"

"She's dead. She'll live on in our memories."

That's not really living. I knew that then as much as I do now. Being remembered isn't the afterlife. That's others using their

3

working brains to think about you. When you die, you won't know if somebody's remembering you or not. I told her something like that, in a way that an eight-year-old would say it, and then my mother just shrugged it off. She told me that my grandmother didn't know she was alive before she was born, she wouldn't know she was alive after she passed away, and that's the way it was. That's the way it was for everybody.

"Are you trying to make me feel better?"

"We all share the same fate, son. Isn't that comforting? Isn't it nice to know that we're all in the same boat?"

That's one fucking shitty boat, I thought.

For years after that, I'd lie in bed and I'd think about what my mother had said, and it would keep me up all night. I'd get out of bed and wander the house aimlessly. I remember one night, I ended up by the front windows of our house, staring up at the sky, at the stars, at the moon, and then past all of that. I held up my hand and looked at my palm in the moon's soft light, looked at all the tiny lines that covered my skin. They were as small to me as I was to the world, as the world was to the universe, as the universe was to eternity, and I felt crushed by the weight of it all.

On nights like that, I'd crawl into my parents' bed. My dad would be awake. I guess he came to expect that sometime in the night, I'd wedge myself between him and my mother. He'd put his hand on my stomach, all those little lines on his palm pressed against my skin, and tell me to raise his hand, then lower it, with my breath.

"Like this?"

I'd breathe into my stomach. I'd watch his hand rise, then fall.

"Like that."

My pulse would slow. My breath would slow. I'd watch his hand until my eyelids grew heavy.

When I opened my eyes, it would be morning.

And I think about that. I think about how we sleep one-third of our life away. Life's already so short I'm afraid that if I close my eyes, it'll be too late to make things right with you. I've already been asleep for so long.

1

The automatic doors whirred to life and parted, allowing Holly to enter Pan Am Pool. She had her hair in a loose ponytail, her backpack hung from her shoulders, and she was wearing a team track suit that was only mildly embarrassing (maroon was not her favourite colour, but it looked good on her). She checked her watch as a gust of warm, humid air, heavy with the scent of chlorine, struck her face.

The city championship for high school water polo was in an hour, 3:00 p.m., and her parents said they'd leave early to get a parking spot nearby. Aquatic events—water polo games, swim meets, synchronized swimming, and diving competitions—filled the parking lot to the brim, like a distracted waiter pouring coffee. It was possible, Holly warned her parents, that they'd have to walk from Taylor Avenue, the opposite end of the parking lot, to get to the pool. The distance was equivalent to a city block.

She hoped more than anything to see her father in the stands. Up until this point, he had not attended one game this season despite his promises.

She pushed through the turnstile, walking past the front desk clerk, and turned to enter the women's change room. In spite of herself, she felt hopeful. She even had a smile on her face—confirmed when she saw her reflection as she walked by a mirror in the change room. She was excited to look into the stands and see her parents, who'd wave at her, prompting her to act humiliated to her friends, but she'd always liked it. Every kid liked to see their parents in the stands, no matter what they said. Her mother came to her games whenever she could. Her father used to, but his presence had become like a dream she had once.

This one mattered, though. She knew that if something was really important, he'd be there. Showing up was the thing. Holly wasn't sure what had happened to her father, why he was so different now. It's like everything about him had slipped away. He may have been in front of her, but he was barely visible, and he didn't see her anymore. She and her mother both felt it.

When she was younger, he made a point of telling her that he was the first person on earth to see her, so he'd known her the longest. He and her mother were so happy she'd arrived, after they'd miscarried three times, that they called her Hallelujah. Holly for short.

Last year, her mother and father were tied up with one thing or another, and she'd had to take the bus to swim practice. It was a long bus ride. Holly stuck earbuds in and, with her eyes closed, listened to music. Listened to every word in every song. This was something she'd inherited from her father. It felt like music was what connected them. Music and her grandfather, who made them go for walks together when they visited him. But those visits had become less frequent.

Holly fell asleep, missed her stop, and passed by several more stops before she was nudged awake by an old lady who'd become worried that she'd not gotten off when she should have.

"I make a point of doing that, dear," she'd said to Holly. "Some people get annoyed at me and some people thank me. I never know how they're going to react."

It took her close to an hour before she arrived at Pan Am, and by the time she got there, her father was waiting for her inside the automatic doors. He took her into his arms and hugged her. She couldn't remember the last time he'd hugged her. The smell of chlorine stuck to his clothing like campfire smoke.

He didn't say anything then, but that night, sitting at the edge of her bed, he explained to her why he'd come to the pool so fast after hearing from the coach that she hadn't shown up for practice.

"You're a young, beautiful, Indigenous girl, Hallelujah," her father had said. "You're way more at risk to get killed or kidnapped than a non-Indigenous girl." He looked her in the eyes, in the half light, and she felt safe. "I couldn't lose you. You're one of the only things that keep me . . ." He stopped. There was a long silence before he took a deep breath, tucked her in, and repeated, "I couldn't lose you."

He couldn't lose her, but then she watched him walk away, and it turned her sense of safety to a chill.

"Dad," she'd said.

He stopped at the door. He was silhouetted by the light in the other room. When he left, he would shut the door behind him, and she would be alone in the dark.

"You're not going to lose me," she'd said.

It didn't look as if he wanted to go. His hand was on the door frame, his fingers curled around it as if holding him there, as if something were taking him against his will, taking him from her, but he didn't want it to. Then why did he let go? Why did he leave?

Holly walked onto the pool deck at 2:50 p.m., and before joining her team for the huddle, before jumping into the water with her hands tight against her hips and her feet pointed down as though to show the way, as though there was anywhere to go but down, she looked into the stands.

There were so many parents there, kids running up and down the aisles, teachers who'd come to watch students try to win their school a championship. Holly looked from face to face, searching the steep stands that reached all the way to the roof. Her mother and father weren't where they typically sat, in the front row near the exit ramp. When Holly got called into the huddle, she continued to scan the crowd until her eyes met with her mother's. Holly's hope rose. She looked to the right of her mother, to the left, but didn't see her father.

Her mother's face looked apologetic; Holly could see that.

She mouthed, "I'm sorry."

But she didn't need to be sorry. It wasn't her fault. She wasn't the one who had flaked on her daughter's game. She wasn't the one who had stayed home, and to do what? Probably lie on the floor and stare at the ceiling. She wasn't the one walking from room to room, so lost in himself that he walked right by her. Walked away, again.

"I couldn't lose you," he'd said.

When the game was about to start, Holly finally got into

the pool. She slapped her hands against her thighs and jumped, pointing her toes toward the bottom, showing the way, as though there was somewhere else to go but down. In the next moment, the noise, the crowd, everything was replaced by Aqua Velva blue. She let herself sink to the bottom, bringing her hope with her, and when she sprung back toward the surface, she left her hope at the bottom of the pool, settled there along with all the lost quarters, nose plugs, goggles, locker keys.

Drowning.

2

Matthew woke up on the couch, fully clothed, his head resting on a throw pillow. Claire had told him on several occasions not to use the throw pillows as actual pillows, but he always did. At some point, she stopped asking him to stop. At some point, she gave up, and resigned herself to the inevitable argument after he was found in the morning with his head on one of the outlawed pillows. Their argument was rote, as though they were in a play, endlessly reciting practised lines.

"*Matthew*, these are decorative and you know that."

She would have a throw pillow clutched in her hands, as though it were a prop in their play.

"*Claire*," he would respond, "why would you buy a pillow as a decoration? By definition, a pillow is for somebody's head."

"Would you eat artificial fruit on a dining room table?" Claire would ask.

Usually right at this moment, she'd replace the throw pillow she'd used demonstratively, and with the utmost precision.

"Of course you wouldn't," she would continue. "They're for decoration. They're for ambience."

Matthew would sit up and mould the pillow he'd used back

into its original shape and present it to her with both hands, as though he were not in a play but on a game show exhibiting a prize she had a chance to win if she correctly guessed its price.

"Don't patronize me," she would say. "How do you patronize somebody without even saying anything?"

"Why would you even buy an artificial apple when you could buy a real one?" Matthew would ask.

"Because you would fucking eat it."

"No shit, I would eat it. An apple is for eating, Claire. It's like decorating the table with a bowl of lasagna and asking Garfield to leave it alone because, hey, *ambience*."

"I'm glad this is such a joke to you," she would say, and then storm out of the family room with her arms crossed, or her hands in her hair.

Matthew opened his eyes cautiously after realizing where he was, noting the firm cushions, the backrest, the afghan covering his body, a few of his fingers and toes sticking through the knitted fabric.

He couldn't remember getting the afghan or curling up underneath it.

Claire was absent. The television was still on. He couldn't remember what he'd begun to watch in the middle of the night before falling asleep. There was static on the television screen now. *Oh god*. Matthew realized that he'd turned it to a public broadcasting channel. It felt like a new low. The program he'd watched had ended, and, undoubtedly, the Canadian national anthem had played over scenes of eagles flying, whales swimming in the ocean, Niagara Falls, a lighthouse on the East Coast, mounted police charging toward the screen like stereotypical savage Indians, a beaver swimming, horses running in slow motion through shallow water, clouds rolling over mountains, a soldier cradling a baby in a war-torn country, an Inuk carving out a block of ice for an igloo, a settler letting a baby feed them corn, a black kid and a white kid hugging. After that, the one-note tone had begun to play and those coloured bars popped onto the screen— white, yellow, light blue, green, pink, red, dark blue. And then the static. Late-night, white-noise television static as he slept. It must have been too early for the station to sign on for the day.

Matthew pushed himself off the couch and took a few minutes to stretch out the stiffness, something that he'd found age had a proclivity for. The other day, he'd been on social media and a picture of him from three years ago popped up. He could hardly recognize himself. He was thinner. His hair was black. He'd always been sure that his hair would be as dark as a crow until he was well into his sixties, like his father, but now he had too many grey hairs to count. He had a salt and pepper beard, and a streak of white hair on the right side of his head like Reed Richards from the Fantastic Four. He had bags under his eyes that wouldn't go away. He'd been horrified to find hair growing out of his earlobes the other day. Earlobe hair was a death rattle.

Across the family room, outside the window that looked over the backyard, it was snowing so thickly that if Matthew didn't know better, he would've thought it was another television screen turned to the same channel, showing the same static, waiting for the morning sign-on.

Waiting to come alive.

When Matthew fell asleep on the couch, he often had to search for his phone when he woke up, like people search for remote controls and spare change. He started by slipping his hand between every cushion, then got on his knees and looked under the couch. After both attempts turned out to be fruitless, he chose the nuclear option and took off all the cushions, but the phone was nowhere to be found (ironically, he did find the remote control and a couple of dollars in change). Desperate, he decided to extend his search to the entire house, save the basement, the only place he knew with absolute certainty he'd not been last night. The basement was, in effect, his daughter's bedroom. Over the last while, he'd been increasingly less welcome in Holly's space.

When Hallelujah was nine, she'd said to Matthew that she would never be embarrassed to hold his hand anywhere, including at school, in front of her friends. "When you're a teenager," he'd said, "you won't even want me to drop you off at the front of your school, whether your friends are around or not." Holly was undeterred and made a bet with Matthew that, up until the age of eighteen, she would gladly hold his hand at any time, in any place, no matter who was around. The bet was for a hundred dollars. Matthew won the bet, but he did not collect his winnings.

Matthew's phone was not lost or hidden. He found it in the master bedroom. What was of concern to Matthew, what made his heart drop into his stomach, what made his body catapult into fight or flight mode, was that his phone was on the nightstand, plugged in to charge, beside a sleeping Claire.

Matthew rushed over to his phone and unlocked it, finding that it was open to a text conversation with Jesse, a woman from his work. It started off innocently, but escalated quickly.

Jesse: *I'm going to get sushi for lunch, want some*
Matt: *Uhhh let me think about that yes*
Jesse: *K*

Matt: *I'm so excited!*
Jesse: *I just can't hide it*
Matt: *I know I know I know I know I know*
Jesse: *I want you*
Matt: *I want you too.*

I want you too. Matthew had ended the conversation with a blushing emoji, like a teenager would. It was one of several texts between him and Jesse that turned inappropriate, and one of the milder exchanges. He tried to convince himself that Claire may not have seen anything, that she may have picked up his phone, seen that the battery was low, and taken it with her to charge for him. But there was a tissue box cradled in her arm, and littered all around her were crumpled-up tissues, stacked up like drifts of snow, as though the blizzard had raged inside the house as well, all through the night.

Everything had changed. Absolutely nothing had changed.

Matthew plugged his phone back in and positioned it just how he had found it. He took off his clothes in the ensuite bathroom, mere feet away from where Claire was sleeping, feet that felt like miles, and ran the shower. While waiting for the water to heat up, he leaned forward over the bathroom sink and stared at himself in the mirror. The bags under his eyes. The streak of grey. The salt and pepper beard. The emptiness.

"You're such a fucking prick," he said.

Steam crept across the mirror. Soon enough, his reflection was a blur. Soon enough, nothing was clear anymore, and all he could hear was the shower. It drowned out every other sound.

3

Holly's parents seemed to be deliberately avoiding each other this morning. She noticed it as soon as she got up, when she found her mother sitting at the dining room table with a cold cup of tea in front of her. On first glance, she looked sick, like she'd woken up with a cold, but the longer Holly sat beside her mother, eating toast with peanut butter that she'd made herself, the more she knew that wasn't the case.

"You okay?" Holly asked.

Her mother glanced up to look out the living room window, where batches of tossed snow periodically came into view. Holly went over to the window and saw her father shovelling the front walk, building up snowbanks on either side of the path. It had been snowing most of the night, a few feet of snow had accumulated, and he'd shovelled halfway to the sidewalk so far. She could see that his earbuds were in and he was stabbing at the snow. Judging by his body language, she guessed he was listening to something like Rage Against the Machine.

"You want something done around the house?" her mother had said once. "Piss off your father."

This was what he did when he was angry, at others or at

himself. His usual method of shovelling was to first pack down the snow by walking over it. He never shovelled unless her mother made him, and by then he'd have to use the ice scraper. Snow would lift off the concrete in heavy bricks. Her father said it was satisfying, when the packed-down snow came off the front walk like that.

"That's why I leave it for so long," he'd told her.

Her mother said that he was just lazy.

When her father came inside, covered in snow and sweat, ice hanging off his beard, his breath was short and heavy. The air between her parents was so thick that it felt to Holly as if she had to wade through it, like she was walking through water in the shallow end of a swimming pool, and she couldn't wait to leave the house, go to school, get away from it. Whatever it was. Who knew anymore? It could've been something that had happened between the two of them, or that her mother was mad that he'd not come to Holly's water polo game. The ride home from Pan Am Pool yesterday was spent listening to her mother apologize.

After school, nothing had changed—her parents were being distant and weird, and it was worse than if they'd been totally at each other's throats. Holly decided to go out with Charmaine and Christian even though it was a school night. She didn't ask her parents for permission—like they would notice anyway. Before leaving, Holly rummaged through her parents' liquor cabinet and found a bottle of spiced rum that had been at the back of the cabinet for as long as she could remember. There was a thin film of dust on the bottle's shoulders, and she was certain that by the time her mother and father noticed it was gone, they'd no longer care she'd taken it in the first place.

The liquor cabinet was in the dining room, underneath shelving occupied by porcelain angels kissing one another, a miniature ship, and family pictures. Holly called them "pictures of the dead." They were of her grandfather on her mother's side (heart attack), her uncle (HIV/AIDS), her great-grandmother on her father's side (COPD), and her great-grandfather on her mother's side (Ford Crown Victoria). It was a particularly sad shelf. It hung on the wall tilted forward, as though it could not take the sadness, as though it were trying to make the pictures slide off its surface. Every once in a while, her father would correct it, but he could never fix it permanently.

Holly removed the bottle from the liquor cabinet gingerly, as though playing a game of Operation, trying her best not to disturb any other glass object and alert her parents of where she was and what she was doing. Once it was free and clear, she slid the bottle into her purse. As she was leaving the room, she spotted her father's cellphone lying on the dining room table, and stopped. She wondered if there was something on his phone that would reveal what the hell was going on with her parents. Curiosity got the best of her.

It took her exactly one attempt to unlock the device. The code was the year of her birth: 2006. Holly's second guess would've been her mother's date of birth, then her father's. He was self-centred enough to have used his own date of birth, but he'd opted to use hers. For the briefest moment, though she was still angry at him for missing her game, she felt contented. And what a stupid thing to feel pleased about, so after that moment, the feeling was gone, because in the end it meant nothing, just that her birthdate was easy to remember.

Holly found the cellphone's contents mostly dull. There was a golf game he played that he, according to Claire, spent too much money on. There was a movie app, where the viewing history was mostly independent films like *Beasts of the Southern Wild*. There was the internet, which had no websites of note in the browsing history. There was Amazon and eBay, a banking app, Wikipedia, podcasts, Spotify, and many more that revealed nothing to Holly. She checked her father's messages last. She had begun to scroll through her father's text conversations when a horn blared from out front of the house.

Charmaine had arrived.

Holly scrolled through her father's messages hastily. Her parents' texts were disappointingly boring. There was the odd snarly message (her mother was not happy, for example, that he'd not come to the city championship, or that he'd forgotten to put towels in the dryer before going to bed, meaning that she'd have to run them through the wash again in the morning). But mostly, it was them communicating obligatory information. Where her father needed to be and when he needed to be there, what chores needed to be done (that he, she noted, likely wouldn't do anyway, so *Why am I even reminding you?*), that he should try to stretch or read a book if he had trouble sleeping rather than pace all over the house for most of the night.

It was the text history with a stranger named Jesse, somebody Holly had never heard of, that caught her attention. More than that, once she'd read through some of the texts, she gasped, and then cupped her mouth to shut herself up. Charmaine honked again, pressing the horn for longer this time. Holly wanted to read more. She wanted to read the messages over and over again ad infinitum, drilling them into her brain, torturing herself and, at the same time, presenting her with the impossible decision of whether to show her mother or not.

"*Thanks for this afternoon it's good to have another body to keep you warm on a cold day?*" Holly whispered to herself. "What the fuck is this?"

How could she not show her mother? Holly's hand was still over her mouth, but now it felt as though she had it there to keep herself from vomiting. She took a step toward her mother's bedroom, her father's cellphone clutched in her hand so hard that it was a miracle the glass didn't crack. But she stopped after taking only one step.

"It's none of your fucking business, Hall," she said, trying to convince herself to let it go.

Charmaine honked a third time, jolting Holly into a decision to leave it, at least for now. If Charmaine honked a fourth time, her mother would be angry, possibly keep her from going out at all, and the only thing Holly was sure of was that she needed to get drunk.

Reluctantly, she locked the phone and put it back where she had found it, then took a swig from the dusty bottle to numb the shock. After a quick and dangerous coughing fit (spiced rum was awful—she could see why it had gathered dust), Holly put the bottle back into her purse and ran out to meet Charmaine and Christian, who were waiting impatiently for her in Charmaine's old white sedan, which seemed to glow orange like embers under the street lights.

There was never a plan when Holly, Charmaine, and Christian went out; they were impulsive, and Holly didn't expect tonight to be any different. Especially because it was particularly cold and had started to snow again. Coupled with a strong wind, snowflakes felt like shards of glass against her skin. But they drove past where they should've turned if they were going to hang out at Charmaine's place and, soon after, took a left onto Portage Avenue, rather than a right, which would've brought them to Christian's house. There was never a plan except, it seemed, tonight. It wasn't long before they were speeding down the perimeter, outside the city, through increasingly bad weather.

"So where are we going?" Holly asked.

She took a swig of the spiced rum before passing it to Christian, who shrugged with a mischievous grin before downing a significant portion of the bottle as though it were water.

"You'll see," Charmaine said without taking her eyes off the road, but if she had, Holly thought it wouldn't have made a difference; all she could see in front of them were snowflakes lit by the car's headlights.

It looked as if they were driving into a swarm of locusts.

Holly grabbed the bottle back from Christian, spilling some on his jeans, and drank. It burned her throat and made her face scrunch up as if she'd shoved a thousand sour candies into her mouth all at once. At least she was starting to get a buzz. If she kept going, by the time they went into the ditch—and she was positive they were going to hit a ditch at some point if they stayed on the perimeter—she'd either be passed out or too drunk to notice. She chased one pull of rum with an even bigger one, then Christian grabbed the bottle. He didn't drink any, just screwed the lid on and placed it securely between his thighs. Holly tried to take it for another chug but couldn't move the bottle.

"Holy fuck, I guess the ThighMaster's been working out for you," Holly said.

"Very funny," Christian said.

She placed her hand around the bottle's glass neck and unsuccessfully tried to move it again.

"I'd have better luck lifting Thor's hammer. I'm not worthy."

She gave the neck another shake right after that, trying to catch Christian off guard, but no luck.

"Stop it, you're turning me on," he said.

"No hand jobs in my car!" Charmaine said, glancing back.

"Seriously, though," Holly said to Christian, "if I want a drink, give me a drink. You're not my dad."

"No shit," he said. "Your dad's not even acting like your dad, according to you."

Holly turned away from Christian and stared out the window and watched the snow whip by. She imagined it hitting her skin. She thought it would eventually stop stinging. Eventually, she'd just go numb. She wouldn't care about what Christian had just said. She wouldn't care that he was right. She wouldn't feel the need to make him feel bad, as though he were wrong. She wouldn't have cried for an hour after the water polo game, even though they'd won, because her dad hadn't come to watch. She'd be able to forget the messages she'd found on his phone.

"Hey." Christian nudged her on the shoulder.

"Yeah?" Holly looked away from the window, to Christian, and forced a grin.

"I'm sorry," he said. "That was a shitty thing to say."

He handed her the rum. She took it from him. She placed it at her feet. The car was unsteady. The bottle immediately tipped over and began to roll around on the floor mat.

23

"It's okay," she said. "No fucks given, right?"

"Right." Christian smiled at Holly like he thought he could get a genuine smile in return, but when he didn't get one, he slapped his hands against his thighs as though he could reset the entire conversation, as though he'd clapped the slate board on a movie set to start the scene over again. "Anyway, I just want you to be able to keep your wits about you for where we're going."

"To keep my wits about me?" Holly laughed. "What are you, seventy?"

"Where we're going it's kind of like Bloody Mary on steroids," Charmaine said.

Holly had never done the Bloody Mary thing. It wasn't something that had ever scared her. It seemed stupid to believe that if you said something three times while looking at a mirror, a ghost would appear. But if it meant that they were going to do something other than drive, something that offered a tangible fear, Holly was for it. They couldn't get there fast enough.

A few miles later, and by some miracle still alive, they turned off the perimeter and drove north along an unpopulated country road, where to the left was the Red River, and to the right was a thickly forested area. Somewhere around here, northeast of the city, was Selkirk, and she guessed they were headed in that direction, but what was scary in Selkirk? There was a giant catfish in the middle of town. Catfish were scary as fuck, the wide mouth and whiskers, but the statue was not. The statue was no more frightening than any other town statue, like the Happy Rock in Gladstone, literally a big rock with a smile painted on it. In Melita, a town situated in the banana belt, there was a statue of a banana wearing a belt. People didn't try anymore. If they were to come across a real catfish as large as the Selkirk statue, that would be another story, but catfish weren't that big, at least not in the city. She'd been fishing with her grandfather on the river and had caught a few; none were more than a foot long.

Holly crawled into the passenger seat, leaving Christian alone in the back. She watched the road ahead, not bothering anymore to ask where they were going, because Charmaine and Christian were too committed to the surprise, too satisfied with themselves. The snow had eased off, the wind had not, and endless wisps of snow were sliding over the concrete like snakes. Holly found it oddly calming, so when they stopped abruptly, it was jarring.

"My dear Hallelujah," Charmaine announced, "we have arrived."

Holly looked out the back window, out the side windows, out the windshield, and saw only black.

"Arrived where exactly?"

Holly reached back, patted her hand around the floor mat until her fingers touched glass, picked up the bottle of rum, and drank. It didn't burn as much now.

"Since we're not doing anything," she said, holding the bottle in the air as though asking for a toast. She took another swig before Christian snatched the bottle away. "Okay, *Dad*."

"Just cool it, all right?" Christian said.

"You're no fucking fun, you know that?" She turned and looked away. "Where the fuck are we?"

Holly's words were slurring. She was mildly aware of this.

"Turn your flashlight on and shine it over there," Charmaine said, pointing at something outside the passenger window.

Holly pressed her phone against the glass and shone the light toward the woods, only there weren't just woods where they had stopped. There was an old church sheltered within the trees. It had peeling white paint, a boarded-up front door, a sagging roof that looked as if it might cave in at any minute, a steeple leaning to the side, and at the top of it all, above the trees, reaching to the heavens, an impossibly perfect (given the condition of the structure) cross.

"Okay," Holly said, "you got me. Why are we at a really old church?"

"Because we're going to try to see the devil," Charmaine said, as though it were a foregone conclusion. "I've heard that if you run around it three times, that's what you see."

"Are you for real?" Holly asked, and when Charmaine nodded that yes, she was for real, Holly turned to Christian. "Is she for real?"

"It's an urban legend," Christian said, sounding unsure of what side of the fence he should be on, as though it had seemed like a good idea earlier, but now, not really.

"This is *exactly* the same thing as Bloody Mary," Holly said. "Do something three times and then something scary is supposed to happen."

"Yeah," Charmaine said, "I told you that it was like Bloody Mary on steroids. Instead of standing in the bathroom in the dark and saying a name three times in the mirror, you run around a church three times."

"And instead of encountering the ghost of Mary Tudor," Holly said flatly, "you come face to face with the devil himself."

"Exactly. Now, come on, live a little." Charmaine stepped outside and then leaned inside the car, bracing herself with the driver side door while cold air rushed into the vehicle. She'd been blasting the heat ever since leaving the city, but now it had been bullied away. "One dance with the devil and we'll go home."

"I'm in." Christian hopped out of the car as if they'd driven to the beach in the middle of summer. He wasn't even wearing a winter coat, just a fleece.

"Fuck it," Holly said.

The drinks were starting to hit harder now, and it took the bite out of the cold. It made minus twenty degrees Fahrenheit feel like plus five. Reverse wind chill. She opened the passenger side door and climbed out. The snow was deep. It reached above Holly's ankles. She, unlike Christian, had worn a jacket but hadn't bothered to wear boots. Converse sneakers offered little protection from the elements. She hugged her arms against her chest as though that would help with the feet situation. There was a sign to the right that looked like it had been knocked over at some point, the wooden post fractured like a broken bone. The sign itself was bronze, partially snow-covered, and while nobody wanted to wipe away the snow because nobody was wearing mitts, you could make out that it was a Catholic church. Saint something.

"Let's get this over with."

Nobody argued with Holly. Christian had brought the bottle, and they finished it between them, passing it back and forth. Christian tossed it into the forest and it landed silently, as if it had been swallowed up by the darkness. The group walked to the front of the church and stopped before the steps that led up to the boarded-up door.

"I think you have to go clockwise," Charmaine said.

"That makes sense," Holly said. "My grandpa says in sharing circles they go around clockwise. Actually, I'm not sure at all why that would make sense."

"Maybe it's universal," Christian reasoned. "Like how the number thirteen is unlucky in any context."

"True," Charmaine said. "They don't even make thirteenth floors."

"Okay, I hate repeating myself but: let's get this over with." Holly grabbed on to Christian's arm to keep herself steady. "I'd like to puke in your toilet," she said to Charmaine, "and then pass out on your couch. I love your fucking couch."

"Mi casa es tu casa," Charmaine said.

Christian counted down from three, and then they took off running. The snow got progressively deeper around the back of the church. By the time they rounded the corner to the last side, Holly was already out of breath, having had to high knee run to get through the snow. She had her hands wrapped around Christian's forearm about as tight as Charmaine's hand had been wrapped around the steering wheel. Holly wished that she could climb onto Christian's back and have him carry her for the last two laps, but she kept going with the other two, finishing another lap in twice as much time.

With half of the final lap remaining and, according to urban legend, the devil waiting for them on the front steps of the church, Holly collapsed. Her hand slipped off Christian's arm, and she rolled onto her back. The sky had cleared and the stars were brighter than they ever were in the city. Holly lay there, unmoving, counting constellations. She heard Christian stop and walk toward her. She heard Charmaine keep running, committed to finishing.

The sky began to spin as though Holly were not lying in the snow but rather on a merry-go-round that had been spun violently. The stars smeared into lines as if they were beings of light engaged in a round dance, something her grandfather had spoken about and Holly had seen once in a mall, had even taken part in.

It was beautiful, then and now. She stared up at the trails of light until darkness covered the stars, one by one, like spilled ink. Until there was only black, and she heard voices fading to whispers as she lost consciousness.

"What do we do with her?"

"Get her into my car, obviously. Can you carry her?"

"Can you?"

"Fuck off, Christian."

"We going to your place?"

"She loves my couch, doesn't she?"

Hallelujah came to in a car, infested with spiced rum that had soaked into her blood. The world was still spinning, but it wasn't so bad when she had her eyes open, and so she kept them open. It wasn't so bad that she couldn't tell where she was. Somehow, from lying in the snow behind the church, she'd ended up sprawled out in the back seat of her father's car. She didn't know if she'd been passed out for that long, whatever time it was now, or if she'd gotten so drunk she couldn't remember. It didn't really matter either way. She had ended up where she was now, so who gave a fuck how she got there. Her father was driving, and there was no doubt that he was taking her home. She pulled herself up into a sitting position and leaned against the door, pressing her temple against the cool glass of the rear passenger side window. She watched the late-night traffic. She watched cars drive in clusters, driving beside them, driving away from them, driving toward them. She watched their headlights. She watched the dotted white line. She rolled down the window for fresh air, not caring how cold it was.

Her hair got caught up in the wind, first flowing behind her head as though she were swimming, then swirling over her head like a miniature tornado, each strand dancing to an unheard song.

"Hey."

Holly turned toward her dad, who had been watching her. She watched him watching her until he turned back to the road.

"Could you close the window, Hallelujah? It's freezing."

She remembered the texts she'd seen on his phone more clearly than should have been possible, given how drunk she was. Thinking about them was sobering. She rolled up the window. Her hair fell back into place over her shoulders.

"I guess I did end up seeing the devil," Holly said, her speech still slurred, glaring at her father, her jaws clenched so tight her teeth were about to shatter.

"What was that?" her father said.

She must've whispered it. Her head hurt too much to speak loudly. She didn't repeat herself. She returned her gaze out the window, at the snow swirling like ghosts, there then gone. At the dotted white lines guiding them home, there then gone. At the headlights, there then gone.

Nothing was permanent.

"I didn't say anything," she said.

"Okay," he said.

They drove in silence until they turned off Portage Avenue and onto a side street. They'd be home soon. Holly couldn't wait to crawl into her bed. She'd have a huge glass of water before passing out again, and then in the morning, she'd make herself some greasy food before school. Somebody had told her once that greasy food helped get rid of a hangover. It was an experience she'd not had. Charmaine, Christian, and Holly had drank before, but Holly had never had as much as she'd had tonight. It struck her that her mother might smell the spiced rum on her.

"Hey, you're not gonna tell Mom, are you?"

They met eyes in the rear-view mirror. He hesitated.

"If I don't tell her, you won't be the only one in trouble."

"Come on. Do me a solid."

"Sorry, Hallelujah. I'd love to, but I can't keep a secret from Mom."

"Don't call me that. I hate that fucking name."

Holly wiped away the fog that her breath had made on the tempered glass. They were passing her old elementary school. She used to walk there in less than ten minutes. He used to walk with her.

"Don't swear."

"Whatever, *Dad*."

"And don't say *Dad* sarcastically, like it doesn't mean anything."

"You're right, I should've said *husband* sarcastically. My bad."

Holly couldn't tell whether this was her or the spiced rum talking, but quickly determined that it was both, that the spiced rum had enabled her to say what she wanted to say to her father.

"What's that supposed to mean?"

"Well, you're not that good at either of those things lately, Matt."

"Okay, for sure you're not going to start calling me Matt. You can call me Father, Dad, sir, whatever, but—"

"*Sir*," Holly said, "pfffft. Okay."

"I think you should think twice before drinking this much again, Hallelujah."

"I said, don't fucking call me that!" Holly lunged forward and gripped her hands around the front passenger seat. Her nails dug into the fabric. "And if you want me to stop drinking this much, then I'll make you a deal: how about you stop texting some bitch that isn't my mother!"

Her father immediately pulled over and stopped the car. They were two houses away from home. Holly thought about leaving right then before hearing what her father had to say, because what could he say? She thought about running off anywhere but home. She'd heard once that doctors said if they had to die by suicide, they'd drink a ton of alcohol and fall asleep in a snowbank.

Holly wanted to find a snowbank.

When her father didn't say anything for a minute that felt more like an hour, as though everything had started to move in slow motion, Holly said, "If you're so bad at keeping secrets from Mom, then how the fuck are you keeping *that* secret?"

Her father sighed heavily, as if he'd been holding his breath for hours. Years. He collapsed forward, pressing his head against the steering wheel, and stayed like that for another period of time that seemed longer than it really was, before lifting his head and turning toward her. He looked tired and lost all at once. Holly almost felt bad for him, pitied him. He looked so fucking pathetic.

"I didn't do anything," he said. "I wouldn't have done anything."

"But you did do something," she said.

Another, deeper sigh. "I know. I know I did."

"Why?"

Her father wiped at his eyes. Funny. She'd not seen a tear. She'd missed the tear. He pinched the top of his nose, between his eyes, and lowered his head. He was breathing deeply, in and out, trying to calm himself. He shook his head, as though whatever he was going to say, there was no way to say it.

Holly saw tears then. He didn't wipe them away. It was odd. Tears indicated emotion, but his eyes, when he looked at her, were empty more than anything else. She did pity him. At least for tonight. That very well could have been the spiced rum, too, but even if it was, the pity felt real.

"I guess I was trying to fill a void," her father said.

Holly looked at her father for another second, before turning away, before looking out the window. To the right, on the passenger side, there was a park. There was a park, then some trees, then a riverbank, and then the frozen river. She couldn't see any of those things in the dark; she just knew they were there.

"Yeah," she said, "I guess I was, too."

4

In the gloaming, with Claire asleep and Holly in the basement, Matthew got out of bed. He had stared out the window long enough, waiting for sleep that never came. He stood in front of the bathroom mirror and inspected the minutiae of his face, trying to see what his daughter saw when she looked at him.

One side was sharper than the other.

"You could never be a model because your face isn't symmetrical," a girl had told him when he was younger.

He hadn't cut his hair for almost a year. He'd not shaved for months. He sported a full beard, which was impressive for a forty-year-old man with Cree heritage. Most Cree, after months without a shave, would've looked as though they'd transplanted a few pubic hairs onto their chin. It must have been the Irish in him on his mother's side. There were stray hairs on his cheeks. The longer he locked eyes with his reflection, the more they nagged at him. Soon, they were all he could look at. The entirety of his lopsided, bearded, olive-skinned face became a handful of stray hairs. He knew that a single human hair was approximately ninety thousand nanometres wide. There were 25.4 million nanometres in one inch, and the average human face was about fifty-eight square inches. How insignificant was that? What was one human life against the enormity of infinity? As Matthew turned toward the medicine cabinet to fetch his safety razor, it occurred to him that this was a good example of why he'd always had trouble sleeping.

One thought became the fucking big bang.

The safety razor had been dormant for months, unless Claire had used it to shave her legs. For some reason, she liked to use his razor, not hers. In closely examining the razor, Matthew couldn't be sure whether she'd used it or not. There were old hairs and dried-up shaving cream and miniscule flakes of skin caked on either side of the blade, top and bottom.

It wasn't fit for use.

In the medicine cabinet, beside the bag he kept his safety razor in, were extra blades individually wrapped within a plastic container that gave out one thin blade at a time like a Pez dispenser. Matthew slipped one blade out with his thumb, pinched it between his index finger and thumb, and placed it on the bathroom counter. He unscrewed the handle on the safety razor, which released the mount, the old blade, and the cap. He unwrapped the new blade, then wrapped the old blade in the wax paper and tossed it into the garbage. He rinsed the handle, mount, and cap thoroughly under hot water, until every last trace of dried shaving cream, every severed hair, every skin cell, had been washed away. The mount was placed atop the handle, and Matthew picked up the new blade, intending to rest it on the mount, but in the process, he nicked his index finger. He dropped the blade, which, weighing next to nothing, fell back onto the counter in a whisper. Matthew reflexively stuck his index finger into his mouth. After a few seconds, he took his finger out to see the wound sucked clean, before it welled up with crimson again. He watched until the blood had formed a drop that slipped off his fingertip and ran down his finger, then across the back of his hand. Before it reached his wrist, he wiped it away with a single sheet of toilet paper. He used the same sheet of toilet paper to press against the cut until the bleeding stopped.

While waiting, he returned to staring at his reflection, scanning every detail of his face, everything he had noticed before and new details that presented themselves the longer he looked: the grey hairs in his beard, the permanent creases between his eyes and on his forehead that Claire said made him look perpetually angry, the bags under his eyes. How tired he'd become. How many thoughts he'd had. How many hours he'd stayed awake, staring out the window.

Matthew took the toilet paper off his fingertip, tossed it into the toilet, and flushed it away. His fingertip looked like a clown's nose, dyed red from his own blood. He picked up the blade with his other hand, held it to the light, with the flat side facing him, then rotated it 90 degrees, and it disappeared. It was almost as thin as a strand of hair, so narrow that when turned sideways, it was as though it didn't exist. Matthew imagined being small like that. He rotated his other arm so that the dorsal side of it was facing him. There was a spot near the base of his thumb where two blue veins met, then carried on together toward his elbow. It formed the shape of a Y. He thought of how if he were to lay out all the veins in his body, they would stretch to sixty thousand miles, but that spot, that one intersection, that blue-shaped Y, was less than half an inch in length. How utterly small.

If you were to cut it in half, you would die.

The bathroom's vanity lights glinted off the razor blade and across Matthew's face. He lowered it to his arm and touched the corner of the cool metal to the spot where the veins intersected. The Y shape. He pressed it down lightly, too lightly to break skin, but then harder, and the blade penetrated his skin. A small but steady stream of blood slid down his arm from the cut. He never would have expected that such a thin cut could yield so much blood.

Matthew watched the delicate red line flow down his forearm and gather into a single drop of blood that clung to his elbow like dew at the tip of a leaf. Matthew watched the droplet fall and splash against the white porcelain sink, then another. He placed the blade on the counter and took a few sheets of toilet paper, folded them together, and dabbed at the blood all the way up his forearm. He held the folded toilet paper on the incision for a few minutes until the bleeding had stopped, then took it away, leaving a red slit no wider than a hair. Under the generous vanity lights, surrounded by sky-blue walls, looked down upon by a lightning-shaped crack in the ceiling, Matthew unfolded the paper to reveal a blot of red that had perfect bilateral symmetry, like a Rorschach test.

He looked at it intently, trying to figure out what he saw in the shape.

Matthew tossed the blood-soaked tissue into the toilet, flushed, and watched it dance in circles, in swirling white lines, then disappear. He affixed a bandage over the incision he had made just as more blood began to pool, ready to paint another bright-red line down his forearm. He returned the safety razor to the medicine cabinet, having not shaved off a single hair, took one last look at himself in the mirror, and then turned off the bathroom light, thrusting the bathroom and bedroom into darkness.

He stood in the doorway, allowing his eyes to adjust, and while waiting, listened to Claire's measured breaths and tried to find the same rhythm. She was calm when she slept. When she slept, it felt as though everything that had happened between them could be forgotten as easily as a dream. A square of soft white light from the window stretched from one side of the bed to the other. He looked at Claire, the empty space at her side, the impression of his body, then left the doorway, left the bedroom, and began to wander.

Matthew had just entered the kitchen, had just stood in front of the kitchen window, had just begun to gaze at the stars, challenging himself to find constellations his father had told him about as a way to distract himself, when he heard voices coming from the basement. He recognized Holly's voice, but there was another, male voice. At first, Matthew thought it was coming from the television, but it became apparent that this wasn't the case. Matthew, though wide awake for the past few hours, had not heard anybody come inside the house, but there was a burst of laughter, which was irrefutable evidence that a boy was in the basement.

He left the kitchen, walked past the pantry, and stood at the top of the stairs, where he listened, intending to eavesdrop, to hear what they were saying to each other. But his daughter's and the male's voice stopped. They were engaged in an odd standoff, but Matthew knew he was destined to lose a battle of wills with his daughter. The best parts of Holly were from Claire, including Claire's stubbornness. He was sure that Holly would sit there in the dark, in the silence, until morning if she had to, so long as Matthew refused to leave. Recognizing the futility of it all, he gave up and descended the stairs, taking normal steps, loud enough for the pair to know that he was coming, but soft enough that he didn't appear angry, whether he was or not. He couldn't decide. It surprised Matthew how much it bothered him, to find a boy in the basement. It surprised Matthew that his deliberate steps quickened until he reached the bottom. A dark figure got up from the couch, clearly the boy, and another figure, Holly, got up immediately after. The math wasn't hard; the boy had been on top of his daughter, and though it was dark, he could see that Holly was putting a shirt on.

"Who's this?"

Matthew flicked on the basement light just in time to see Holly straightening out the shirt she'd thrown on.

"Jesus, Dad," Holly said.

"Oh hey, Mr. McIvor," the boy said.

Showing hubris, he approached Matthew with his hand extended. Matthew glanced at it but didn't shake it straight away. He looked at Holly, who was now finger-combing her hair. She had bed-head like Matthew. The boy's hair was no tidier than Holly's, his face flushed from making out with her, not likely from being scared of Matthew. Matthew wasn't imposing.

The boy's hand was still extended. Was he as stubborn as Holly? Matthew figured that the quicker he shook the kid's hand, the quicker he'd leave. While shaking the boy's hand, Matthew noticed the bandage on his wrist had come loose. There was a trail of blood down his arm, and a pool of crimson had coagulated around the slit he'd made with the razor blade. He ended the handshake and clasped his hands together behind his back, trying to make it seem as though he was displeased.

39

"And you are?" Matthew asked the boy.

"Christian."

"Oh, you were there when I picked up Holly from Charmaine's last night."

"Yeah, that was me."

"It's time for you to go home, Christian. That is, unless you've been drinking with my daughter again."

"*Dad*," Holly said.

"Need a ride?" he asked Christian.

"No, I'm good," Christian said, then turned to Holly. "I'll see you tomorrow?"

Holly nodded.

"Good night," Matthew said to Christian as the boy brushed past him and hurried up the stairs.

Matthew and Holly stared at one another while listening to Christian put his shoes on, open the front door, then close it. A few moments later, there was the faint sound of a car starting, then driving off.

"Really? On the couch?" Matthew said.

"Oh, where'd you want us to be, on my bed, Dad?" Holly said.

"I would've liked for him to not be on top of you, wherever you were," Matthew said.

Holly started for her bedroom door. Matthew noticed the stench of beer. *No, I'm good*, that little shit had said. The creases between Matthew's eyes deepened. He wondered where the bottles were. He thought of where he would've hidden them when he was her age. Behind the couch, he figured. Somewhere that Holly probably hoped they would stay hidden until morning, at which time she'd dispose of them. Kids think parents have no sense of smell.

"We're not done, Holly."

She stopped. "What?"

"You can't just have a boy over in the basement this late at night without telling your mom and me. You're sixteen."

"I know how old I am, thanks."

"Good." Matthew crossed his arms. It felt like an arm-crossing kind of moment. "Then you know you're too young to be making out with some guy on the couch, especially after he snuck in here."

"*Sneaked* in here," Holly said.

"It can be either, actually, and you know . . . you're not supposed to be drinking beer in the basement, either, or anywhere for that matter. Especially not two nights in a row. Did you forget how shitty you felt yesterday when—"

"Alcohol's meant to make you feel like crap after it makes you feel good," Holly said. "It's a trade-off."

"You said you weren't going to drink again," Matthew said. "You promised me every time you came up for air when your head was stuck in the toilet."

"I wouldn't be the first person in this house to break a promise, would I?" Holly said.

She continued to the bedroom door, walked through the doorway, and put her hand on the side of the door, primed to slam it shut.

"Hey!" Matthew rushed over to Holly's bedroom. "You can't talk to me like that."

"Why?" Holly said.

"Why? Because I'm your dad, that's why."

"You can't just suddenly decide to parent and think I'm going to respect you. Where've you been the last few years? Where were you two days ago?"

41

"I was right here," Matthew said.

"Exactly! Probably on your phone being shitty because nobody was around to see it. You'd rather talk to whoever the fuck Jesse is than come to my game!"

"That's not fair."

"This isn't fair to me, and shouldn't that matter more?"

Holly slammed the door, and it stopped an inch from Matthew's nose, shut hard enough that it thrust a breath of air across his face. An inch between him and the door. A few feet between him and his daughter. Such a short distance, but somehow infinite. As though he could travel a lifetime, and not close the distance, because he had spent so long creating it.

Holly pressed her palm against the door so firmly that her fingernails began to turn white, anticipating that her father might try to come inside. With her other hand, she cupped her mouth to muffle the sound of her whimpering, furious tears. She collapsed to the floor, crouching, tears pooling along the side of her hand, tears curling down across her fingers.

Matthew put his hand on the door, as though Holly might do the same on the other side, like people do in prison movies against thick glass, phones pressed to their ears.

* * *

It wasn't more than a few seconds later that she removed her hand. She trained her eyes on the door, waiting for him to come in. Waiting for him to walk away from her. Waiting for something. Waiting for anything but silence. When nothing happened, she decided that she would break the silence herself, maybe even just fucking break something. There were her water polo and swimming medals, each one of them thumbtacked to the wall. But she was proud of them, didn't want to ruin them, and wasn't sure if she could anyway. There was her collection of snow globes, which she'd collected until last year, when she decided she was too old for them. But as upset as she was, if she were to break them, the cleanup would be a nightmare. In the end, she retrieved a stuffie from her bed. It was a dinosaur that her father had bought her at the Original Pancake House when she was five. It hit the drywall with a disappointingly soft thud, then fell onto the mattress, almost exactly where she'd picked it up from.

Holly pulled out a photograph she'd placed in her bedside drawer the other night. It was of her, as a toddler, walking on a trail with her father. She slammed the drawer shut and tossed the frame across her bedroom. Almost before the picture came to a stop after skidding across the carpet, she was on the floor beside it. She picked it up and ran her thumb along a crack that had bloomed in the glass, a razor-thin crack, almost imperceptible, but she knew it was there. To her, it looked like a canyon. Her heart began to pound and her breath became short. An overwhelming sense of fear came over her, but she didn't know what she was afraid of. She was just afraid.

She sat there with the picture, leaning against the wall, the frame clutched against her chest, imagining the walk she'd taken with her father, because she couldn't remember it. It came to her in images, like frames in a film reel that had been cut up and dropped into her arms. She looked at the photo again, as though she were there, as though she were walking with her father, as though he would walk with her.

Matthew could hear Holly breathe deeply, trying to calm herself. There came a distinct sliding sound. She was taking a record out. He heard her place it on her portable record player, the one he and Claire had gotten her for Christmas. The needle scratched against the black circle. The static sound of a stylus moved gently on the vinyl across the etched grooves. An electric signal was fed to the amplifier. A song began to play.

Holly lay on her bed, curled up into a ball, the picture still in her arms, mouthing the words, listening for more than the music.

Matthew stood there, listening to the music, reciting the lyrics without uttering a sound, just moving his lips. Holly had been right. It wasn't fair. He stayed there with his hand pressed against the door until the music cut out, until the static sound came, until all he could hear was Holly's breath.

Ashley and I used to fill a backpack with beer and walk all over River Heights, down back lanes, breaking basketball rims and taking random things from unlocked cars, like cassette tapes, loose change, and manuals. One night, when we hit Taylor Avenue, we'd already walked a couple of miles and were looking for different shit to do. Back then, there was a pitch-and-putt golf course on the other side of Taylor. We decided that we were going to break in and hit balls in the dark, aim at passing vehicles. I never said I was smart at your age. Sometimes when I get upset with you, it's because I did the same things.

Ashley ran across Taylor Avenue without checking traffic. A white sedan missed him by a few feet, but he made it. I, unlike Ashley, checked for traffic. There was a van coming from the right, but other than that, it was clear. I ran across the street, intending to stop on the boulevard, wait for the van to pass, then meet Ashley on the other side.

I thought there was a boulevard, but it was farther east. I just wasn't paying attention. The van flashed its brights at me and honked at the same time. It ended up missing me by less than an inch; I felt its side-view mirror brush against my shirt. If I'd run a split second sooner, if I'd run faster, the van would've hit me head-on. After it *passed me, it kept driving and honking, as if there were more idiot kids running dangerously across the street.*

When my feet were safely on the grass on the other side of Taylor Avenue, Ashley and I collapsed, laughing hysterically. We never did break into the pitch-and-putt. We didn't dig in the sand like kids at the beach with shovels and pails, didn't swim in the man-made pond, didn't hit balls over the fence and try to hit cars. We lay on our backs on the south side of Taylor Avenue for an hour and stared at the sky. I looked past the moon, past the stars that looked like reflections of build-ings and cars, and into the deep endlessness of space.

That was the closest I'd ever felt to it.

5

Matthew woke up early in the morning, well before the sun rose, and lay there staring out the window as colour announced itself gradually, grey to warm, as though increasing the saturation of a photograph. Claire, who'd never had trouble sleeping, who could put her head down on anything and fall asleep in seconds, was dead to the world. She'd always told him that if he was up, he should get up and do things around the house.

"Things need to be done, and I can't do all of it all the time," she'd said.

"What does Holly do around the house?" he'd said.

"Holly's a teenager. Teenagers don't do anything around the house. No teenager ever in the history of the world has done anything around the house, and they shouldn't be expected to. You're an adult."

"Yeah, and I work. I pay for this house."

"I know you do. Just clean a fucking bathroom once in a while."

Claire had had a point; she always did. She was mostly always right, but Matthew could never bring himself to admit it. Each morning, he intended to get up, no matter how early he woke, sometimes before four in the morning, but each morning he stayed in bed, watching the colours change, watching the sunlight slide over the darkness like a cinematic wipe in slow motion. He told himself that he was trying to get back to sleep, but really, he just didn't want to get out of bed, so he didn't until he absolutely had to. What was there to look forward to? Sitting at a cubicle surrounded by grey walls, pummelled by fluorescent lighting, playing solitaire.

Matthew waited until Claire got out of bed, and then he got out of bed. When he stood up, he noticed that his arm had continued to bleed, albeit lightly, and some of the blood had stained the white sheets. He covered the stain with the comforter, making one half of the bed, and not very well. When Claire noticed the literal half-assed job, she sighed and proceeded to make the entire bed as though she'd been in the military. Matthew watched with a quickened heartbeat when she readjusted his side of the bed, because the stain came into view momentarily, but she didn't see it. He relaxed then, as much as he could. He was still unsettled about last night, having the door slammed in his face, and about the last couple of days, with the text conversation both Claire and Holly had discovered. He carried that anxiety with him to the dining room, to what promised to be a supremely awkward breakfast.

Matthew's expectations were met. After all the work Claire had put into making breakfast—baked oatmeal with fresh berries and maple syrup—nobody had taken one spoonful of it. Matthew, Holly, and Claire seemed to be doing their best to ignore one another with as much intention as they were ignoring their food. Matthew kept glancing back and forth between Holly, who refused to look at him at all, and Claire, who was hard to read. Did she know what had gone on last night? Had Holly

48

told her? Matthew hadn't, but Holly and Claire exchanged texts as much as they spoke face to face. It was very likely that Claire knew, and because she wasn't trying to make things right, something she often took it upon herself to do, she sided with one of them. Undoubtedly Holly.

Feeling strongly that he needed to be heard, Matthew decided to break the silence that had draped over the breakfast table like a pall. He took a bite of the baked oatmeal first, as though this might win him favour with Claire, then dabbed at his mouth with a napkin and cleared his throat.

"Look," he said to Holly, "it's not that I don't want you to have a guy over; it's that he sneaked . . . snuck . . . sneaked . . . Claire, it's either, right?"

"I don't think it's relevant, Matt."

"I just want to lecture you with proper grammar, that's all," he said to Holly.

She rolled her eyes.

"Anyway." Matthew tried to gather himself. The ice had firmly not been broken. "You can't have a guy in the basement and not tell us. I don't even care that you guys were, you know, making out."

When neither Holly nor Claire said anything, when they only shared a look between the two of them, he continued.

"Just let me know, and then I won't hear a strange voice in the basement and feel the need to check it out and find my daughter playing tonsil hockey with a dude."

"Tonsil hockey?" Holly said, but not to Matthew, to Claire.

She was looking straight at her mother, her spoon dangling between her index finger and thumb. Matthew found himself entranced for a moment by the pendulum swing of the utensil.

"Who says *tonsil hockey*? Do you see what I have to deal with? When he decides to pay attention to me, I have to listen to his fucking '90s terminology like he's trying to relate to me or something. Is that even from the '90s? Maybe it's from the '80s."

"I know," Claire said quietly. "I know, just . . ."

She didn't finish the sentence. She picked up her spoon, then put it down delicately, perfectly in place, as if she were setting the table for a fancy dinner, the same way that she made beds.

"I'm sorry," Matthew said to Claire, "but is it suddenly okay for our daughter to have boys over late at night? And be drinking? Again?"

"Can you tell him that I'm sixteen and I can kiss a boy if I want?" Holly said to Claire.

"Are you listening to me?" Matthew said to Holly. Then, considering that Holly wasn't speaking to him directly, he decided that he, too, would make Claire the go-between. "Is she listening to me?"

"Matthew, let it go." Claire was doing her best to stay measured. "She *is* sixteen."

Claire and Holly exchanged another glance.

"Are you guys in some secret club now? Is there a handshake? Can I see the handshake? Is there a fist bump explosion involved?"

"Can you tell him to grow up?" Holly said to Claire.

There were levels of calm at the table. There was Claire, who was still holding it together, there was Matthew, who was upset but not raising his voice, and there was Holly, who looked as though she wanted to throw her baked oatmeal at his face.

"How grown-up do you think it is to ignore me when I'm sitting right beside you, and for you to talk to your mother instead of me, like I'm a ghost."

"If the shoe fits," Claire said.

Holly stifled a laugh, as though she didn't want to show a crack in her hard exterior.

"And you're enabling her," Matthew said to Claire. "You're not helping. Like, at all. You're acting like a teenager. She used to be . . ." He turned to Holly, unwilling to play her game. "You used to be a real sweet girl, you know. I remember that."

"Maybe I've made some not sweet friends," she said.

Matthew wasn't sure if she was addressing him directly or through Claire. Either way, she was looking down at the baked oatmeal. She pressed her spoon deep into the food, then pulled it out.

"How would you know either way?" she said. "You remember me from when? In a few years, will you remember me now? Could you?"

"At least I don't walk around here acting like a zombie, Matthew," Claire said. "You're here, but you're not really here."

"If I'm not really here, then where am I?" Matthew asked.

"Do you want to go there right now in front of our daughter? Do you want to actually talk about it right now?"

Matthew didn't tell Claire that Holly knew what she was referring to.

"No," he said. "No, I don't."

Claire put her face in her hands and sighed. Matthew shoved some baked oatmeal into his mouth. Holly slid her bowl away from her, to the centre of the table, and then stood up aggressively. Her hips collided with the edge of the table and made all their plates shake. A bit of Matthew's coffee spilled over the edge of his cup. In the ensuing silence, with Holly standing and looking over them, with Claire's head in her hands, Matthew watched a drop of coffee slide down the white porcelain. He unconsciously began to rub his thumb over the bandage on his wrist. The droplet met the kitchen table and left, in its wake, a thin line of dark brown. He placed his thumb on the rim and then slid it across the warm, smooth surface of the cup, wiping away the trail.

"Can I be excused?" Holly asked Claire.

"We're not done here yet. We haven't even talked about the real issue," Matthew said.

"Yes, you can," Claire said to Holly.

Matthew watched Holly leave the dining room. When she was out of sight, Matthew turned to Claire, who, as though she were putting on some kind of performance, lifted her face and met eyes with Matthew. If Matthew were a zombie, they at least, for the moment, had something in common: Claire had dead eyes, as though she couldn't allow herself to show any emotion, or had none left to give.

After a drawn-out silence, the kind desperate for interruption, Claire said, "She's right. You've not been present. Even before . . ."

"She knows, you know. When I picked her up the other night at Charmaine's, she—"

"She feels," Claire interrupted, "that it's offensive to have you get after her about something like a boy when you never do regular things with her."

She lifted Matthew's coffee cup and, with her napkin, wiped the coffee ring that had been formed by the spill.

"You've got to spend time with her. You're missing so much right now, and whether you believe it or not, she misses you. And for what? For who? Who's more important?"

"She is. You are."

"Matt . . ."

"We haven't talked about what happened. We should talk about it."

Claire's face disappeared again. She spoke while facing the table, her forehead pressed against her palms.

"All she wanted was for you to go to her game. She didn't want the moon."

Matthew shook his head, as though she could see him.

"A fucking water polo game, Matthew. You couldn't've just went? You had to . . . what? What was so important? You had to text your little—"

"No."

Claire stood up, gathered the untouched bowls of oatmeal, then disappeared into the kitchen.

"I'll talk to her," Matthew called out to her. "I'll apologize before she goes to school angry."

Claire popped her head into view, followed by her entire body. She came to stand in the doorway and looked vaguely apologetic.

"She doesn't want to talk to you," Claire said. "Like, not even a word."

"What?" Matthew sat up and leaned forward. "What do you mean? I'm not allowed to talk to her?"

"That's what she told me."

"She told you to tell me," Matthew corrected.

"Yes."

"Well, fuck." Matthew threw his arms out. He felt his heart quicken along with his breath. "How long's this going to last?"

Claire shook her head. "Until she's ready to talk to you."

"So, I can't just go down there and say I'm sorry and make it right?"

"See, that right there"—she pointed toward him, as if the words he'd spoken were tangible, as if they could read them over and over again—"that's why she's not talking to you. You don't get it. You can't force it. You just have to let her be."

"This is so damn . . ." Matthew trailed off as though he wasn't willing to have any more of his words scrutinized. "I never do anything right."

"The first thing you need to do, Matt, is stop making everything about you. You did this. You did all of this. But you did it to Holly. You did it to me. The . . . Jesus Christ, Matt, the world doesn't revolve around you. The world doesn't revolve around anybody, just the sun."

6

It was a frigid morning. Matthew's father had once told him a word in the Swampy Cree dialect for how cold it was. *Kisinaw.* "It is bitterly cold." His father had never taught him the language when he was a kid, but as an adult, Matthew had picked up a word or two and had come to understand that Cree was a descriptive language more than a prescriptive one, like English. One word often stretched out into a sentence in English. Cree was an economical language and, Matthew thought, a pretty one. He regretted not being taught it, but after his father had told him about his time at residential school, he understood why. It was as though his father had left the language on the land, on a long-lost trapline he spoke about, rather than bring it with him to such a cold, dark place. And when his father found it again, he thought it was too late to teach Matthew.

Kisinaw.

Matthew had been sitting in his car, waiting for it to heat up, pressing down on the gas pedal to rev the engine and speed up the process, coax warm air into blowing through the vents. He blew warm air into his hands, as though trying to show the vents what they were supposed to do. He'd forgotten to bring mitts and had no intention of going back inside. He was glad that he couldn't even see outside; the windshield was covered in milky frost.

Matthew stared at the glass, replaying the events of the night before and this morning, as, bit by bit, the windshield cleared in the shape and movement of a rising sun.

Or an atomic bomb.

The rear glass cleared in strips, until it looked like partially opened blinds. Minutes later, with the windows safely cleared, Matthew put his car in gear with a shaky hand and, still distracted, backed out of the driveway, almost hitting an elderly man who was walking his dog. He announced his presence by whipping Matthew's bumper with the end of the dog's leash.

There were two ways to get to work, and Matthew chose the route that brought him around the perimeter, rather than through the city. He didn't much like traffic; rush hour made him feel claustrophobic—a tall man inside a small car, and, to compound matters, a small car lost within a parade of vehicles. Conversely, the perimeter, at this time of day, was near-empty, as if the highway had been cleared just for him.

He'd travel for a couple of miles, then turn off the highway onto a long back road that led into the city and, eventually, his office.

There was nothing to see on the drive. Everything was familiar. To the left, a trailer park and then a newer development with its cookie-cutter houses, put together with as much care and speed as the prefab houses he'd seen on-reserve. To the right were the prairies, the monotony broken only by the Assiniboine River, which curled its way through the city until colliding with the Red River at the Forks, one of the only tourist attractions in the city. Ahead, the highway appeared to get smaller and smaller, as thin as a razor blade, or a strand of hair, before disappearing into the vast horizon.

He felt an apology was in order.

Matthew, with one hand on the steering wheel, reached blindly for his cellphone, which he'd shoved into his pants pocket. He had to lift his ass off the seat and arch his back to retrieve it— an acrobatic feat. He glanced back and forth from the highway to his phone, his pupils darting side to side as though he were in REM sleep. He tried to pay attention to the road while unlocking the device with Hallelujah's birth year. As he approached the turnoff to the back road, the kind of road you'd find in the country, he scrolled through his messages until he found Hallelujah's name, then opened their ongoing text conversation. Calling their low volume of messages a conversation was a stretch; the last text he'd sent Holly was from the night she'd been drinking, asking her, near morning, if she was okay, if she needed anything. She'd not replied.

"Texting isn't talking."

Matthew convinced himself that sending her a message was not breaking the newly established rule that he wasn't to say anything to her, but he still opted for a one-word text: *Sorry*. He wasn't certain of his own logic and felt this was a reasonable compromise.

As he finished typing out the word and was about to press the send button, Matthew felt the car shake and looked up to find that he, at over seventy miles per hour, was headed off the highway and toward the guardrail. He dropped his phone, leaving it to bounce off the passenger seat and onto the dirty floor mat, gripped the steering wheel with both hands, and jerked it to the left, guiding the car back onto the highway just before it hit the guardrail. The car likely would have broken through the barrier and crashed onto a set of railroad tracks below.

Matthew kept driving and reached the turnoff where the off-ramp curled away from the highway and led to the back road. He pulled over around where his car would've landed, and stopped. His hands were still gripped around the steering wheel, white-knuckled. He uncurled his fingers, let go of the wheel, and placed his hands on his lap. With his phone on the floor mat and the text to his daughter unsent, Matthew began to laugh hysterically until his stomach hurt and tears were rolling down his cheeks.

He had to wipe his eyes with his jacket sleeve to see clearly, because tears had blurred his vision. Then he sat in the silence, interrupted infrequently by a passing vehicle. He'd almost gone over the edge of an overpass. But sitting there, now that the laughter had passed, he was oddly calm; the near-death experience had been the equivalent of taking a Xanax.

Matthew shook his head, bewildered, then put his hands back on the steering wheel, positioned at ten o'clock and two o'clock. He looked at his knuckles. They were dry. They were always dry. Claire had told him a number of times that his skin was like a reptile's, because its dryness looked like scales. They were light brown, not white any longer. He decided that he'd clutched the wheel out of instinct, nothing more. Sitting there now at the side of the road, he didn't feel fear, but at the same time, he didn't feel grateful to be alive. What was there to feel grateful for? A daughter giving him the silent treatment? A wife who seemed too exhausted to care about closing the expanse that he had created between them?

He was surprised by how empty he felt.

A crow landed on the hood of his car, startling him. It looked

THE THEORY OF CROWS

ahead at first, as though considering where Matthew was headed, but then, in a jerky motion, looked at him. Its eyes seemed almost human, with deep-brown irises and knowing black pupils. It tilted its head, and Matthew found he was tilting his head in response, almost as if they were communicating. But when it shuffled its talons around on the hood of the car, and he worried that it might scratch the paint, he laid on the horn, and it took off into the sky.

Matthew leaned forward and craned his neck to watch it fly off, and when the crow was out of sight, he put his car in gear and continued on his way to work. He was on the back road now, and there was even less to see than on the highway. The same development remained on his left, as though inescapable; this road, too, disappeared into the horizon; and on the right, a snow-covered farmer's field was sparkling under the generous light of the rising sun. A sun dog had climbed above a row of trees east of the farmer's field. Crescents of refracted light created by ice particles in the atmosphere hugged the sun on either side, perfectly symmetrical. It was an easily explainable weather phenomenon, more common than a rainbow.

Holly was confident her father was as worried as he'd been frustrated over breakfast. She checked the time on her cellphone: 8:17 a.m. He'd still be driving to work. He'd be thinking of her. After last night, Holly had told her mother that she had no interest in talking to her father, in him talking to her, for the foreseeable future. It shouldn't be him who had the right to decide when to pay attention to her and when to ignore her. To crouch beside her in the basement bathroom while she puked her guts out, holding her hair out of her face so she wouldn't get vomit all over it, but a day before that, to stay home texting some bitch home-wrecker rather than come to her water polo game. She'd brought up finding the messages, too, but her mother stopped short of discussing it with her.

"But it's all related, Mom," Holly had said. "It's got to be."

"I don't know," her mother had said, sounding completely worn out. Shattered. She'd tried to hide it but couldn't. "Maybe."

The walk to school was quiet and cold. When Holly breathed in, the air burned her nostrils. When she opened her eyes for too long, it made them tear. She had to wipe the tears with the sleeve of her jacket to clear her vision, and before they froze, binding her eyelashes together as though they'd been Krazy Glued. She walked while being serenaded by the crunch of her boots against packed-down snow, the hypnotic sound interrupted only by passing cars from the nearby through street.

Holly noticed that she was gripping her phone in her jacket pocket hard, as though she were trying to keep it warm in the cold. She realized that she had been holding it tight the entire walk, and wondered why. The answer, after reflection, was obvious: her cellphone was on vibrate, and despite what she'd asked of her father, through her mother, she expected the phone to shudder in the cold and for a message to come through. The closer she got to school, the harder she gripped her phone, as though she could will it to movement.

She entered a large field that housed two soccer fields, a baseball diamond, and two hockey rinks, and continued through the deep snow on her way to school. The crunching sound grew louder; her phone remained silent. Ahead of her lay a blanket of untouched snow, and the clear sky above allowed the sun to strike it unimpeded. The path was beautiful and blinding. Her eyes began to tear again, but from the brightness. Soon, upon entering the school, Holly would hardly be able to see anything, and it would take several minutes for her vision to correct itself.

When she was a child, her father had made her a pinhole projector so that she could view a solar eclipse. He'd warned her that if she tried to look at the sun without it, she would damage her eyes. When he wasn't looking, she'd lowered the box and looked at the sun with her naked eyes, because it was just that beautiful and it seemed a shame to witness it through something that made it less brilliant.

Nothing that brilliant should be made to be anything less than it was.

Her father had caught her staring up at the sky, the box at her side, and covered her eyes with his hand. She remembered the feeling of his skin against hers, warm and calming. She remembered that he smelled like coffee grounds and new-car scent. She remembered that it took a long while before her vision corrected itself.

It's odd how easy it is to write these letters when I couldn't even send you a one-word text the day I almost drove off the road. I tried to send that text all day, my thumb hovering over the send button but unable to press down on it, like there was an invisible barrier. It makes me wonder what I'm going to do with these letters, if I'll have the courage to give them to you. Not sure if courage is the right word. Not sure if it's the right thing to do. It feels like dumping all my shit off on you, to make myself feel better. At least, sometimes it feels like that, anyway, rather than explaining to you why I've been the way I've been. Or maybe it's both, and that's okay. Or maybe it would be better if I just started acting like the dad you deserve to have. Do you need an explanation? Do you want one? Did you need an apology? Because I am. I am sorry.

I dated this girl in grade eleven, when I was around your age. We only went out for a week, but it felt like a month—as a kid you measure relationships in dog years. During that week, I never hung out with her outside of school, and not really while we were in school, for that matter. Being her boyfriend was like being part of the monarchy—a largely meaningless title. She liked that I was on the basketball team, and that I had blue stitches above my eye from an errant elbow. I guess it made me look tough.

I spoke to her once over the phone. She'd asked me to call her when we passed each other on our way to separate classes. I freaked out all day about having to call her. We didn't know each other, we'd never really talked to each other, and I had no clue what I was going to say to her. At school, there are enough distractions to be comfortable in the silence of a young relationship. A friend passes by. A fight breaks out. The bell rings to start class. Over the phone, silence is all-encompassing. Silence is a black hole.

During English class, I scripted out the phone call. I wrote everything I was going to say, made a list of her potential responses, and follow-up talking points based on each response. It looked like a family tree that went generations back in time, or a murder board. I was a pretty good writer in school—English language arts was my best subject—but that night I found out I was a terrible actor. When I got older, I told myself that it hadn't been as bad as I thought it was at the time, but it was so fucking bad. The next day, her friend told my friend that she wanted to break up with me, and I spent the lunch hour drinking beer in a park down the street. I played basketball drunk after school, and to this day I can't believe my coach didn't smell it on me. Then again, maybe he did and just didn't want to kick me off the team.

Regret covers everything. It's thick like fog. It's hard to see through. Your grandfather says that he doesn't regret anything because you can't change what happened. I don't know if I believe him. I think we all wish that we could go back and do at least one thing over again. I wish I would've sent you that text, Hallelujah. I wish I would've sent you that text even though you had told me not to talk to you. Because I was a coward and you deserve better. Because I wouldn't have done what I did next. Because I wouldn't be blaming myself for something that may have happened anyway. I think it's my penance. How fucked up is that? We can drown in regret.

7

Matthew parked at the back corner of the parking lot at work, by a broken fence that no longer served a purpose and a patch of trees with naked branches that reached into the sky like cracks spidering across glass. A snow-packed pathway led through the broken fence to another, larger parking lot for several manufac- turing businesses, where a broken-down truck with a red roof had been sitting for as long as he could remember. In the summer, people without homes squatted in the abandoned vehicle.

Matthew exited his car and uncoiled the extension cord he'd wrapped around the driver side mirror, then brought it with him to the front of the car. He plugged one end to the block heater, and while struggling mightily to plug the other end into the electrical outlet, his unprotected hands quickly freezing in the cold, he noticed something that he'd not seen before, which was strange considering how many lunch hours he'd spent in his car overlooking this exact spot.

A cross was propped up against a bush that resembled a tumbleweed. It had, intentionally or incidentally, been formed out of wood from a broken pallet that lay nearby. It could very well have been fortuitous—pallets, after all, were made of planks of wood facing this way and that, and two pieces could easily have shifted to form the shape they were in now, the wind blowing it to where it had settled, right in front of Matthew's car—but even still, considering what he'd been going through, the coincidence seemed a little too precise to be dismissed. Claire had read the texts on his phone, Hallelujah wanted so little to do with him that she was refusing to speak to him, and in his pocket, still typed out but not sent, was the word *Sorry*. He'd written the text for Hallelujah but wondered if he shouldn't be sending the same message to Claire. Wasn't Christianity founded on the hope of forgiveness? His father, an ordained minister, certainly thought so.

"Fucking hell," Matthew whispered, blowing into his hands, which by now had little feeling to them. He looked skyward to the heavens. "That's a little obvious, don't you think?"

He crouched down and engaged in a staring contest with the cross. He had a mind to break the symbol, to pick it up and snap it in half over his knee. He reached forward and put his hands on the wood, on either side of the cross, deciding what to do with it. He lifted it off the ground and held it there, in front of his face, until his shoulders grew tired. Then he placed it back where he had found it and turned away to head into work, sucking on his finger after discovering a splinter that had embedded itself in his skin.

"You haven't been texting me back."

Matthew almost fell backwards into the wooden cross, but stayed on his feet. He put his hand over his heart, which had jumped from being startled. Jesse had managed to approach him, unseen and unheard. He took a deep breath, put the hand that had been over his chest into his pocket, and, for the first time

65

since nearly driving through the guardrail, locked his phone, as though there was something secretive about a text to his daughter, about apologizing to her for everything he had done.

For this. For Jesse.

All he could think of was that one word.

"Sorry," he said.

Jesse put a hand on his arm. She rubbed it softly.

"You don't have to apologize," she said. "I'm sorry for sneaking up on you like that."

"Yeah, I—"

"I thought you'd lost—" She chuckled. "Sorry, go ahead. I interrupted you."

"I didn't lose anything." He looked at the cross, then at Jesse. "I just saw something interesting, I guess." Why did he always feel nervous around her, like a boy about to ask a girl to slow dance in a school gym? "Coincidentally interesting," he added. He glanced at the cross once more. "A sign."

He raised his eyebrows sarcastically, trying to brush off the real significance he'd found in the wood planks.

"Found art," Jesse announced, her breath hanging in the air like cigarette smoke.

"Something like that," Matthew said.

He broke eye contact with her, looking away until she touched the side of his chin with two chilly fingers, compelling him to meet eyes with her, and to stay like that. She kept her fingers against his chin. He felt her fingertips warm against his skin, until he took her hand and moved it away.

"What's wrong?" she said.

Most of their colleagues thought something was going on between them. They took coffee breaks together, sometimes sitting next to each other in the lunchroom, sometimes driving to get coffee that didn't taste burnt. They'd come back late because they'd park somewhere to talk, actually talk, but Matthew knew, and so did Jesse, that people thought they'd been fucking. They'd go for walks through the nearby park and sit on a metal bench by the duck pond until their asses were frozen. It had never gotten that far. It had never gone further than texting. But for Claire, that was far enough.

"Everything," he said, and felt a tear pool at the corner of his eye. Did she see it? He could feel it freeze as it dropped; it didn't make it more than halfway down his cheek.

He looked up. It had started to snow. A million snowflakes covering the sky like stars. He thought of stars and their constellations. He thought of his father, because his father was inexorably tied to the stories Matthew knew of the constellations. Whenever Matthew looked up at the stars, he heard his father's voice, felt his father with him. The same was true when he and Claire and Hallelujah used to go camping, when they used to do things with one another as a family. Staying in the wilderness, setting up a tent by a river, listening to the water rush by at night, made him think of his father, because while they stayed on the land for a few days, his father spent the first ten years of his life in the bush. Out in the forest, far from the city lights, stars were crisp and bright and countless, like a detonated glitter bomb. Matthew then began to see constellations in the snow, as though he were standing in a clearing in the bush, not in the middle of a parking lot. He saw Matootisan, the Sweat Lodge, a constellation that explained how the sweat lodge ceremony came to be. He heard the story roll off his father's tongue like poetry. Seven uncles' spirits were captured by Mistapew, a giant, and placed into seven grandfather rocks.

The uncles' nephew released their spirits by heating the rocks, bringing them into a domed structure, and splashing water over them. Matthew thought of Mistapew. It was a Cree word. The word in Anishinaabemowin was *sabe* and was associated with honesty, one of the seven sacred laws. He thought of honesty. He saw his phone on the nightstand by Claire's side of the bed. The last text he'd sent Jesse was a GIF pulled from a *Big Hero* 6 scene, of Baymax hugging Hiro. Matthew had typed, *I could be your Hiro baby*, underneath the image. He pictured Claire seeing that GIF.

Matthew looked away from the sky, at Jesse, and his heart began to jackhammer. His pulse was fast and heavy, as though a switch had been flicked. He was struggling for each breath. It felt as though he'd just finished running a marathon.

"Matt?" Jesse said. "Are you okay?"

She put her hand on his arm again. He turned away from it, away from her.

"I . . . I don't know, I . . ."

Matthew knew what was happening; it had happened several times before. It didn't make the panic attack any less terrifying in the moment. He couldn't remember it being this bad, but he knew that he wasn't going to die.

"I need you to go," he said. "Please."

"But why? What happened? Did I do something?"

"We did something," he said. "We've been doing something, and we can't . . . I can't anymore . . . Please."

Matthew's teeth were chattering, his fingers were trembling. Jesse had come unseen and unheard, but the sound of her footsteps leaving was clear, heading toward their office from the side of his car. When he heard the door of the building open, then close, he fell on his knees, in front of the car, facing the cross that had been made, intentionally or otherwise, out of a wooden pallet. He reached forward and placed his hand on the surface of the cross as though it might steady him, as though it might keep him from floating away and disappearing completely. With his other hand, he unlocked his cellphone and dialed his parents' number. His father answered.

"Tansi, my boy," he said.

"Dad," Matthew said. "It's happening again, and I don't know what to do."

"Yes, you do," his father said. "You've done it before."

He imagined his father's hand on his stomach, watching it rise and fall, how his careful touch brought calm. But he couldn't feel it; there was only panic.

"No, I haven't. Not without you." Matthew's heart was racing, and even in the cold, his face was flushed. Sweat formed and instantly froze. He was crying. His eyelids iced together. "What if I need you?"

"If you need me," his father said, "you know I'll be here."

Matthew hung up with a frozen, rigid thumb, took one last look at the cross, at the rotten boards, and retreated into his car rather than the office. He turned the ignition and, with the engine having been started recently, warm air shot through the vents.

You've done it before.

"Okay," he said in response to the remembered words. "All right."

He plugged his phone into the auxiliary cable, swiped away from his text messages, from the unsent text to Hallelujah, and turned on a playlist. It was funny. He and Holly listened to the same music by the same bands. They shared that. How could you share something like that and still be so far away from each other?

69

Nick Cave and the Bad Seeds started to play. Matthew turned the volume up to fifteen, reclined the driver seat, and stared at the car's headliner. He focused on a stain from water damage. He didn't know when it got there. A song ended, and another began. Matthew Good. "Everything Is Automatic." He slipped a pill onto his tongue. It dissolved into nothing. Nothing changed.

He dialed his parents' number again.

"Dad," Matthew said. "I'm sorry. I can't do this alone."

I'm sorry. They were so easy to say, those two words. Why were they so easy to say?

"You know that I'm here."

"Feel like an early lunch?"

8

When Holly entered the school after walking across what amounted to a field of diamonds, it was like she'd gone from life to death. Outside, the sky was a pure, effervescent blue, and gazing up at it, she felt as if she were hovering above the water at Clear Lake. Not one cloud in the sky. Not one ripple. Only the sun and, if you were to look hard enough at the horizon, the translucent setting moon, hovering above a line of houses to the west. There were tears frozen against her cheeks that she noticed upon stepping on the rubber floor mats inside the back doors of the building. She thawed them by pressing her fingers flat against her skin, and waited for her eyes to adjust in the process.

Inside, throngs of students hurried to their lockers like cars in rush hour. The metal doors of lockers urgently opened and shut. The crowd buzzed like worker bees. The floor tiles had once been gleaming white, but had long been sullied by countless thousands of sneakers. The walls were a muted brown; Holly had once remarked to Charmaine that it was as though they'd been painted with liquified shit. And above it all was a perfectly aligned row of fluorescent lighting that stretched all the way from the back door to the front, the bulbs protected by thick metal wires, because over the years, students had made a habit of breaking the lights, desperate for release from their dull, mind-numbing glow.

"They're not that bad," Charmaine had said to Holly once.

"They're not that bad," Holly had repeated, imitating Charmaine's tone, then took a slow-motion video of the hallway, of nothing specific, and replayed it so that Charmaine could see the strobe-light flicker.

"Fuuuuuuuck," Charmaine had said in a profanity-laced sigh. "They're that bad."

"They're that bad," Holly had said.

Or kids just liked breaking stuff.

As she navigated her way through the hoard of teenagers, she thought about how she'd much rather be standing in the middle of the field under the sun, blinding herself. However, her parents had surprisingly promised that if she maintained an A average (which she had) and perfect attendance (which, so far, she had as well), at the end of grade ten, they would buy her a car. The caveat seemed to be that they'd not specified what type of vehicle—she may very well be driving to her first day of grade eleven in a K-car, for all she knew—but she reasoned that a car was a car, and having your own in the eleventh grade was inarguably as cool as it was convenient, for both her and her parents. No more bus rides to the swimming pool for water polo practice, which meant there'd be no threat of falling asleep and freaking her father out. Though she'd liked his reaction, it wasn't enough for her not to feel excitement at the prospect of avoiding the bus, which was often littered with fast-food containers, empty cigarette packages, obscene graffiti, and the faint aroma of piss. And from time to time, there were creepy old men that she knew were checking her out, mentally undressing her. So, rather than turn around and head back outside, she forged ahead, toward her locker.

Christian was there before her. It looked as if he'd been waiting there all night, since they'd been caught on the couch by her dad, as though when she heard his car drive away, he'd come straight here and camped out on the floor near her locker. There were bags under his eyes, and his hair was tousled in the best possible way, like Christian Slater *circa* 1989, like all they had to do now was find a couple of mean girls named Heather.

He'd been leaning against her locker, one foot propped up, hands in his pockets, eyes searching, and when he saw her, he came to attention. She greeted him with a smile and a shove, moving him out of the way so she could get into her locker. He placed his hand on the small of her back, underneath her jacket, which sent a shiver up her spine that radiated across her body. She sorted out what she needed for first period, before stuffing her backpack into the cramped, modestly decorated space. A mirror no bigger than a credit card. A bottle opener fridge magnet that her uncle had brought her from Mexico.

"She doesn't drink, Joel."

"It's for Pic-a-Pop bottles, Matty."

"They twist off."

"You're no fucking fun."

Joel had slipped it to her when her father wasn't looking. Now it held up a faded printout of Bon Iver's self-titled LP cover.

Holly closed her locker, secured her textbook and binder between her right hand and hip, and moved to slide Christian's hand from her back and take it in her own. They'd not travelled more than a few steps when he stopped suddenly and directed her toward the side of the hallway, against a set of unoccupied

73

lockers. He put his hands against her cheeks and kissed her. It gave her flashbacks of last night. Seeing her father at the bottom of the stairs. Putting on her shirt as he turned on the lights. She pulled away and clutched her books against her chest as though they were armour.

"What's wrong?" Christian asked.

"Nothing," Holly said.

"Nothing?" Christian said. "Sure, buddy."

"Okay, everything," Holly said. "Is that better? Everything is wrong."

"Is this about last night?"

"Of course it's about last night, Chris. Do you think anything else significant has happened in my life over the last few hours?"

"Jesus, I'm sorry."

Holly had her back against the lockers, and Christian had his back to the thinning crowd.

"I don't know," Holly said. "Maybe it's more than that. I don't know."

"Is it about me? You're not going to dump me, are you? I'm sorry about the rum the other night. I should've let you drink the whole goddamn bottle. I just didn't want you to."

He moved his hand toward her cheek as though intending to stroke it with the back of his fingers, but she recoiled.

"Does every single guy think everything is about them?" Holly pushed Christian away with her books, then walked past him, toward her class. She'd not gotten far when she felt his hand on her shoulder. She spun around and threw daggers at him with her eyes. "You're all fucking narcissistic pricks, you know that?"

"What the fuck, Hall? You're projecting!"

"What are you, my shrink?"

"Just because your dad's an asshole doesn't mean I'm an asshole, too."

"And yet there you were, monitoring my alcohol consumption."

"So, this *is* about me."

"Are you listening to a word I'm saying?"

Holly felt her eyes fill with tears. Her heart was hammering against her ribs. She felt flushed and was sweating profusely. Her grandfather once told her that tears were pain leaving your body. In science class, she'd learned that tears and sweat both have sodium chloride, which is why they taste salty. They were the same thing. Pain was dripping from every pore, from every tear duct, and she couldn't stop it. She wanted it to stop. How much had she held inside, and for how long?

"I don't feel good," she said. "I don't feel good. Something's not right. Why the fuck is this happening?"

"What's going on?" Christian said. "What should I do? Should I call somebody?"

"My dad's not an asshole!" She could hardly speak through the rising panic. "He's fucked up, just like me. When you put two people together who are both fucked up, shit's going to get even more fucked up. It's fucking math."

"Okay, I—"

"Do you know why I drank all that rum?"

The colour had drained from Christian's face, and he looked like he was in shock, as though he'd been told that a close relative had died. He just shook his head.

"So that my dad would have to come pick me up, so that he'd . . ." She took a deep breath. She pinched the bridge of her

75

nose with her thumb and index finger, then spread them out, running her shaky fingertips along the skin below her eyes, wiping tears away. ". . . pay attention to me. And then he did and I fucking . . . what? The very next night, I slam a door in his face."

Christian sighed. "So it's not about me."

"Oh my god! I am crawling out of my skin!" Holly rushed past Christian again, and when he tried to grab her arm to hold her up, she slapped it away. "Get the fuck away from me!"

"Holly," Christian pleaded, and reached for her again.

"Get. The fuck. Away!"

The bell rang for first period, but there were still students in the hallway. It should've been frantic, like there was a bomb scare and kids were rushing for the exits. It should've been loud. The shrill screech of sneakers, rubber against tile. The drone of pubescent angst, desperate not to be late and trigger an email to their parents notifying them of their child's tardiness. The swoosh of fabric, pant legs, and rubbing shoulders, like rustling leaves. But it was as though the world had been put on pause. Everybody in the hallway had stopped and was staring at her, including Christian. Christian worse than anybody else. He looked confused and horrified. Holly couldn't stand one more second of this sort of attention, and so she ran into the girls' bathroom and hid in the farthest bathroom stall, where there was a hazy beam of morning light above her head from a privacy window near the ceiling. As she caught her breath, she lifted up her hand and watched dust swirl around her fingers, as though dancing in the strange light.

At a certain time after the bell rang, halfway into first period, Holly realized that her mother would have received an automated notification from her teacher that she'd not shown up for class.

Dear Parents/Guardians,

Your student, Hallelujah McIvor, was marked absent January 15, 8:52 AM.

If you are AWARE of this absence, please provide the reason immediately by contacting the school.

Thank you.

Holly's parents had not received that notification previously—all her absences had been planned due to water polo—but Charmaine's had several times, and on occasion, she had shown Holly the message as though it were a badge of honour, and so Holly had memorized the verbiage.

She stifled laughter while repeating, "If you are AWARE of this absence,'" punching the word *aware* with a sarcastic tone.

"'AWARE,'" she repeated.

She lowered her hand and reached into her right jeans pocket. Her fingers were still quivering. She knew that this was because of the panic attack she'd had, that she was, in all likelihood, still having. She knew because she'd had one last night, and she'd seen her father have them, too.

This, at least, they had in common.

This, at least, made her feel more connected to him, in some fucked-up way.

So, too, did the medication she pulled out of her pocket, which she'd stolen from her father and stored in one of those cylindrical plastic travel containers for Tylenol.

She opened the lid and tapped the edge of the container against her palm until one pill tumbled out, settling in the middle of her palm. Anti-anxiety medication. A small, white, oval tablet, with a line down its middle for half-dosages, that she knew would calm her within minutes, as though it were made up of all the dust travelling along the beam of light overhead.

"They're aware now," she said, and then raised her palm to her mouth, tilted her head back, and let the pill roll onto her tongue.

She sat there and stared at the white-tiled wall, reading graffiti, line by line, while the pill dissolved, returning to the dust from which it had been made.

Some of the lines were gross: *When did I eat corn?* One was of a ghost with a speech bubble that read, *Have a good pee! Don't be afraid to poo, if it's natural to you. Boo!* Another read, *Don't beam me up, yet, Scotty. I'm taking a shit!* Neatly written with black Sharpie on one single tile was *This I hate:* 1. *Vandalism.* 2. *Lists.* 3. *Irony.* 4. *Lists.* 5. *Repetition.* 7. *Inconsistency.*

By the time the medication had kicked in, it was too late to go to class. Holly didn't want to be a spectacle, to have a classroom full of eyes on her, and in her estimation, the damage had been done anyway. If she was going to be late, she may as well be really late.

Thankfully, if Christian had been waiting for her outside the girls' bathroom as he had been waiting for her at her locker, he'd long since given up and gone to class. The hallways were empty, the school deathly quiet. It was as though every student, every teacher, had been plucked from existence, like the rapture had come and they were, at that moment, all floating to the heavens to meet Jesus in the cold winter air.

And then there was the agnostic Hallelujah.

Alone.

It was enough to make a girl a believer.

But that wouldn't do. Holly didn't like the thought of being on her own. She may even have freaked out if it wasn't for the anxiety medication, which had prevented whatever was in her brain from affecting her body. The pills worked like that. She'd overheard her father talk about the meds with her mother, when he'd first filled the prescription. The doctor had told him that they didn't stop him from thinking the way he did, but they might stop how his thoughts made him feel.

"And I was like," her father had said, while Holly pressed her ear against her parents' bedroom door, "don't you have anything that can just stop me from thinking that way?"

"There's no pill that can do that," her mother had said.

"Yeah, that's what he said. He said, 'You can't magically change the way you think.'"

"That's what psychiatrists are for."

"I told him I wasn't going to see a shrink."

"It might help."

"I'd rather take this whole bottle and see if these little white fucking tablets might fill me up."

"You really feel empty like that?"

He didn't answer her. Holly had stayed at the bedroom door for a few minutes, listening to silence, waiting for them to say more to each other, until she heard footsteps coming toward her and hurried away. The next night, after her father had fallen asleep on the couch in the living room, she sneaked into his bathroom, rummaged through her parents' medicine cabinet, and took a couple of pills in case there came a day when she felt the need to have one.

Today was that day.

Of course, she knew that the teachers and students hadn't literally been sucked up into the sky, but regardless, she felt an impulse to get out of the building, as though it might get taken, too, and her with it. She couldn't die in the middle of giving her father the silent treatment, as much as he deserved it. Christian was right; he was an asshole. At least, he had been an asshole for what seemed an unreasonable period of time. But he hadn't always been, even recently. He'd come to get her at Charmaine's, and had held her hair while she got sick. He'd come to the basement when he'd heard a boy. Misguided attention, but attention.

It was an odd thing to have all these thoughts racing through her mind and for her to feel nothing from them. It was an odd thing to have the thoughts she was having in the first place, as though the medication had caused the anxiety that her body needed protection from. It was an odd thing to be numb in this way.

Holly had left her textbook and binder on the floor of the farthest bathroom stall, under a line of graffiti that read, *Your smile could save somebody's life.* Just think, one gesture could do something like that.

It was the medication talking.

There wasn't a thought given to her locker, or of putting on her jacket, which was stuffed on top of her backpack. She made a beeline for the back door. Once there, she pushed it open, and a rush of winter air struck her. She stepped outside, and chills coursed over her body. Her teeth were chattering; her fingers were trembling. She ran until she came to the middle of a soccer field, and there she collapsed to her knees and took out her cellphone.

She dialed her father's number, but it went to voice mail.

There was the agnostic Hallelujah—alone in the middle of the soccer field on the coldest day of winter, the moon having now dipped below the houses to the west, the sun having now risen higher but offering no more warmth—sure that she'd just received a sign, and so she didn't bother dialing her father's number again. She knelt there for as long as she could tolerate before returning to school.

The bell had rung for second period, and the halls were full of students rushing from one class to another like dust particles swirling under the strange, dim light.

I know you remember the lake. We didn't stop going all that long ago. When you turned thirteen, you told me and your mother that you'd grown out of it. I understood. Your mother did, too, even though she was upset. Your mother likes bringing family together. We went on that road trip instead. One of these days, maybe you'll want to go back again. If you've inherited some stuff from me, I think you will. When I was thirteen, I was over the lake, too. I wanted to spend the summer with my friends, not my parents. So we stopped going for a few years, and I fucked around over the summers. Spent time with the handful of friends I had. Got a job at the community centre's canteen. But when I was in my early twenties, I missed the lake.

When I started going up with your grandparents again, I had this whole new appreciation for it. I brought your mother up after we'd been dating for a few months. That's when we got to know each other. Really got to know each other. We used to sit by the fire at night, eat a bag of chips, drink, and talk. We'd talk until we ran out of firewood and the fire went out, and it was the kind of dark you can only find at the lake. I think she married me because of the lake.

We used to rent an old place a bit of a ways out of town, one of a few cottages built within a wooded area. The ground was always covered in old pine needles and roots. There were so many roots they looked like snakes, like we were staying near a snake den or something. Somewhere off near the main road, which you couldn't see from where we were, was a pool. You could hear it, though. You could hear kids playing. Their laughter would drift to us like fresh air off the lake. It would be the only thing that made you realize that you weren't out in the wilderness somewhere, away from the world.

The cabin was a faded pink colour, and there was a firepit outside and a little sandbox that seemed out of place, but that you liked to play in. One day, we were playing in the sandbox together. You were building castles, and I was helping you wet the sand just enough that when you put it into those plastic moulds, when you tipped it over, the shapes would stay together. Sometimes you'd get me to tap the top of the moulds so the sand would come out perfect. You liked stomping all over the castles when you were done, even though you'd spent so much time putting your kingdom together. We were about halfway done making castles when we both heard a huff and looked up to see a black bear walking toward us. It was still a safe distance away, but it had gotten pretty close before we'd heard it. I picked you up and rushed you into the house.

Your grandfather was reading a book in the living room when we got inside. I put you in your bedroom with a board book and closed the door, trying to get as many barriers between you and the bear as I could, just in case it decided that it wanted to come inside. I whispered to your grandfather that there was a bear outside, all while keeping an eye on it through the window. It kept coming toward the cottage. By then it was walking around the sandbox, like it didn't want to ruin your castles. I must've sounded panicked even though I'd whispered. I must've looked panicked.

"It's okay, son," your grandfather said.

He put his book on the coffee table, calm as can be. There wasn't an ounce of worry in his voice. And it wasn't like he was acting cool for me. The fact that there was a bear right outside our cottage didn't bother him one bit. To him, it was like there was another cottager walking by on the way from the pool.

"Did you hear me?" I said. "There's a bear. Outside. Like, right outside the cabin."

It was sniffing at the ground between the sandbox and the cottage and looked like it was going to make itself comfortable. I picked up the phone and started to dial the owners, so they could get park rangers down there, but your grandfather put his hand on my arm and shook his head.

"The bear is our relative," your grandfather said.

"The bear is our what?"

Your grandfather repeated himself, and then he got up and walked out the front door.

"What are you doing?" I said.

He didn't answer me, and I wasn't going to follow him outside. I thought, Well, it was nice having a dad. I was sure that he was about to get mauled. I dialed the owners anyway, despite what he'd told me. I figured that if they got the park rangers down there fast enough, they might get there in time to save your grandfather. The phone rang while I watched him walk deliberately toward the bear, his arms at his sides. The owners weren't picking up. They didn't always. Sometimes they were at the pool. Sometimes they were cleaning a house after people had left.

Your grandfather stopped a few feet away from the bear. The bear stopped sniffing the ground and looked up at your grandfather. He started talking to it. I couldn't hear what he was saying, but it looked to me like the bear was listening to him. One time, the bear even nodded. I swear to god, that bear nodded.

"Hello? Hello?"

The owners had picked up, but I didn't care about them anymore. I was enraptured by what was happening outside. I hung up the phone and went to the window and just . . . watched. Your grandfather and the bear were having a conversation. It lasted for a minute or so. Then the bear grunted and went on its way, back into the forest. Your grandfather watched the bear until it was out of sight, and then he came back inside.

"Dad, what the fuck just happened?"

I think that was one of the only times I swore around your grandfather.

"I told him that you were nervous and he should probably leave, if he didn't mind," your grandfather said.

"If he didn't mind," I repeated.

"Yeah," your grandfather said. "If he didn't mind."

Your grandfather sat down, picked up his book, found his place, and started reading again, like nothing particularly amazing had happened. I stood there for a long time, glancing from him to the spot outside where he'd carried on a conversation with that bear, and back to him.

"That's the problem," your grandfather said after a while, without looking away from his book. "You don't believe in things like that."

I brought you out of the bedroom after that, when everything was safe. You ran to each window, looking for the bear. When you'd been to the last window, you looked back at me quizzically; it was your way of asking where it had gone. I looked at your grandfather for some help because I didn't know what to say.

He shrugged and said, "Tell her the truth." So that's what I did. I told you exactly what had happened.

You couldn't talk much back then, being just a little girl, but your face said a lot. Your face said more than any word. After I'd recounted the whole story to you, you tilted your head to the side like it'd been weighted more on one side than the other. Your brow furrowed and your eyebrows kind of collapsed together. Then you shook your head.

"Bears can't talk, Daddy."

"Not most bears, no," I said. "But that bear we just saw, that one wasn't most bears."

"Can I talk to it?"

"Oh, honey, I think we best leave the bear-talking to Moshom."

You asked me about that bear all day. You asked me about that bear when I was tucking you into bed that night. When me and your mother and your grandfather were trying to play cribbage later on, you were still awake, asking about that bear from the other room.

I went in and sat beside your bed. I looked around really carefully, like I was making sure nobody was around, that nobody was listening, that whatever I was about to say was our little secret.

I leaned toward you and whispered into your ear, "I talked to the bear and he said that you should go to sleep."

You went to sleep right after that. It was kind of like a boogeyman story, or the northern lights coming down to get you if you whistled at them. It was a cautionary tale. That's how I got you to go to sleep for a long while, but when you got a bit older, it didn't make you sleep anymore. You knew I'd been lying to you. You knew I'd been lying about the whole thing. But the thing was, that's the only thing I was lying to you about.

Everything else was the truth.

9

Matthew's parents lived close to the office, less than a ten-minute drive. It seemed to take longer than that, though Matthew rushed. In fact, he'd left work so frantically that he'd forgotten to unplug his car. When he finally arrived at his parents' house, he saw the extension cord, which was normally wrapped around his driver side mirror, on the ground, extending the length of his car so that the plug trailed underneath the rear bumper. He realized then why people had been honking at him. He'd been wondering how he could have pissed off so many drivers on the short trip and had driven more self-consciously with each passing moment. It had made him feel far more nervous than he'd felt this morning, when he'd almost driven off the highway. Of course, there was the whole matter of his panic attack, which hadn't improved. He wanted desperately to see his father.

At least he was here now, and the sight of the house he'd grown up in had a calming effect. It wasn't only his father waiting for him inside, but also memories of better times.

The snow was drifting over the front yard in waves. He used to play soccer there with his next-door neighbour. He'd guard a makeshift net on the side of the yard closest to the other next-door neighbour, an old lady named Dorothy. Her skin had been textured like a raisin. She yelled at him whenever she caught him on her property, like when he let in a goal and had to retrieve the soccer ball. It wasn't like he was ruining the grass; she just hated Matthew. He never knew why until one day when the soccer ball rolled to her feet. Instead of kicking it back to him, Dorothy crouched down, her knees cracking on the way, and made him come take the ball from her hands. When his hands were around the ball, she hissed at him, as though she were a snake, "Take your ball and bring it back to your teepee, you little savage."

When Matthew turned nine, Dorothy had a stroke and moved to a nursing home, and their soccer games were much more fun after that.

On the first step of three that led up to the door, underneath a layer of packed-down snow, Matthew's initials were carved into the concrete beside a clumsily drawn heart. He'd gotten in trouble when his father saw it, because he'd spent "an arm and a leg" to pay for the new front steps. But, over time, the initials, and even the heart, had become an important relic of Matthew's childhood, like the measurements of his height on the kitchen door frame, taken every year from when he was one until the day he'd moved out with Claire. If his parents ever moved out of the house, which seemed unlikely at this point, he was certain they'd take that side of the door frame with them. Sometimes he wondered if they'd find a way to take that section of concrete as well. They were sentimental like that, about the vestiges of youth. His mother still wore her mother's gold necklace every day, which had a Victorian locket that held faded pictures of her parents within it. His father still had *his* father's cane, which he didn't even need to use; he just kept it propped up against the wall in his study. His father, Matthew's grandfather, had carved an intricate bear's head at the top of it.

The front door was blood red; it helped to distinguish the house from the cookie-cutter bungalows that lined the street, until the houses became two-storeys about halfway down toward the older section of the neighbourhood, as though they'd grown with age. Having a blood-red door was tradition on his mother's side of the family. The house she'd grown up in had had a blood-red door, and the first house she'd moved into with Matthew's father had incidentally had a blood-red door, which his mother had taken as a sign to buy the house even though it was far too small to raise a family in. His father had described it as a walk-in closet. Matthew had driven by it on a historical tour of his parents' life one day, and saw what his father had been talking about. The house was dwarfed by others on the block, as though it had been built for little people, or Memekwesewak, creatures that his father swore he'd seen as a child on the trapline.

His parents' second house was the one Matthew had grown up in, the one he was walking up to presently. They had painted the door red before doing anything else, before they'd moved one thing inside of it. When Matthew was a toddler, a kid around his age was kidnapped a few blocks over, and Matthew's mother became a block parent. All the parents on their street told their kids that if they were playing outside and saw the big blue van that had been described by police, they should "Run to the red door." The red door meant safety—even Dorothy said so. Before that, she'd not been a fan of it, said that it was an eyesore. Dorothy had been so mad about it that she tried to, as his father described it, "racist it away," so that his parents would paint it another colour.

"That's a good colour for you and your boy," Matthew had heard her say to his father once.

His father didn't acknowledge the comment, just replied, "Your lawn's looking nice today, Dorothy."

His father had told him that Dorothy's lawn was as patchy as her skin.

"Your skin," he'd said to Matthew, "is perfect, and don't let anybody tell you otherwise."

Matthew opened the screen door, raised a trembling hand, and knocked three times. He didn't have to wait long before it swung open, sending a breath of heat across his body. Standing in the entryway, awaiting his arrival, was his father.

"You knew I couldn't make it on my own, right?" Matthew said.

"It's not that." His father shook his head. "Everybody needs somebody sometimes."

Matthew thought back to his youth, the nights where he'd find himself wandering the hallways, wandering the empty rooms, staring out the front window, feeling crushed by infinity, realizing that he was not significant. He thought of how he'd crawl into his parents' bed. His father would be awake. His father would be waiting for him. His father would help him breathe.

"Well, thanks," Matthew said.

His father looked worried, which was disconcerting, because he was usually unflappable. It was in his eyes, which were wider than normal, and his eyebrows, which were slightly cocked.

He had his hands in the pockets of his navy slacks—Matthew had never seen him wear jeans in his entire life. He was wearing bear paw moccasins, a pair he'd owned for decades. They'd been made authentically by his sister, Matthew's auntie. He had a white T-shirt on underneath a light-grey V-neck sweater that matched his salt and pepper hair. His glasses had fallen to the tip of his nose.

Matthew did his best to hide the panic, because it was still present, coursing through his veins like blood. He was inside, in the warmth, but felt shaky. There was a cold sweat across his forehead. His heart was thumping just as hard as it had been in the parking lot at work; he could feel it in his neck and chest.

"So, what's for lunch?" he said, forcing a smile because it was nowhere near lunchtime, but trying to ignore the awful sensations that were taking up space in his body.

He wanted to sit down at the kitchen table with his father, eat whatever he'd make, talk about shit that didn't matter, and then he'd feel better.

But his father wasn't so easily fooled.

"We can eat in a bit," he said.

He guided Matthew over to the couch on the opposite side of the living room, the one he sat in to watch sports, or do his crossword puzzle in the morning. Matthew sat down in the middle of the couch, directly underneath one of the many paintings that decorated the walls of the house, each one of them created by an Indigenous artist. The one Matthew sat under now was of a mother holding a baby in her arms, and both mother and child were reaching toward something that was out of sight, somewhere off in the distance, far from the canvas. You were left to wonder what they were reaching for, the mother and the child. You were left to wonder what they needed that they didn't already have.

Matthew's father sat down beside him and groaned in relief, as if he'd come to rest after a marathon. He didn't ask what was wrong. His father was about to do what he always did, no matter what had worked Matthew up to the point of panic—a kid stealing his toy on the playground, nobody attending a party he'd planned in grade four, the police bringing him home because he'd set fire to a garbage can, his first serious girlfriend cheating on him while she was at an outdoor festival that he'd not been allowed to attend, the principal suspending him from school for three days because he'd had the shit beat of him for no reason other than he was a "dirty savage." Half the school had yelled war cries while Curtis Gill pummelled him like an MMA fighter. Whatever the trigger, the manifested panic felt the same each and every time. Matthew, sitting beside his father, couldn't decide what was better: panic or numbness. The kind of detachment that didn't allow you to care if you almost drove off an overpass onto a set of train tracks.

"Just hold still, son," his father said, reaching toward Matthew's stomach cautiously and quietly, as though there was something there to swat away.

Could anxiety be shooed away?

Matthew did as he was told. He watched his father's hand inch closer toward his stomach in complete silence, and noticed in the process how his chest was rising and falling rapidly, but not so much his stomach. Then his father placed his hand flat against Matthew's abdomen.

"I want you to stop breathing into your chest, and start breathing into your belly," his father said.

These were instructions that Matthew had heard on several occasions, but they always felt new. It could've been because he'd tried to calm himself on his own previously, but had never been successful. It was as though his father had to be part of the process. Having panic attacks at home sucked, infrequent though they were, because his parents lived too far away, and so Matthew would be forced to wait them out. Take a Xanax. Drink a shot or two of whiskey.

Was there really much of a difference between calm and numbness? It was the nomenclature of panic.

Still, Matthew much preferred this. He'd taken a pill, but his father was able to ease him out of panic faster than Xanax, and without giving him a buzz.

Following his father's instructions, Matthew focused on not breathing into his chest, but into his stomach, making his father's hand rise, then fall, as if riding on the crest of a wave, like the snowdrifts covering the front yard. Matthew imagined the snowdrifts moving as he watched his father's hand rise higher with each passing moment, until Matthew noticed that his breathing had evened, the sweat on his forehead had dried up, his hands had stopped trembling, and he could no longer feel his heartbeat. He sighed, then looked from his father's hand to his father. They met eyes. His father had tired eyes; he'd seen Matthew through this many times before.

"That's better, eh?" his father said.

"Is it that obvious?" Matthew said.

"Fight or flight," his father said.

His father had a way of being cryptic and simplistic at once; Matthew always felt the need to decipher what he meant. Fight or flight. Matthew had come into the house feeling like somebody had a gun to his head. You experience a certain brand of terror when a gun is held to your head, not that he'd ever had a gun held to his head, but he *had* almost driven off an overpass onto a set of train tracks and figured that if he had, it would have done as much damage. When the fight or flight response is over, when the threat is gone, naturally you look more at ease. How could you not?

"I don't know how you do that," Matthew said.

His father put his hands on his knees and, with an assist from Matthew, got up from the couch. He looked outside at the snowy waves rolling across the front yard, at snowflakes whipping off the white surface like a dust cloud, at a man trudging down the street, holding his arm over his face to protect himself from the wind and cold.

"We don't really need to eat lunch, you know," Matthew said. "It's not even ten."

"How about brunch, then?" his father asked.

"That either."

"Why don't we have something and take a walk before you have to go back to work?" his father said. "I didn't really have breakfast."

"Neither did I," Matthew said. "But, Dad . . . take a walk?"

He looked outside and wondered if his father had seen a different world than he had. This was possible. He knew that his father had lived out on the land during the winters when he was a child, and as a result, the cold had never been as intimidating to him. He was getting older, he was getting frail, his hair was turning grey at an alarming rate, he was almost at the point where he would need to use the cane with the bear's head, but at the same time, he was a different kind of tough. That old-school "I walked fifty miles to school in the winter, uphill both ways" kind of tough.

What could Matthew say?

His father made his grilled cheese special: two pieces of bread slathered with butter, two slices of cheese, and between the cheese, fried Klik. To Matthew, Klik tasted as though somebody had eaten several hot dogs and then puked them up into a can, but he knew that it was comfort food for his father, so he ate it without complaining. He'd had worse. There were few things that made his father look more content than when he was eating Klik, and it was a rare treat, because Matthew's mother didn't typically allow his father to have it.

"Do you know those old commercials with the egg, where the narrator would say, 'This is your brain,' and then the egg would get cracked and start frying on a pan, and the same narrator would say, 'This is your brain on drugs,' or something like that?" his mother had said one day when she'd come upstairs from sorting the laundry and saw Matthew and his father eating, appropriately, over-easy eggs with a side of Klik that had been fried in butter.

Because Matthew liked to get a rise out of her, he did his best to look as though he were eating his favourite food as he chewed a forkful of Klik, and said, "Actually, isn't it some settler white dude who fries the egg? He takes the egg from the carton, says the thing about the egg being your brain, then points to the pan and says that the pan is drugs. *Then* he cracks the egg and—"

"You get my point," his mother said.

"Anybody watching that commercial who liked fried eggs probably went out and bought an ounce of weed," Matthew said.

His father, usually quite stoic and reserved, almost spat out his food.

"What I'm saying is that this"—his mother pointed to the Klik—"is a visual representation of a heart attack."

"So, you're saying if they'd made a commercial about the dangers of Klik, the egg would've been your heart, the pan would've been Klik, and the fried egg would've been a heart on Klik?"

"Oh, shut up and eat your lunch," his mother said, smiling, before leaving the kitchen.

Matthew chased her down and lifted her off her feet with an enormous bear hug.

On the trapline, his father and his family never ate Klik. They ate what they caught, like fish and muskrat and prairie chicken, or picked berries. The only things they ate that weren't right off the land were sugar, lard, and flour. His father would spend the better part of the year on the trapline, the one he wasn't sure how to get to anymore, and come home for two months in the summer before heading back onto the land. When he was home in the community, Klik was a delicacy to him, but only when fried.

Matthew tore through his sandwich and the side of beans his father had cooked, while his father picked at the food and ate only a few bites. They cleaned up after themselves and then bundled up for the walk. Matthew borrowed an old coat of his father's that was too big for him now, because Matthew's jacket wasn't the kind for walking through a blizzard.

"You can keep it," his father said while Matthew was slipping his arms into the coat.

With their jackets zipped up, their hoods on over thick toques, scarves tied across their faces all the way up to their eyes, and their hands protected with mitts his auntie had made, Matthew and his father stepped out into the cold.

They reached the end of the front walk and turned to head up the sidewalk in the direction closest to an intersection, where Matthew planned to have them turn back, because he knew his father was too old to walk far in weather like this, no matter how tough he was. Almost to prove Matthew's point, his father struggled to find his footing his first couple of steps, as if he were walking on thin ice and had to be careful not to fall through. Matthew's hands were already sweating, which was remarkable given that the weather reminded him of Hoth from *The Empire Strikes Back*. Only a few steps farther and he'd be looking for a tauntaun to cut open and sleep inside. The mitts were made traditionally, like his father's moccasins were, constructed with great skill out of moosehide and rabbit fur. He had gloves from Mountain Equipment Co-op that weren't nearly as warm. It was further testament to his auntie's handiwork that while Matthew had also borrowed a pair of Sorels, not bothered at all that he had to scrunch his toes up so that his feet could fit inside the boots, his father hadn't changed out of his moccasins.

"They're warmer than anything else I could put on my feet," his father had said at the front door before leaving, when he saw Matthew staring at the leather footwear.

After another few feet, his father cleared his throat and spoke. "What's bothering you, my boy?"

Matthew didn't respond right away. His father became unsteady, and Matthew had to put his hand around his father's biceps. He wasn't sure what to say about how he'd been feeling for as long as he could remember. His father and mother had already noticed something was wrong, but they weren't sure why, because Matthew had never been able to articulate it. How could he talk about what an asshole he'd been to Claire? Texting with Jesse from work. Not quite sexting, but definitely flirtatious enough to warrant the crumpled-up tissues on the bed beside Claire. What could he say about how he'd been acting around Holly? The word *Sorry* was still on his phone, unsent. Sorry for what? For pushing her away, like he'd pushed Claire away? How do you articulate something you don't understand? Why had he started texting with Jesse and withdrawn from the people who really mattered?

He gave up trying to make sense of it and said, "I feel like nothing matters. I feel small. We're all so small. We're just on this rock spinning into infinity." He shrugged. "It makes me feel empty. Empty and afraid." His father stopped walking, and so did Matthew. He looked Matthew straight in the eyes with the sort of intensity that only a father could muster, and it made the cold, the wind, the snow, fall away. It was only them. They were all that mattered in the moment.

"How do you feel all of that, and empty?" his father said.

Matthew couldn't think of a response. The admission had surprised him; he'd not intended to say those words. He'd not been aware that he felt that way until he heard himself speak, as though he were outside of his body, watching, and there were two Matthews. Maybe that wasn't far from the truth. He'd always felt detached from reality but, at the same time, trapped within it. He'd learned how to function despite how this had haunted him, to just hold all the confusion and emptiness in when people were watching, then dwell on the questions he had, the unresolvable questions, alone at night. During the day, he pushed those questions down to the pit of his stomach, like a seed planted in the dirt. But over the years, the seed had grown, and whatever it was, it came to its maturation and exploded within his body, and he was no longer able to put on an act for others. For Claire and Holly.

Because of this, he had pushed them away and, instead, pulled somebody else closer. Now his daughter wouldn't talk to him, and if she had a choice, Matthew was positive that Claire wouldn't either. But having a child seemed to mandate some form of communication between parents.

Matthew tried to explain all of this to his father, only stopping short of telling him about Jesse and the troubles he'd caused with his wife. That was a shame he wasn't willing to disclose, even to his father. At some point during Matthew's rambling exposition, they started to walk again, out of necessity more than anything; standing still in the cold invited more of it, and by now, their eyelids were coated like hoarfrost on blades of grass, and even moosehide was having trouble warding off the freezing temperature. The stop sign looked as though it were a mile away, but they carried on, Matthew holding his father tighter with each passing step.

Matthew used his tendency to drink lately, which wasn't a lie, as a proxy for Jesse and his inappropriate text exchanges. He'd dipped into the liquor cabinet more and more in the preceding months and, even without his father's counsel, thought that his drinking and the texting were somehow related. He thought that discussing one issue with his father might help him understand the other and, in so doing, help him understand what the connection was.

"It feels like, all that drinking, maybe . . . I don't know . . ." Five words—*It makes me feel empty*—had come without a thought before, but now his subconscious offered no help.

Luckily, he had his father, who, as part of being an ordained minister, had trained as a counsellor. Finishing Matthew's sentence, his father said, "You're trying to fill that emptiness you've been feeling."

"Yeah," Matthew said. "Yeah, I guess so." He pulled his scarf up so that it covered half his eyes; it had slipped under his mouth. "And it's like I want to stop having to drink in order to feel . . . something. I want to be able to say sorry to Hallelujah, and to Claire, for . . ." He stopped himself from divulging the information he'd withheld from his father. "For being so distant. I feel like I've left them behind in this fucking . . . sorry . . . in whatever this is."

They'd reached the stop sign now, and Matthew's father took

a step forward as if he wanted to keep going, as though the distance between the house and the intersection wasn't enough space for them to have the conversation they needed to have. They had their best conversations while walking, not confined within four walls. But Matthew could tell his father was getting worn out despite his determination, and gently, but firmly, guided him away from the intersection, back toward the house.

"You're worried about the outcome of whatever you're feeling," his father said.

"Of course I am," Matthew said. "Wouldn't you be? If I don't get my life together, aren't you worried about not spending eternity with me?"

"You don't believe in God," his father said.

"Yeah, but you do, and don't you want to hedge your bets? Shouldn't you be wanting me to stop all the crap I'm doing and repent, accept Jesus, even if I don't believe? You're down with Pascal's wager, aren't you?"

His father didn't respond immediately. They kept walking. They passed several houses. They were almost turning back onto the front walk, heading toward the door, when his father said, "I know, as a minister, I'm supposed to say that accepting Jesus is the way to heaven, but I don't think that's true, son. I can't imagine a god that would lock the gates to heaven because you didn't accept Jesus into your life. I think that's cruel."

Matthew helped his father up the first step, then the next two. They stopped at the front door, where they were somewhat shielded by the wind and so the cold wasn't as bad.

"So what? Live a good life, all that?" Matthew said.

"That's simplifying it," his father said. "But if you feel that you need to, that's one thing to work on. Are you living a good life?"

"I . . ." Matthew felt as though he'd breathed in a lungful of cold air.

"I think you're asking the wrong questions of yourself," his father said. "I was telling you that you were focusing on the outcome. Your drinking, for example. That's not how you're going to get through this."

He said this in a way that made Matthew wonder if his father had seen through his lie about drinking, if he knew there was something else he was holding back. He was intuitive like that.

"What do you want me to do, keep drinking?" Matthew said. "Isn't that what I should be trying not to do?"

"Of course I don't want you to keep drinking," his father said. "I've been down that road. I thought it could numb my pain from going to that place up north, that place they called a school. It got so bad that I used to fall asleep beside the road. In the fall, I'd cover myself with leaves to keep warm."

"How did you stop?" Matthew said. "I mean, how did you get out of all the . . . destructive stuff?"

His father shook his head, as though he, who seemed to know everything, didn't know this one thing. But then he shrugged.

"I passed out in a ditch in the middle of winter. I had no business waking up. Probably would've died there. Seen the yellow. When you see the yellow, you're dying. But I looked up at the moon. The stars. I remembered the stories. Not any one in particular, just how stories can heal. And I knew that wasn't who I was as an Indigenous person. From that day, I started walking the Red Road, the road I'd been travelling on as a kid. I'd lost my way, or was led away, but I found my way back."

"The Red Road," Matthew said.

He recalled his father talking about it before. It was the way of Indigenous people across Turtle Island. Their connection to the land, to spirituality, to relatives, to traditions and ceremony.

"But, okay," Matthew said, "so the outcome was drinking for you, but you said not to focus on the outcome."

"That's right." His father looked away, down the street, following the footprints they'd made in the snow as they'd walked to and from the stop sign. "I had to think about where the path started to know where the path was going to take me."

"I feel like you're being purposefully ambiguous," Matthew said.

"Son," his father said, looking back at him, putting his hand around Matthew's arm as if he were the one who needed support. "You said you feel empty. You have to figure out why. That way, you can fill it with good things, not things that are going to harm you." He paused, wiped the frost away from his eyelashes. "And your family."

"How do I figure that out?" Matthew said. "Just be direct with me, Dad. No riddles or Yoda talk. I know you don't want me to find Jesus."

"You need to walk the Red Road," his father said. "You've never believed any of it. You question everything, which is good. You need to think for yourself. But you believe in nothing."

"What's there to believe in?" Matthew said. He wiped tears away as they fell, with the moosehide mittens, before they froze against his skin, froze his eyes shut.

"The land has all the answers," his father said. "When it's summer, we'll go. I haven't been for so long. You can take me before I can't go any longer. We'll find my trapline, and I'll teach you what it was like out there."

"And the crows will welcome us, right?" Matthew said. "You told me that before."

"Whether you believe it or not, make fun of the way I used to live or not, that's where your healing is," his father said. "If you want to get rid of your emptiness, the land will fill it, and it will stay full. That's what got me through all the hard times, and that's what led me back to mino-pimatisiwin."

"The good life," Matthew said.

"Ehe," his father said. "The good life."

"Okay," Matthew said. "I'll take you. We'll find your trapline."

"And when the crows welcome you, you'll remember yourself, I promise," his father said. "They'll carry the old you away, and you'll find something new."

Matthew nodded but was unconvinced. He wasn't sure if he could remember himself. He wasn't sure if he ever knew who he was to begin with.

10

Holly had no intention of going to class when she walked inside from the cold. By then, second period had started, the halls were empty, and this felt appropriately analogous to her own state of being, or maybe it was just that the drug had reached its peak efficacy. Either way, she stayed in the emptiness for as long as she could, until a teacher asked her to return to class. She walked in that direction as long as she felt the teacher's eyes on her, and when she looked back to find the teacher gone, she continued to wander the hallways. For a while, she followed the fluorescent lighting's dim reflection with her arms stretched out, pretending that she was balancing on a narrow path of white light, and if she fell off, she would fall into the void. It made her feel almost child-like, like pretending the floor was lava. She played the game until she'd walked the length of the school, from the back doors to the front doors, and then grew bored of it and simply wandered aimlessly, lost in thought, until the buzzer sounded and second period came to an end, at which time she ducked into the girls' bathroom and found the stall she'd hid in earlier that morning. She lay on the floor, curled up into a ball, and stared at the same hazy beam of light, the dancing particles of dust, until her eyelids grew heavy and she fell asleep on the cold floor, using her sweater as a pillow.

She came to in the back of her father's car. The daylight had faded, giving way to darkness. She was lying across the back seat, her head resting near the passenger side door, tilted upward, so that she could see out the window. The black sky was interrupted every few moments by an orb of light the colour of the sunset rising from the horizon until it was out of view, over and over again, as though the world was spinning that fast, spinning out of control. Her head was pounding. She sat up, leaned her head against the window, and the cold glass felt soothing against her forehead. The earth kept spinning. The sun kept passing by. She counted the days. One. Two. Three. Four. Five. Six. Seven. One week passed in seconds. Her father was in the front seat, his eyes on the road ahead, oblivious. They hadn't spoken for days now. They hadn't spoken for weeks now. Before she knew it, years would pass in silence. Before she knew it, they would be gone. Before she knew it, they would be particles of dust dancing along a beam of light as the earth continued to spin.

"Could you open the window, Dad?"

"It's cold out. You'll be too cold."

"I don't mind the cold."

"I don't mind it, either."

The rear passenger side window jerked to life, and a whirring sound filled the car as the glass lowered halfway down. A rush of air shouldered its way inside. Her father had left papers by the rear driver side. When she'd been lying down, her legs had held them in place. Now free from that security, the papers burst to life, swirling frantically all over the back seat of the car, a sheet or two flying out into the night.

"You should close the window," her father said.

Holly breathed in the cold air, and it stung her nostrils. It made her head hurt differently, as though she'd chugged a Slurpee. It was a good kind of pain.

"I like it," she said.

"Then we'll keep it open for a little while longer."

"Just a short while."

Her hair was dancing, too. It was dancing as though there was music playing, but the radio was off, and the car was silent except for the wind, which sounded like a river with a strong current. It was dancing over her head, dipping and churning and twirling like a miniature tornado, as though she were submerged in water, weightless.

"Your grandfather used to talk about the crows."

As though signalled by the words, as though his words were lyrics to an unheard song, her hair began to dance in circles over-head, and with each passing second, dance lower, lower still, until each black strand of hair spun around her body like the earth around the sun, that glowing orb of light. And then each strand of hair became the body of a black bird, and each sheet of paper became a wing, turning white to black as though absorbing the darkness. Soon, Holly was encased in raven black, in the dance of crows. She felt her heart pound like the beat of a drum. She felt cold air rush into the car through the opened window. She heard the song that the crows were dancing to. She heard her father's voice above all else.

"Your grandfather used to say that you could remember the land, even if you'd never been on the land before. Your grand-father used to say that the land could remember you. It works the same way with crows, Hallelujah. They remembered him, they would remember me, and they remember you. They pass these things down through the generations."

Her father wasn't there any longer. There was nobody driving the car. It barrelled forward through an intersection, where it narrowly missed hitting several cars. Holly felt herself rise off the back seat as the crows began to spin faster. She recognized where they were, a stretch of road called Grant Avenue that cut through Assiniboine Forest, one of the routes her father took to work. The car veered off the road as though steered in that direction, and as it approached the trees, jumping a walkway, it came apart, piece by piece. The doors and hood broke off, got caught up in the wind, and rose into the sky, turning into enormous crows, the kind that she'd seen far up north in Thompson. Up there, they called the crows "Thompson Turkeys." The roof was next, exploding into the air like a black carrion bird pecking at roadkill and getting interrupted by approaching traffic. Part by part, the car turned into a flock of crows, each one of them soaring into the night sky before diving back down to earth and joining the dancing swarm around Holly's body. Part by part, until, like her father, the car was gone.

She was upright, hovering above the ground, moving forward at the same speed the car had been travelling, heading straight toward the forest. Before she hit the trees, the crows carried her up, then over Assiniboine Forest, higher and higher still, until the city below looked like nothing more than a model, somebody's idea not yet realized. The cars speeding down Grant Avenue looked like a child's toys. The trees, brilliant green and plastic. And a figure standing on the boulevard between the forest and the street, looking up at her, reaching toward her, but too far away.

Her father.

Holly could see everything, but he was all she cared about. She stretched her arms toward him, as though she might be able to touch him, despite the distance between them. But as more crows joined in, spinning wildly around her, dancing to the beat of the drum, their feathers blotted out her vision until she could see nothing at all. Not the cars, not the trees, and not her father. Then her stomach dropped, as though she'd been in a roller coaster cart at the pinnacle of the ride, teetering over the edge, and it had now begun its descent. She plummeted toward earth, the crows flew away, and before hitting the ground, she startled awake.

It took Holly a moment to gather her bearings, to realize that she was still on the bathroom floor, curled up against the corner of the farthest stall from the door. She rubbed her face, expecting to feel cool skin, but found warmth. The dream had felt real, every part of it, beginning to end, as if she'd really been carried away from the world, then dropped from such a great height. She patted the floor around her body to ensure that this was real, that it wasn't an *Inception* thing going on. She took inventory of the bathroom stall: The porcelain toilet with its ebony lid. The beam of light. The particles of dust. The graffiti on the wall.

Holly blindly reached for her cellphone. She could feel it bulging in her front right pocket. She pinched the top of it between her index finger and thumb and wrangled it free, then held it inches away from her face without moving from the spot she had claimed on the tiled floor. There had been no text or call from her father. She thought, for a moment, that the dream had meant something, that there was a reason it had seemed real. It had already begun to fade, as dreams do, but one image remained clear: her father, standing on the boulevard between Grant Avenue and Assiniboine Forest, watching her being carried skyward, reaching out for her. The absolute least it could have meant was that he had sent her a message.

Next, she checked the time and was surprised to find that she'd slept for a long while, it now being well after lunch and into fourth period. She noticed a small collection of drool on her sweater, where her mouth had been.

"Gross," she said.

Holly wondered if she had snored while napping. Those Xanax knocked you the fuck out; it helped her understand, or allowed her to excuse, some of her father's behaviour, if he'd been popping them. If she'd been snoring, had anybody peeked underneath the bathroom stall door? She couldn't have been the first exhausted, or medicated, teenager to fall asleep in a school bathroom. There was another line of graffiti just above the bottom of the door, with an arrow below it, pointing toward the space between it and the floor, a distance of about two feet.

Beware of limbo experts.

"No shit," Holly said, as though she could converse with the author of the note, as though she'd found herself in the bathroom-stall version of a movie like *Frequency*, where two people were able to speak to each other across time.

Holly placed her palm flat against the tile and pushed herself up. She was sore all over. She felt like her father's age. If she'd not checked the time, she would've been able to guess, by her stiff joints, that she'd slept for too long. It was a matter of convenience that she'd fallen asleep in a bathroom stall, because she now had to pee, and so she stood up, shuffled over, and sat back down again. In the middle of doing her business, she continued to read the graffiti on the walls, in all different fonts, in all different colours, with so many things to say.

She reached into the pocket of her jeans, crumpled up around her ankles like a compressed accordion, and pulled out a Sharpie. She found a clean area, a blank slate, took the cap off the Sharpie, and wrote:

A careful dance with practised steps,
This life a wheeze inside my chest,
 The shredding tears, numbing rain,
Prescriptions filled to stop the pain,
The tortured love of missing parts
The echo of my beating heart.

Holly decided to skip the rest of her classes, because what more damage could be done? She was already going to hear it from her parents, or at least her mother, who, as opposed to her father, had texted her several times while she slept, wondering where she was and why she hadn't gone to class.

I just needed the day, mom. Sorry.

The dream she'd had had left an impression on her that she was quickly becoming obsessed with. She'd been in the back seat of her father's car, hungover, like she had been the other night. In this way, it had started off more like a memory. She'd rolled down the window, and her hair began to whip violently from the rushing air. It had turned into crows that eventually lifted her off the ground. Her father was reaching for her, and then she fell earthward. How would she ever figure that out? A memory that turned into some messed-up hallucination, like a bad acid trip. Who could tell her what any of it meant, if it had meant anything at all, if it hadn't just been a Xanax-induced experience?

There was only one person who came to mind. Holly dialed her moshom's phone number, and paced back and forth within her bathroom stall (she felt as though she could lay claim to it as hers by now) while the phone rang. After several rings, and when Holly was about to hang up, her kōkom answered.

"Tansi," she said.

"Hey, Kōkom," Holly said. "What's up?"

"Shouldn't you be in class?"

"Just on a bathroom break and thought I'd call."

"You know I love to hear from you, nōsisim, but you don't usually call during the day," she said. "Is something wrong?"

Was something wrong? Was anything right? Holly ran her hands through her hair and bit her lip. She focused on an imaginative bit of graffiti to distract herself enough so that she didn't cry over the phone.

Don't force it.

"Is Moshom there?"

Her kōkom's voice lowered. "He's having a rest, my girl. Your father came over earlier and—"

"My dad was over there? He was working today, wasn't he?"

"You know he isn't far from here," her kōkom said. "He wasn't himself, either. They went for a walk down the street."

"In this weather?" Holly said.

"That's the only place they seem to be able to have a conversation," her kōkom said. "Anyway, it tired your moshom out, and he's been sleeping since."

Holly punched the concrete side of the bathroom stall, the one that had the privacy window, and the one with the most graffiti because it was harder for the custodian to clean off. She instantly regretted it, because while it let out a hollow thud, a sound that her kōkom failed to pick up, it hurt like hell. She made a *tsssss* sound while shaking her hand vigorously as though trying to dry it off, like the pain could be gotten rid of so easily.

"Are you sure everything's all right?"

No, it sure as hell wasn't. She wasn't on speaking terms with her father, she'd blown up at her boyfriend whether he deserved it or not, she'd just had a weird dream, she'd slept on the floor of the bathroom for hours, her knuckles were probably broken, and the one person who could offer some kind of help was sleeping. And why? Because her father had worn her moshom out with his own issues. It was like the arguments she'd heard her parents have on several occasions—whenever something was wrong with her mother, whenever she wasn't feeling well or she was upset, her father magically felt worse or was even more upset than her.

"It's like I'm not allowed to feel shitty, because you'll just feel shittier, and then you know what? Somehow, I end up having to look after *you*."

She would laugh even though she was crying.

Instead of her father owning it and apologizing, because she was right, he'd get defensive and say something like, "Do you think I'd actually choose to feel this way, Claire? I wouldn't wish it on my worst enemy."

Her father clearly didn't get women, and if she was to be honest with herself, she'd kind of been counting on that. It was reverse psychology. She thought that if she said not to talk to her, it would make him pay attention to her again. A part of her didn't want him to talk to her, and she didn't want to talk to him, but there was a part that wanted him to. There was a part that wanted him to see her. To really see her. But if he couldn't see her mother, then she couldn't expect him to be any different with her, and it was just as well.

The end result was that he was once again hogging the spotlight, even though he wasn't aware of it.

"Holly?" her kōkom said. "Are you sure—"

"Yeah, I'm sure," Holly said, then sighed. "I'm sure. Can you get him to call me when he gets up? Like, if he's up before school's out?"

"Of course, nōsisim," her kōkom said, not able to mask the concern in her voice, and added apologetically, "I'd get him up, but he's been so tired lately. Your father had to practically carry him up the steps."

"I totally get it," Holly said. "Let him sleep. It's not a big deal. I love you."

"Kisakīhitin, my girl."

Holly ended the call, slipped her phone back into its spot in her front pocket, then left the bathroom stall for the first time in hours. She may have felt as though she owned the stall, but that didn't mean she wanted to spend another moment in it. She had an impulse to change her clothing. It didn't matter that all she had were gym clothes in her locker. At least they weren't covered in bathroom floor germs.

On the way to her locker, she had to pass by the office, the staff lounge, and the Elder's office. When the whole reconciliation thing had gained steam in Canada, what she'd heard her moshom and kōkom call Turtle Island, the school hired an Elder to provide counselling for all students (but especially the exactly three Indigenous students who had self-identified), to provide cultural awareness workshops for the school, where students learned about things like residential school history and pre-colonial life, and to conduct sharing circles and morning smudges. The Elder, a Cree woman from up north, was named Rebecca. She was short, had light-brown hair that was always braided and reminded Holly of sweetgrass, and always wore brilliant colours. With her slightly hunched back from age and maybe a hard life, she sometimes looked like a rainbow. Holly had always liked her from an outsider's perspective (she'd never spoken to her directly herself), and as she walked past Rebecca's office, she stopped suddenly and turned toward it. Her moshom was a recognized Elder, and seemed to always be Elder in Residence for one thing or another, and for that reason, along with the added bonus of him being her grandfather, Holly had wanted him to interpret her dream. It felt like an Elder sort of thing. But since he was napping, Holly figured it was worth a shot to talk to Rebecca.

Holly took a couple of steps to the office door and stood there for a moment, eye-level with the nameplate that read "CULTURAL ADVISOR," and wondered if the advisory job extended to dreams and whether she should even bother. She imagined "DREAM ADVISOR" being on the nameplate instead, embossed in gold against the black background, then quickly dismissed the thought as stupid. She almost walked away. She turned in the direction of her locker, then stopped.

"You're making excuses," she said out loud.

The only person she ever opened up to, really, was her moshom. There was something about him that was comforting and safe, like you could tell him anything in the world and he wouldn't judge you. He'd listen, sit there quietly and reflectively, reaching back into the many teachings he'd been gifted through-out his long life, and then say something profound, even though he'd always use an economy of words. With him, less was always more.

"People talk so much but say so little," he'd told her once while they were watching a political debate.

It was why he'd never gone into politics, though he'd been asked by parties to run for them. He was well known and respected in the Indigenous community, and he walked a delicate line, finding the same amount of acceptance in the Western world.

"Walking in two worlds," he'd explained to her, going on to tell her that the starting point was acknowledging that no matter what your background, you shared something with everybody on the planet: "That you are human."

"So, why'd you never run?" she'd said to him.

He told her that he thought he could make more of a difference away from the world of politics, but he admitted that the propensity to speak a lot but say very little existed in the church as well. Holly thought that her moshom was a different kind of minister. She'd sat in the church more than once just to listen to her grandfather speak (she was not sure of the existence of God). The congregation, she noticed, had as many white faces as brown. The community must have felt the same way she did: her moshom was comforting and safe, and also pretty fucking smart.

Holly thought of the times she'd seen a lineup of students at the Elder's door, as though they were waiting to buy tickets to a concert. All kinds of students—as many white faces as brown. If they were so eager to talk to her, there had to be a reason for it. She had to be pretty good at her job. So Holly did an about-face, mustered the confidence to step up to the door again, and knocked rhythmically, as though she and Rebecca had already established a secret code.

Rebecca greeted Holly with a warm smile and led her into the office. They were deep into the school year, but it looked as though Rebecca had only recently moved in. This surprised Holly. She'd expected the office to be more cultural, she supposed, for lack of a better term. She'd pictured dream catchers and eagle feathers and sweetgrass braids hanging all over the place like Christmas ornaments on a tree, Indigenous art plastering the walls, so much tobacco that the room may as well have been a smoke shop, and a plate of bannock sitting on the coffee table between them. She'd expected the office to be dripping with Indigeneity. But instead, there was one single dream catcher hanging perfectly centred in front of the window, a smudge bowl on a small, circular table beside the Elder, with a ball of sage in it and a book of matches at its side, and on the ground, a medicine wheel throw rug. Holly figured, though she hadn't been explicitly told, that the medicine wheel rug was not to be stepped on, like a team logo in a dressing room, so she walked around it to get to her chair.

"What's troubling you, my girl?" the Elder said.

Holly liked that the Elder called her "my girl" like her kōkom. It set her at ease. Rebecca was no Moshom—nobody was—but she was giving off some strong auntie vibes.

"Can I level with you?" Holly said. "Like, do we have confidentiality by law or whatever?"

The Elder chuckled, but not in a way that made Holly feel as though she were being made fun of.

"It's between us," the Elder assured her.

"Okay, good enough." Holly leaned forward in her chair and rested her elbows on her knees. She looked down at the rug. She looked, specifically, at the white section of the medicine wheel, which was divided into four quadrants: white, black, red, and yellow. She pictured herself back in her dream, looking down at the world. The trees, the road, the grass, her father. "If I told you about a dream I just had—"

"Just had?"

"Yeah, long story and not important," Holly said, then continued on as though there'd not been an interruption. "Would you be able to interpret it for me? It's just . . ." She mimed her head exploding. "I can't stop thinking about it."

"I'll do my best . . ." The Elder paused in order to prompt Holly to tell her her name, and Holly did. "Holly," the Elder said after being told, and then looked at her curiously before adding, "McIvor?"

"That's right," she said. "How the fu—um, how did you know that?"

"A Cree can always spot a Cree," the Elder said with her trademark chuckle. "Your moshom wouldn't happen to be Charlie, would he?"

"Yep, that's him," Holly said. "Charles McIvor."

Rebecca went on to tell Holly how they went way back, how she'd grown up in Norway House as well. Her last name was Balfour. There were a lot of Balfours around Norway House, just like there were a lot of McIvors. She told Holly about how she used to swim with her moshom in the lake behind his house, and then, when they were older, how they used to watch their children swim, Holly's father and Rebecca's daughter.

"So much is passed down from one generation to another, my girl," the Elder said. "Stories and traditions and ceremony and even activities. *Kapasimo*. That means 'swim' in Cree."

"Cool," Holly said.

"But listen to me go on. I'm telling you about all these memories, and you want to know about your dream." She reached to the side and picked up the smudge bowl and the book of matches. While lighting the sage, she said, "Sometimes, when enough time passes, memories feel like dreams. They fade like dreams fade, too."

The sage started to burn, and then the Elder blew the flames out. A trail of smoke rose from the sacred medicine, billowing toward the ceiling gracefully, and it reminded Holly of the crows in her dream, how they were dancing to music that, initially, she couldn't hear. The smoke seemed to hear its own song.

The Elder extended the smudge bowl toward Holly and fanned the smoke toward her. Holly had smudged occasionally, during school events like Orange Shirt Day, and knew why it was done and what to do, so she went through the motions but didn't feel as though it accomplished anything. It was more to appease the Elder, who explained that the act was one of purification, that it gave them the ability to centre themselves in the moment.

Holly cupped her hands together and washed the smoke over her head, over her eyes, over her mouth, over her heart, and pushed some down across the rest of her body. After she was done, she nodded, and Rebecca asked if she would fan the smoke toward her in turn, and Holly did. The Elder mirrored Holly's movements, only when she smudged, there was a poetry to it, a truth that Holly, when seeing the actions, wished that she had.

When the ceremony was over, the Elder picked up a stick from a desk behind her that was otherwise as bare as the rest of the office. The stick was about two feet in length, and at the handle, leather had been wrapped tightly around it, while at the opposite end, there was a tuft of white fur, probably from a rabbit.

In the middle of the stick was a thin strip of leather, the ends of which were decorated with beads that matched the colours of the rug—black, red, yellow, and white, in that order—and two small feathers. It was a beautiful piece of wood, as pieces of wood went, and when Rebecca offered it to Holly, she was glad to take it, although curious as to why it had been offered.

"What is this?" she said, gripping the handle with one hand and rotating it so that the fur tickled the fingertips of her other hand.

"It's a talking stick," the Elder said. "Usually, in a meeting, it's passed around and the person holding it has the right to speak."

"Oh," Holly said. "So do we have to pass it back and forth, then, if we're going to talk to each other?"

"No, we don't have to do that. I offer it to kids, and staff, who come to visit me, to calm them. And it helps for focus."

"Kind of like an ancient fidget spinner."

"Yes." Rebecca chuckled again, which Holly found to be as comforting as the talking stick at this point. "I'd say it's exactly like an ancient fidget spinner."

"Well, thanks," Holly said, continuing to rotate the talking stick in her hand. She'd moved her fingers down now, so that the feathers brushed against her palm with each rotation, like brushes in a car wash. "Cool."

"So," Rebecca said, "tell me about this dream you had."

Holly fiddled with the talking stick for a second longer, moving the beads along the leather strip as though it were an abacus, then clasped it with both hands as one would wield an axe, and rested it on her lap. She recounted as much as she could remember about the dream to the Elder, beginning with her waking up on the back seat of her father's car, and ending with her plunging to earth toward her father and his outstretched arms. She even, unprompted, connected it to the night her father had come to pick her up after she'd drunk herself into a stupor, showing how the dream had matched real life to start and then veered into the bizarre. When she finished talking, it felt as though she had been telling the story for a long time. She'd been staring at the stick for the duration of her monologue and expected to find the Elder sleeping in her chair when she looked up, but she was not.

The Elder nodded her head and threw a mischievous expression Holly's way. "It sounds to me like you've got daddy issues," she said.

If Holly had been drinking water at that moment, she would've spit it out. Thankfully, she wasn't. She just laughed in shock.

"What kind of Elder are you?"

"What did you expect an Elder to be?"

"Touché," Holly said. "I've got to say, I'm pretty confused. You said the daddy issues thing, and then you did the shrink thing of answering a question with a question."

"I am a trained counsellor, like your moshom, but sometimes you need a bit more than a talking stick to set your mind at ease."

"Fair."

"It does seem, though, my girl, that this dream you had has a lot to do with your father."

"You're not wrong."

"Can you tell me a little bit more about that?"

The Elder shuffled to the edge of her chair, as though Holly was telling a suspenseful story. The smudge bowl had been resting at her side, on the table, and smoke was rising from it. It gave off a pleasant aroma, like a scented candle. Holly breathed it in as though taking in fresh air, closing her eyes. She didn't open them when she answered Rebecca's question.

"If I had a Facebook account, and my dad friended me, we'd set our relationship status as complicated. If you get the reference."

"I have a Facebook account," the Elder said. "That's how a lot of community members speak with each other and get their information, like when bingo night is."

Holly laughed again.

"Just kidding. Bingo's on the local radio station every day."

Holly wished that she'd come to see Rebecca earlier in the year, but she had wanted to avoid dealing with the negative attention of being Indigenous. She'd already, albeit infrequently, dealt with racist remarks, or ignorant ones. And tokenism. The tokenism was more common. When any Indigenous subject was brought up in history or social studies, the teacher always asked Holly about it first. One time, she'd been sent to the office when she snapped, "How the fuck should I know?"

Holly told Rebecca about how her father had held her hair out of her face while she was sick, and how he'd come to pick her up at the pool after not hearing from her. Then Holly said, "He wouldn't come to my water polo championship, he walks around like a zombie most of the time, and then last night"— Holly seethed at the memory—"last night, he fucking—" She cupped her mouth after swearing, as though she could catch it and put it back.

"It's okay to be emotional," the Elder said. "It's not the first time I've heard a swear word."

"Sorry," Holly said, regardless. "Last night," she continued, "he comes downstairs when I'm with my . . . when I'm with a guy, and acts like he cares all of a sudden."

"Do you think he doesn't care?"

Holly felt an impulse to break the talking stick in half over her knee, but just gripped it harder.

"I know he cares. I just think he's going through his own shit, whatever it is, and he . . ." She sighed, loosened her grip, and began to turn the stick in her hand again, letting the soft fur brush across her fingers. "It feels like he cares more about himself."

"Have you talked to him about any of this?" the Elder said.

"Not exactly." Holly told Rebecca about how she'd done the exact opposite, how rather than talk to him about how he was making her feel, rather than ask why he was acting the way he'd been acting, something she'd not thought of doing, which made her feel vaguely narcissistic even though he was the adult, she'd asked him not to speak to her and had vowed not to speak to him until he'd gotten his shit together. "Maybe we both need to get our shit together." She glanced at Rebecca. "Sorry about the *shit* thing."

"I've heard that word, too."

"I don't know," Holly said. "I feel like, you know, he's broken, I'm broken, and can two broken people really fix their own relationship unless they've fixed themselves? Does that even make sense?"

"Yes, my girl." She paused thoughtfully, looking off to the side and watching the ever-thinning trail of smoke. "Do you think," she said, returning her attention to Holly, "the dream is really about wanting to connect with your father somehow? Hearing you talk about him, it's clear that you love him, but the distance in your dream—I understand it now."

"What do I do about it?" Holly said.

"I think, if you're ready to, if you feel that you're able, you should talk to him," Rebecca said.

Holly leaned back in her chair, shook her head, and waved the stick around as though she were conducting a symphony. Then she placed it back on her lap and kept shaking her head. "Well, I can't do that. I just . . . I'm not going to do that. I can't do that. It's just the principle of it, Elder."

"Why?" Rebecca said. "You can't let pride get in the way of healing."

"It's not pride that's the thing."

"Then what is it, my girl?"

"It's . . ." Holly handed the talking stick to the Elder. Her shoulders slumped, and her voice seemed to slump as well, because she thought she knew the answer, as painful as it was. "I want him to care enough to talk to me first. I don't want to, like, let him off the hook. I want things to change. I want them to change for me, and I want them to change for my mom. Something has to give."

"Maybe he wants to, but he doesn't know how," the Elder said.

"Maybe he does. Men can be pretty dumb. But even still . . ." She thought of everything that had gone wrong with him, with them. She thought of all that he'd done for her during that time, the little glimpses of hope. She thought of the times before that, like when they snuggled up together while watching a movie, like when he took her to the field so they could hit golf balls together. Those good times were as clear as the bad, no matter how far away they were. That gave her hope, and resolve. "He's going to have to figure it out."

I couldn't get out of bed the night you won the championship. You'd gone out with your friends, and it was late, and I guess I was more worried about you coming home than I was about my own anxieties. I used to worry about emptiness, but I knew that my life would be emptier without you. I felt it that one day when you fell asleep on the bus and didn't get to practice on time. I felt it when you were so drunk that I worried you had alcohol poisoning. You couldn't even walk. I stayed up with you the whole night, making sure you were sleeping on your side, feeding you water every once in a while like an IV drip.

That one night, I just lay in bed on my side, motionless. I stared out the window, looking past the street lights, looking past the tangled branches that made the navy-blue sky look like a sheet of cracked glass, at the stars. I played connect-the-dots with the stars, finding the constellations that I'd been raised with. I tried to find meaning in the stories I'd been told about them, teachings that would help me understand anything. But it was only desperation. The stories were made up. The stories never meant anything other than what people intended them to mean. Just like all the stories your moshom used to tell me, and not just about the stars. About Mistapew. About

Memekwesewak. About talking bears. About the crows. About all that shit.

I stared out the window, and I listened for you to come home. At some point you did, and I was relieved, like I always am when you come home at night. There's always that worry, a parent's worry, that one night you won't. That's the only kind of worry I should've had. Or rather, the only kind of worry you should've seen. I dragged you into all of my shit. I dragged both of you into all of my shit.

I listened to the front door open, then close. I listened to your footsteps lead down the hallway, to my and your mother's bedroom. It was dark in the house. When the hallway light flicked on, the outside disappeared from view, as though it ceased to exist. When the hallway light flicked on, the window became a mirror, and I saw you standing at the bedroom door, facing your mother and me.

Your mother was sleeping. She had been for a couple of hours. Her breathing had been the soundtrack of my stargazing. When the hallway light came on, she didn't stir. I didn't move, either. I didn't want you to know that I was awake. I stayed where I was, staring at the window, staring at you standing at the bedroom door, staring in my direction. I made myself believe it was in my direction.

Maybe you knew I was awake, like I knew you were standing there, like I knew you'd been drinking. I could smell it on you.

I thought, Is she drinking because of me?

I'd skipped your game, and for what?

I saw your mouth open. I heard the sound of your lips parting. I heard a quick breath, drawing in air to say something. I saw you take a step forward. And then you paused. Stood there for a minute, your hand on the door frame. You moved some stray hairs away from your face, pushed them behind your ear. You turned to leave, then stopped and turned back. Just for a moment. Just for one second. And I wondered, I still wonder, what you were going to say. Was it like me wanting to say something to you a million times, but never saying anything, aside from what was obligatory or for show?

What were you going to say?

Would it have changed anything? Did it? The hallway light flicked off, and you vanished, and the darkness returned. The window was just a window again. The street light with its vague orange glow. And the shattered-glass reaching branches. And the stars. Especially the stars. The endless stars.

I thought, All those stars are already dead.

At that moment, I knew that I was not significant. I felt so fucking small. I kept listening for you. But you felt just as far away.

11

In the mornings, Matthew drove east toward the sun, as though it were his destination. As though, during the coldest days in winter months, the sun dog's crescents of light were arms outstretched, ready to welcome him. In the evenings, Matthew drove west, and if he left early enough, he drove toward a dying sun that painted the horizon red and orange and yellow, as though it were a struck match head lighting the sky on fire.

Tonight, Matthew left late.

There'd been so much on his mind that the day had passed unnoticed; he'd not played one game of solitaire. Matthew had stared blankly at his computer screen, where he could see a faint reflection of himself. He let phone calls go directly to voice mail; he didn't answer any emails. It was only when Jesse came to his cubicle unannounced that he snapped back to reality.

She asked him what had gotten into him, if he'd really meant what he'd said.

He didn't answer immediately. He stared at her as he'd been staring at the computer screen, at the shadowy image of himself, of the man he used to be, of the man he wanted to be, not who he was now.

Claire popped into his mind. She was lying down on the bed, buried under a comforter and a mountain of tissues. An empty tissue box was at her side. Matthew's phone was on the nightstand, opened to the texts between him and Jesse.

"I meant it," Matthew said. He'd never sounded more vacant or tired. He rubbed his hand over his face, from his forehead to his chin. "I'm sorry."

"I'm sorry, too," Jesse said, then shrugged. "It was fun."

That was it. She left his cubicle without another word, just a look of regret. Matthew couldn't tell what that look meant, whether she was disappointed that they wouldn't interact as they had previously, or that their relationship wouldn't become something more, or that something had started that they both knew wasn't right.

It was after six p.m. when Matthew left the office, and the sun had dipped out of sight by then, dousing the flames it had ignited along the horizon. The sky ahead, the horizon in the untouchable distance, was progressively darker shades of blue, and the highway lights were low-hanging stars. He couldn't remember the last time he'd driven home at this time of day. Maybe last year after the staff Christmas party—he'd skipped this year's celebration. In the dark, it seemed like an entirely new route, as though he'd never been this way before, and the road, which felt desolate even during the day, was so desperately empty that it felt as though he shouldn't be on it. But he continued ahead, and got closer to the overpass he'd almost driven off that morning, and the closer he got, the bigger and brighter the high-mast lights on the highway became.

A deer darted across the road, well ahead, and Matthew slowed his car to a crawl. The deer stopped on the shoulder and waited there, looking back across the pavement. Matthew stopped his car entirely, and soon enough, a fawn walked casually in front of his headlights, without a care in the world. Once safely on the other side, the pair leapt off together and disappeared into the night.

Matthew arrived home to find his food on the dining room table; Claire and Holly had long since finished their supper. He sat in the quiet and thought about how it was no quieter than when his wife and daughter were at the table with him. No lonelier. Claire had made pizza. He took one bite, chewed, then spit it out on his plate. Pizza tasted better hot or cold, and this slice was room temperature. Maybe he just wasn't hungry. Maybe nothing would've tasted good to him.

The light in the kitchen was off and the dishwasher was running. He scraped his food into the garbage and placed his plate in the sink. He leaned over and sipped water straight from the faucet. When he stood up, a drop of water rolled from his bottom lip, down his chin. He wiped it away with his sleeve. There was a gust of wind outside that blew snow off the neighbour's roof. The snow fell in slow motion in front of the kitchen window. When the light hit the snowflakes, they looked like a thousand falling stars, like new constellations. Matthew tried to make shapes out of them as people did with clouds, but they were gone before he could think of one. He flicked the light on. Outside, it looked pitch black and endless.

When Matthew was a child, he'd had insomnia. He'd wander the house but always end up by windows. Always windows. He'd stare up at the sky, at the stars. His father used to tell him sky stories when he took him back to bed.

There were no stars tonight. He held up his hand and looked at his palm. He looked at all the tiny lines, the countless lines. There was one that curled around the base of his thumb.

A girl with red hair and braids had inspected his palm once. She traced that line with her index finger and looked up at him with great concern.

"That's your life line," she whispered, as though stunned to near-silence.

"So?" he said.

"Don't you see how short it is?" she said.

She told him that he was going to die young. The lines were as small to him as he was to the world, as the world was to the universe, as the universe was to eternity.

Standing over the sink, with the darkness outside the window, he felt crushed by the weight of it all.

"You're home late."

Matthew glanced to the left, where he could see Claire's reflection in the glass. He'd been so preoccupied with his own thoughts that he'd not noticed her enter the kitchen. He didn't know how long she'd been standing there. Her body language matched her tone of voice. Her arms were crossed. She was leaning against the wall, as far from him as she could get without actually leaving the room. And she wasn't even looking at him. It had gotten so bad that wherever she thought he'd been, she either didn't care or was too disgusted at him to look him in the eyes.

"I know."

Matthew pressed his palms against the kitchen counter, leaning forward. His palms curved around the contoured edge. He stared at the plate in the kitchen sink, the swipe marks his fork had made from shovelling the pizza into the garbage.

"Where were you?"

Only then did she turn toward him. He could feel her eyes on him. He could feel them, sad and pleading and angry all at once. She thought she knew already and was seeking honesty, confirmation. It made the hair at the back of his neck stand, as though a chill had come into the room.

She was wrong, though.

"I was at work."

He turned on the water. He turned the water to hot. He watched the water, slowly rising in temperature, spill over the streaks of pizza sauce. Those tiny lines left behind by his fork. He wasn't sure how long he'd been standing there. He wasn't sure if the sauce had dried onto the plate's porcelain surface. He picked up the scrub brush, dripped dish soap onto the plate, and scoured it gleaming white. He replaced the scrub brush beside the sink. The water continued to run.

"I just got zoned out, that's all."

"Zoned out."

He watched her body shift. She uncrossed and recrossed her arms. She shook her head.

"You weren't . . ." Her voice cracked slightly. She looked away from him. "I mean . . ."

"No. I wasn't."

The water was hot now. Steam rose from the sink. Water hit the plate and spat across the counter. She hated when that happened. She hated when he got the counter wet and didn't dry it. The kitchen window had misted over. It blurred Claire's reflection. She was smeared pastel. She was a figure in a Monet painting. An artist's impression of her.

"I never did." He looked at her, clear and defined and distant. He looked at her reflection. He turned off the water. He reached to the side and grabbed a dish towel. He wiped away the water on the counter, then dried the plate. He placed it beside the sink, on the marble countertop.

"Why didn't you say anything about her? Were you waiting for me to bring it up? Like it's my responsibility?"

"Maybe." Matthew picked up the plate, walked over to the kitchen cabinet, opened it, and put the dish away. He turned to face her and leaned against the counter. He mimicked her body language and crossed his arms. He looked away. "I don't know."

"It's like you . . ." Claire shook her head again and it shook loose tears. He saw them falling down her cheeks. She wiped them away hurriedly, then recrossed her arms. "It's like you saw me cut and just let me keep bleeding." She looked at him. Her eyes were glistening against her will. She was still crying but not wiping the tears away. "It's like you cut me."

"I'm sorry."

Matthew had said sorry to Claire a million times over the course of their relationship, and most of the time he'd meant it. Claire hated apologies. She hated them more than the act for which somebody was apologizing. She had told him and Holly that apologies didn't matter. It wasn't the word, it was the action that mattered. That's what she'd always said about the smallest things—"Don't say sorry about not leaving me with enough gas in the car; just make sure you fill up at night if I'm going out in

132

the morning." She'd said the same about him leaving dirty dishes in the sink when he could have just cleaned them or put them in the dishwasher.

That's what she'd always said about the big things, too.

He took a few steps toward her and stopped in the middle of the kitchen, the track lighting directly overhead.

"I was thinking about you. I was thinking about everything I've been putting you and Hallelujah through the last . . ."

How long had it been? How long had it really been?

"It's been a long fucking time, Matt. It's been too long."

Claire uncrossed her legs, pressed the sole of one foot against the wall, and slid it up. The thin rip in her jeans over her left knee widened, and Matthew could see her skin peek out from between the blue fabric and spiderweb threads. He used to notice these things about her. He used to notice every detail.

The smallest things.

"I know it's been a long time, and I know I haven't been present. It's not how I should have been."

"You've been present for other people."

"That's not where I was."

Matthew took another step forward. One step. He watched to see her reaction. He watched the few strands of hair that had fallen from behind her ear. The contours of her knee. Her toes pressed against the wall, the floor. She didn't move.

"I've talked to her, but we've only talked. I haven't . . ."

"It's not much better. I've been here." She pushed herself off the wall, stood to face him, and took one step toward him. "I've been here, and Holly has been here, too. You've just . . ."

Claire looked at the floor. Directly beneath them was Holly's bedroom. Holly was home. Matthew could hear music playing.

He'd not noticed it before.

"I know."

Another step.

"She needs you."

"I know she does."

"Then you need to talk to her, too. You need to talk to her more than you need to talk to me."

"It never seems like she wants me around."

Matthew looked at the floor. He imagined that he could see Holly. He knew what she would be doing. Her record player would be spinning a black circle beside her bed. She'd be lying down, arms behind her head, eyes closed, singing along in whispers. They used to listen to records together. He used to lie beside her. They used to sing the same songs. They used to laugh when one of them got a lyric wrong. They used to cry at the prettiest words.

"She's a teenager."

"Okay, I'll talk to her. Can I talk to her?"

"Yes, I think you can."

Matthew took another step, this time with the intention of going downstairs to see his daughter. Another step, then another, but he stopped when his cellphone rang. He debated whether to answer it. He slipped it out of his pocket.

12

Holly had waited out last period in the place she'd spent most of the day, and how fucked up was it that a bathroom stall had become her security blanket? The impromptu meeting with Rebecca hadn't provided any answers to the questions she had, but it held her interest. Her moshom said that telling stories is healing, and if nothing else had happened, she'd told a story, and so maybe there was something to it. Maybe there was nothing more to her dream than that she felt estranged from her father and wanted things to be the way they were before. If she were asked to articulate what was wrong in her life, that's precisely how she would describe it.

She'd not gone back to sleep in the bathroom stall, just locked herself inside it, sat on the floor with her back against the wall, and read all the graffiti over and over without any of it registering. Her brain was Teflon for everything that wasn't connected to her dream. When the school day came to an end, she slid under the door to keep it locked, as though nobody would bother to unlock it and her spot would be reserved for her. She imagined writing *Holly's Stall* on the door in Sharpie.

It had grown colder in the late afternoon; the sun had long

since crossed its highest point and was making its descent. The horizon was coloured faintly under the blue with red and orange and yellow all blended together, like drops of food colouring added to water.

Holly liked walking toward the sunset; it made her feel like if she walked long enough, she could reach it. It made her think of the time she'd asked her father that very question.

"If I kept walking, could I get there?"

"We should try it one day," he'd said. "We should walk as far as we can and see if we can catch the horizon. I mean, there's a pot of gold at the end of the rainbow, right?"

"There's no such thing as leprechauns, Dad. That's silly," she said.

"You know, we don't know that for sure, Hallelujah. If there are Memekwesewak, then maybe there are leprechauns, too."

"Maybe. Anyways, I wouldn't really go there, because what if I fell *off* the earth?"

He put his arm around her. "If you fell off the earth, I'd catch you. I'd reach down and grab your hand and pull you right back up."

She held his hand as though she'd fallen off right then and he was pulling her to safety. She thought they should go there on their next hike. She felt good about it then.

When Holly got home, her mother had supper ready and was waiting at the dining room table. There were two plates of home-made pizza at either side of the table, one for Holly and one for her father. Holly took her regular spot to the right of her mother.

She looked at her father's spot, directly across from her, which was vacant. She took a bite of pizza. Her mother was an odd combination of worried and upset, her brow furrowed, her eyebrows slightly raised like a gently cresting wave. Her lips were pursed and her jaws were tight. Holly could see her jaw muscles protruding underneath her earlobes. She was a tight rubber band about to snap.

"Where is he?"

Her mother shook her head slightly. A quick jerk, as though she were flinching from pain. "No idea."

"Well, he's usually here, isn't he?"

"Usually."

"Did he call or . . . ?"

"No, he hasn't called or texted."

"Have you called him?"

"No, I haven't called him."

She hadn't called him, but her cellphone was lying on the table beside her plate like a utensil. To Holly, this was the same as her trying to hide the worry in her voice.

"Why not? What if something's wrong?"

"He's a grown man, Hall," her mother said. "Why haven't you been speaking to him?"

"Good point."

Holly took another bite of pizza. Her mother hadn't touched hers. Holly didn't feel like she could take another bite, either. She tossed her napkin on top of her plate.

"It's good, though," she said.

"Thanks," her mother said.

She told her mother of the dream she'd had, and how she'd spoken to the Elder at school about it because her grandfather had been sleeping. She did not tell her about taking her father's Xanax.

"He went to go talk to Moshom today," she said. "They went for a walk and Moshom got all tired."

Her mother breathed sharply out of her nose. She picked up her phone and checked it, in case, Holly thought, she'd missed a message. Her mother lifted her napkin off her lap and then placed it on top of her pizza, too. She stood up with her plate. Holly followed suit.

"In this weather?" her mother said absently.

"That's what Kōkom said."

"Maybe he went over there after work, then."

"Maybe he did."

Holly went with her mother into the kitchen. As they walked, her mother looked back at the dining room table, where her father's plate of food remained.

"I'll leave that for him," her mother said.

They scraped their plates off into the garbage, one after the other, and then put them in the dishwasher. They stood together by the sink for a moment. Her mother checked her phone once more and then slid it into her pocket. Holly looked at hers, too, almost against her will, just because her mother had, as though she'd caught a yawn. There were no messages from her father, just a thousand from Christian that had gone unanswered. Holly then pocketed her phone and announced to her mother that she was going to her bedroom.

"I'll be here if you need me," her mother said.

Halfway down the stairs, Holly stopped and, without turning around, said, "I know you will."

* * *

Holly shut the door behind her, locked it, and changed into more comfortable clothing, a pair of grey sweats and a ripped Pearl Jam T-shirt, the one with the girl reaching for the gun. Her laundry basket was in the corner of her room. She fished through the pants she'd worn to school before tossing the clothes she'd taken off into the basket with the rest of her dirty laundry. The items she'd taken out of her pockets were on her bed, and she took inventory of them: A receipt from 7-Eleven for a coffee she'd bought on the walk home one day this week. A lighter. Some spare change. Her cellphone and all the messages from Christian it held; she saw a new one that he'd sent since she'd last looked. And the container with two more Xanax pills that she'd taken from her father's pill bottle. She tossed the receipt into the small white receptacle on the floor beside her desk. She used the lighter to light a scented candle and placed it on the nightstand beside her bed. She dropped the spare change into the piggy bank her parents had given her when she was a child. It was a metal, cartoonish dinosaur. She turned off her cellphone so that she wouldn't have to see any more messages from Christian; she wasn't interested in talking to him. She stood facing her bed with the two white pills in the palm of her hand. She stared at them as though they were the sclera of a pair of eyes, as though they were staring back at her.

She used to have asthma attacks that would land her in the emergency room. She remembered sitting on a bed in the ER, flanked by her parents, while the doctor put something over her mouth and made her inhale. Moments later, she could take deep breaths again. Attacks like that didn't happen often. The family doctor prescribed her medicine, which she took every day to ward off the bad attacks. It was coloured green, and it was the worst thing she'd ever tasted before or since. The first time her father had given her a spoonful, she'd thrown up instantly all over his pants. He didn't flinch. He just smiled at her, poured another spoonful, and told her to pinch her nose. He told her that if she pinched her nose, she wouldn't be able to taste it.

"That's a lie," she said.

"No, it's not," he said. "I wouldn't lie to you."

She pinched her nose so tight that her nostrils were two thin lines. Her father placed the spoon into her mouth and tipped it to the side. She felt the cool liquid spill over her tongue but couldn't taste it. She swallowed. She was about to remove her index finger and thumb from her nose, but her father placed his hand over her fingers and told her to keep her nose pinched for a few more seconds because of the aftertaste. He'd put his hand over her fingers and nose so carefully. She remembered not wanting him to take his hand away, for him to stay with her just like that, with puke on his pants.

Holly pinched her nostrils together now, her thumb on one side and her index finger on the other. She pinched her nostrils together until they were razor thin, even though the Xanax pills were tasteless. She lifted her hand, put her palm against her bottom lip, and let the pills fall inside her mouth. She chewed them up and swallowed them. She kept pinching her nostrils closed for another few seconds.

Holly didn't feel at all tired—she'd rested for the better part of the school day—but she lay down on her bed all the same and gazed up at the ceiling as though there was something to look at. She threw memories, better memories, against the white as though it were a movie screen. Her moshom had one of those old screens that you pulled down and hooked onto something near the base to keep the screen from rolling back up. He used to play family movies on it with an old film projector. The movies looked like a filter she had on one of her social media apps, but felt less plastic. Her favourite movie was of her father and her moshom swimming in the lake by her grandparents' place on their reserve. The lake was so big and so blue that it looked like they were flying.

Before long, she fell asleep while playing that same movie on her ceiling, the way that she remembered it.

Holly woke to the sound of the front door opening and footsteps leading from there to the dining room, where they stopped. Chair legs scraped against the hardwood floor, back and forth. There was no noise for a few minutes, until the chair was pushed away from the table and the same footsteps trailed from the dining room to the kitchen, stopping directly above her, about where she figured the kitchen sink was. A cupboard opened. A cupboard was shut. The wind howled outside like a tortured ghost.

A dish rattled in the kitchen sink like chains. She heard her mother's voice, short and sharp. It took her father a long time to answer. She couldn't quite hear what they said, but still, it made Holly uneasy. There was so much dead space between their words. The silence was too much to hear. She put on a record and played it. The black circle spun, static filled the silence, music drowned out muffled words, but Holly cried all the same.

I want you to know what I forgive you for
Now that you're all ashes anyway
Every step into the river pushes you further away.

Every step. One, then another. Her father was moving toward the basement door. Was he going to come down to see her? Talk to her? She sat up in bed, turned the volume down on her record player, and gave full attention, once more, to her parents. At least, if he came downstairs, she wouldn't be on the couch with Christian, her top off. Christian, who by now had likely sent a hundred or so more text messages.

Her father stopped abruptly. Holly got out of bed and walked over to the bedroom door. She placed her ear against the surface and closed her eyes. She heard her father's voice. His tone changed to something more cordial. A greeting. He wasn't talking to her mother. Her parents didn't talk to each other like that. They sounded tired when they spoke with each other.

Holly could hear her mother say, "What is it?"

Something was wrong. Her father sounded like he was in disbelief. He said the same word several times in a row: "What. What. What. What."

He asked the person on the other end of the line what they were talking about. His voice was getting progressively louder and more frantic. Footsteps paced one way, then another. Her father's. Her mother's footsteps followed directly behind her father's. His steps seemed aimless, as if he didn't know where to go. And then, as though his swelling voice had been building to it, a thunderous cry tore through the house. Holly pulled the door open and ran out into the middle of the rec room, where she froze when her father wailed a second time. She didn't know what was happening or why. She didn't want to know. But she started crying, too. Her hands were shaking.

Into the chaos of her thoughts came the memory of a storm.

Her moshom was standing at the side of her bed. He was holding her hand. She could feel the bones through his skin. She could feel his strength. It made her less afraid. Every once in a while, she saw a glint of light, like when the spark wheel of a lighter is turned, but the flame doesn't ignite. Like chewing wintergreen Life Savers in pitch black. Seconds after that light, she heard thunder crack, and it made her entire body shake.

"Don't be afraid," he said. "It's Thunderbird, the beating of its wings."

Something hard hit the ground. A cellphone, Holly thought. Her father cried out again. Something big hit the ground. The crying didn't stop. Holly forced her legs into movement, ran across the basement, and stopped at the bottom of the stairs. She saw her father, crumpled like a paper ball on the floor. Trembling as though he'd just come in from the cold. Trembling like her. His hands were clutched together over his head. His forehead was pressed against his knees. He was hyperventilating. Her mother was on her knees, covering him with her body as though protecting him from a bomb blast. Holly just stood there, looking up at her father, unable to move. She had never seen him like this. She fell to her knees, on the bottom step, hands in her lap between her thighs, cupped together, trying to steady them.

Don't be afraid.

Her mother looked up, met eyes with her.

"What's going on?" she mouthed to her mother.

Her mother's face was pale. She'd been crying, too. Her cheeks were soaked. What bomb had gone off?

Her father screamed like he was in pain. She could feel the vibrations on the soles of her feet.

Her mother shook her head.

"I'll come see you," she mouthed to Holly. "I'll come see you soon."

Holly pushed herself off the step and stood. Her mother turned away. Holly turned away. She took one step, then another, until she was back in her room.

Her father cried out again.

In her room, she turned up the music so that she couldn't hear her father. She lay on her bed, curled up into a ball. A crumpled piece of paper. She closed her eyes, covered her face with her palms, and whispered along to the lyrics.

I was born and you began to disappear.

By the time the last song of the record had played, by the time the final words had been sung, by the time the stylus had ended its journey across the black circle and all that was left was the metronomic rhythm of static, coming and going like soft steps in heavy snow, Holly's father had stopped crying.

Holly stared at the record player. She watched the tone arm undulate over the warped imperfection of the paper-thin disc. She thought the tone arm was rising and falling to the beat of her heart. She thought there was synchronicity between the two. She wondered what that could mean. She wondered if it meant anything at all.

Eventually, Holly heard her parents get up from the floor. She sat up and turned off the record player, replacing the arm in its cradle, the stylus scratching as the needle was lifted off the turntable.

She prepared herself for whatever her mother would come and say.

Footsteps descended the stairs, then approached Holly's bedroom door. With each step, Holly's heartbeat quickened. Droplets of sweat formed. A feeling of dread overwhelmed her. When the doorknob turned, when her mother didn't bother to knock, a rule Holly had firmly established when she'd moved her room to the basement, Holly was glad she'd taken the last two Xanax. How bad would her anxiety have been otherwise?

Now she was face to face with her mother, who was standing in the doorway, looking deathly white, with loose strands of hair glued against her damp cheeks. The strands were razor thin. How odd to notice something that small.

Her mother cleared her throat and met eyes with Holly. Those red eyes. Those apologetic eyes. Her lips were trembling. She cleared her throat a second time.

"You should go see your father," she said in a whisper, as though she were afraid to wake somebody up.

"Why?"

Holly knew the answer would be bad. Of course the answer would be bad. Her eyes welled up with tears and her breath shortened. It felt like she was on the verge of a panic attack, but it refused to come. Those fucking pills.

"Because . . ." Her mother glanced back and forth, from the floor to Holly, from the floor to Holly.

"*Mom.*"

"Your moshom died today. He went to sleep. He went to have . . . He had a nap. He slept a long time. Your moshom. He slept so long. He liked to nap during the day, but not for so long, you know."

"What are you talking about?"

Those fucking pills. She wanted to feel this. She wanted to feel all of it.

Her mother wiped away tears with both hands. She took a deep, stuttered breath to try to calm herself.

"Your kōkom went to check on him just a couple of hours ago, just to see if he was hungry, because he hadn't eaten since he had an early lunch with your father. She . . . and he was gone, Holly. He was just gone. I'm sorry."

Holly wanted her mother to scream the words as loud as she could, so that Holly would wake up and find that this had all been a dream. She thought of the Elder, Rebecca. She wondered if Moshom had been dead when she was talking to Rebecca. She wondered what sort of dream he'd been having. She wondered if he'd been dreaming at all.

"Where's Dad?"

Her father was sitting on the couch in the family room, in relative darkness, staring forward at a blank television screen. A hazy light reflected off it from the kitchen. Holly could see her own silhouette in the reflection, standing at the edge of the kitchen. She walked across the family room and sat down beside him. He didn't look at her, but greeted her all the same. A slight head nod. His eyelids fluttered. A tear fell, curled down his cheek. His arms had been folded, but he unfolded them now. Placed his hands flat against the couch, palms down, on either side of his legs, as though he was trying to brace himself, as though he was about to fall to one side.

Holly reached forward and placed her hand atop his. She curled her fingers around the base of his thumb. She could feel the lines on his palm. She ran her fingertips across them like a needle running over the etched grooves of a record, like she could play a song like that, from the contours of his skin.

They sat there together for a long time, his hand in hers, deep into the night, without a word between them.

PART
TWO

Your moshom used to talk about the trapline like an old friend he hadn't seen for years. He'd made plans to visit, he'd intended to visit, as people make plans to see one another, but never did. They weren't empty promises; he just ran out of time. When we got deep in a conversation, our words always led back to the land. For your moshom, the land was the answer to everything.

The trees whisper answers to any question you could think to ask, by the rustling of their leaves. Your moshom said the land remembered every foot that pressed down on its surface, every set of eyes that gazed upon its ancient beauty, every fingertip that touched its skin, every face the sun warmed. Every living thing—the fish, the four-legged creatures, the birds—was an extension of the land, and when you walked onto it, you became an extension of it, too.

You became the land.

He said you could remember the land even if you had never been there before, if your ancestors lived on it, and, in turn, the land remembered you.

Your moshom used to talk about the crows. They would erupt from the trees like shards of night and circle above in a dance. These swirling lines of black. When they cawed, it would be a song. They would dance to that welcoming song. As you walked deeper and deeper into the trapline, the crows would lower, their music would grow louder, and soon you'd be engulfed by them. It would feel like night, no matter what time of day it was, but you wouldn't be afraid.

I used to try to picture crows bursting from trees, flying in circles, singing a welcoming song, and dancing lower and lower until they held me in their dark embrace. It was hard to believe. Would crows do that? Would they dance in the air? Would they sing? What was the trapline, some kind of fucked-up Disney movie? Could a bird remember somebody even after years of absence? How long did a crow live? Ten years? Twenty? If somebody could remember the land even if they'd never been there before, could it work the same way with crows? Could the crows remember them and their children and their children's children? Could crows pass down that recognition as well?

Your moshom never lied to me, but there were Cree legends he told me that I knew weren't true, that represented something else. Like I know that Canada isn't actually on the back of a turtle. I know that Wisakedjak didn't create humans. He didn't make mud out of dirt and water, mould that mud into a humanoid figure, dry it over fire, and then breathe life into it. The theory of crows seemed equally tenuous, but provable, if you were to go to the place where you would be remembered.

The irony of all this was that your moshom couldn't remember where his trapline was. For all his talk of how the land and the swift water, the birds and the four-legged creatures, could answer any question, remember any person, accept you as a part of it, it was lost to him. Water levels rose and changed once-familiar shorelines. Landmarks fell away like broken street signs. Cabins were destroyed; cabins were constructed.

Maybe if he could've gone himself. Maybe if he could've traversed the same waterways that he did as a child. Maybe he could've found his way there one last time. Maybe he could've seen enough of the path to rediscover the place that he remembered, and it would've remembered him. A waterfall. A bend in the river. An eagle's nest bulging at the top of a thin tree, like a bursting water pipe. A lake with so many reeds protruding through the surface that it looked like hair. A narrow stream no wider than a sidewalk.

Maybe.

Your moshom used to talk about the importance of time. The animals had patterns that you needed to follow, and if you missed those patterns, you ate less, and you were able to trade less. You would be left behind, as though swallowed by the darkness and lost within it.

I've never been to the land. He ran out of time, and because of that, so did I. But I know what that's like. I know what it feels like to know what home is and not be able to find your way there.

13

Hallelujah had said that she wanted to go with Matthew to the funeral home. He needed to go down there to go over the arrangements. That's what the funeral director had called them, the "arrangements," as though she were talking about flowers or edible fruit, not all the decisions that needed to be made following his father's death. The word had seemed cold to him, and while on the phone, his tone was sharp toward her, but she seemed unphased by it. When he ended the call, he admitted to himself that she walked a delicate line. She undoubtedly made calls like this daily and had likely become desensitized to death out of necessity, but she needed to sound sympathetic, just not enough to make it about her. It was not a profession he would've chosen.

Matthew decided to try his best not to get too annoyed by the exchange, and to be cordial when he met her in person. This was one of the reasons he'd agreed to let Holly come with him to the funeral home. If his daughter was there, he was far more likely to keep his emotions in check than if she was not. Over the days since his father's sudden passing, Matthew and Hallelujah had warmed to each other somewhat, far sooner than Matthew would have expected, and through the grief and pain, he'd been on his best behaviour when Holly was around. He didn't want to fuck things up. He agreed to let her come with him and, in fact, welcomed her presence, and not only because he expected that she'd mitigate his emotions. He wouldn't admit it openly, but he needed somebody with him. Matthew's mother didn't want to attend the meeting, and to make sure she was okay, Claire had offered to be with her. That meant the only person left to accompany him was Hallelujah, and though the circumstances were horrible, he was glad for it.

They still hadn't spoken much to each other, but Matthew didn't think it was due to their fight. Holly was stubborn but nowhere approaching cruel. It was more that he'd not had much to say since his father's death, so there wasn't much conversation. He had become lost inside memories and, for the most part, chose to exist within them, like the living version of *Eternal Sunshine of the Spotless Mind*. A part of him was afraid that if he didn't spend his time living in the memories he had of his father, he would lose them. They would slip away.

Then share thy pain, allow that sad relief;
Ah, more than share it! give me all thy grief.

On the way to the funeral home, Matthew turned off the music that Holly had been playing. It was a song that he was fond of, but one that had become difficult to hear: "Naeem." On the night he'd learned of his father's death, after Claire and Holly had gone to bed after spending hours sitting with him in the dark, Matthew played *I, I* by Bon Iver. He wanted to listen to something slow and sad, and it was a good choice. He intended to play the entire album all the way through, on repeat, but after "U (Man Like)" came "Naeem," and he found himself playing that song over and over. He thought he listened to it at least twenty times before falling asleep, and it was still playing when he woke up early in the morning. Some songs become tied to memories. Some songs become memories altogether. "Naeem" became his father's death, just like Pearl Jam's *No Code* had become a weekend at West Hawk Lake with friends when he was nineteen years old.

They drove in relative silence, stealing glances at one another. Each time Matthew looked at Holly, she was staring out the window, but he could tell that she was not looking at anything. Her eyes were blank. She was looking at something in the past. She was lost inside her memories. He often wondered what she had inherited from him. In that moment, he became more aware of what that might be.

If he was lost, that was fine. He'd become used to being lost. He'd become as used to being lost as he had become used to his emptiness, but he didn't want Hallelujah to be like him. She was too young to be lost. She was too young to wander. He knew that she had taken his Xanax. He was obsessive about the number of pills he had left. He counted them regularly to make sure he never ran out. A couple of days ago, he found his pill bottle was three pills short, and he knew that it was Holly who had taken them. Claire wouldn't have. Claire dealt with her anxiety differently than Matthew. Claire was more functional in her anxiety because she had to be, because Matthew was not. He cleared his throat, looked at Holly again, met eyes with her for the briefest moment before she looked away, and so did he.

"You know, it's funny," he said.

She looked at him again and, this time, didn't look away.

"It's the memories that don't seem important that you remember most. Just little moments that you don't ever think you're going to recall, and then years later, they're the clearest. And, conversely, the opposite end of the spectrum, the big moments, the spotlight moments, they don't seem as important when it comes down to it."

"Yeah," she said.

"For a while, I was trying to think of the last thing I said to your moshom, the last, like"—his voice began to shudder, but he caught himself—"the very last moment in our lives together, but I can't fucking remember. Sorry. I can't remember."

"I've heard profanity before, Dad."

"I just . . . it's gone," he said. "And I've been thinking about that. If you're going to remember one thing, wouldn't it be the last moment, the last word, the last . . . Just, that's it. I'll never get to say another word to him, and I can't even remember the last thing I said to him. You know?"

"I can't, either," she said. "I can't remember, either. I don't even remember the last time I saw him, and how fucked up is that? How fucking . . ."

"I know."

"Sorry."

"I've heard profanity before, Hallelujah."

"How sad is that, though? To lose that."

Matthew had been driving at a snail's pace. Winnipeg drivers did not like slow drivers. The car directly behind him had been tailgating him to let him know that he needed to speed the fuck up. Matthew hadn't noticed until now, when the car honked. He pressed down on the gas pedal.

"Know what I've been thinking about? The memory that's stuck in my head? Your moshom and I used to golf all the time. We didn't go as often in the last couple of years, but when he was younger, we golfed a few times a week. He was really good. Just fairways and greens, fairways and greens. He used to say that he played bogey golf, tried to get a five on every hole. Shot for ninety." Matthew pulled into the median lane and turned on his left blinker, waited for traffic to clear. "I didn't have a goal in terms of a score. Ninety, ninety-five, eighty-five, whatever. My goal was always to beat your moshom. It didn't matter what we both shot as long as I shot one stroke less than him." He turned into the funeral home's parking lot and pulled into a spot. He put the vehicle in park but didn't turn off the car. "I never beat him. We played hundreds of games together, and I didn't beat him once."

"I know," she said. "You told me that every time you came home from golfing with him. You'd talk about how you didn't beat him, but how you weren't sure if you wanted to, because if you beat him, it would mean he was getting older. You didn't want him to get older."

"We used to play two courses the most. A few years ago, maybe ten years ago, when he was still hitting the ball pretty far, we both went into the right trees, about the same spot. We drove up in our cart—we were using carts by then because his knees weren't up for the walk—and we were walking around like those guys at the beach with their metal detectors, right?"

"Looking for lost treasure," Holly said.

"Looking for lost treasure." Matthew smiled at the memory, picturing him and his father wandering around in the forest, getting ticks on their legs that they'd have to pull off later. "At one point, I was pretty deep. About to quit looking. I was going to take a stroke and just drop a ball. Take my medicine. Anyway, through the trees I saw your moshom." He shook his head and laughed, then cupped his mouth before the laughter turned into tears. He took a breath and the air filtered through his fingers. "I saw your moshom kick his ball away from the trees and into the rough, where he'd have a shot. I was so mad. I was so fucking mad because the game was close and I thought I might beat him and . . ." Matthew put his hands back on the steering wheel and gripped it until his knuckles turned white. His hands were shaking. "I *am* glad I never beat him. I was glad I couldn't even beat him last year, when he was getting weak, because it made me feel like, I don't know, like he was stronger than he was. But, Hallelujah, that was the moment, that was the exact moment." He took a deep, drawn-out breath. "We think our parents are invincible. We think they're superheroes, at least when we're younger. That was the moment when I knew that my dad wasn't. That he was human. He found his ball in the trees and used his foot wedge to give himself a shot." Matthew laughed, and then sighed. "He probably would've beat me anyway."

Time passed. One minute, then another. Matthew cut the engine. The car started to cool down quickly.

"That's it. That's the memory. Out of all the time we spent together, out of all the moments we had, little things like that stick with us. You just never know, Hall. You just never know. I want you to have moments like that, with me."

Holly nodded. "He was still a superhero, Dad."

Matthew looked to the left, at the funeral home. His father was somewhere inside the building. He still hadn't decided whether he wanted to see him or not. The last time he saw his father, they were walking through deep snow together, just trying to make it to the stop sign and back. He must have been so weak. He must have been so tired. On the way back, he'd stumbled, and Matthew had grabbed his arm. Just once. Just another moment.

"Yeah," Matthew said. "Yeah, he was."

"Thor has his hammer; Moshom had a foot wedge," Holly said.

Matthew got out of the car and so did Holly. They met at the rear bumper and walked toward the building together.

"That goddamn foot wedge."

14

When you walked inside the building, there was a waiting room immediately to the left; there was an actual fireplace lit and crackling; there was a pot of coffee, a kettle, a container with an assortment of tea, cups, a box of sugar cubes, and one of those miniature cartons of milk, all on a stand; there was a painting of a cabin in the middle of a forest with a path leading to it strewn with autumn leaves; and there was a rotating magazine stand, the kind she'd seen in drugstores that were typically filled with comic books. This one was filled with brochures that touted all the additional services that were available. The different styles of urns you could get. The models of caskets that were available to choose from ("With a refined style, premium fabric linings, impeccable finish, graceful curves, and unmatched durability, the MW21 Strafford Classic is a necessity for your dearly departed"). What sort of cremation container your loved one could get burned to dust in. The cost of a funeral if you planned on having it there in the attached church. The room may as well have been a car dealership. Cruise control? Power windows and locks? Remote starter? Directly ahead of them was a staircase to a second floor that was cloaked in darkness and, as a result, creepy as hell. To the right of the staircase was a small, sterile room that Holly could just barely see into from where she was standing. To their right was a narrow hallway that led to two enormous, rustic doors, which opened to the church. The hallway had a fancy red runner with gold trim. Holly hit her father's arm and pointed it out to him.

"That looks like something you'd see at a movie premiere," she said. "Where does the paparazzi stand?"

"The paparazzi are kind of the ones sitting in the pews, aren't they?" her father said.

Holly thought about it for a moment, then nodded. "Yeah, I guess so."

The funeral director fetched them, and they followed her to the meeting room with all the coffee and hot water and brochures. She offered them something to drink. Holly took a coffee with an abundance of sugar, and her father opted for a peppermint tea because, he noted, his stomach had been bothering him.

"Grief does a lot of things to the body," the funeral director said.

"Or he could just be gluten intolerant or have IBS or something," Holly said as they were seated.

She focused on one brochure in particular, about the casket models. SA23 was the model on the front of it. She was surprised to see that coffins were named like luxury automobiles, like you were choosing between a Lexus or a Mercedes-Benz. She wondered what sort of urn her moshom would be getting. She'd overheard her parents talking to her kōkom about it the other day, that her moshom was to be cremated. She heard them talking about urns after that. Her father didn't care. Her mother thought it might be nice to get one of those urns that grew a tree. Holly googled it quickly and said, "A living urn." She didn't hear what her kōkom said on the subject. Her parents must've heard her in the hallway, listening in, and shut the door.

Her father took a sip of the peppermint tea and told the funeral director that it tasted fine, and thanked her. They had a peppermint-centric conversation for the next couple of minutes that discussed the benefits of aromatherapy.

Holly sipped at her coffee, which tasted like black licorice, bitter and sweet and slightly burned. All the money they made selling luxury coffins, and they couldn't afford a better coffee maker.

Her father raised his Styrofoam cup to his mouth and tipped it against his lips without swallowing any hot liquid. Holly heard him smell the inside of the cup. He put it down, directly on top of the ring it had made.

"Sometimes aromatherapy isn't quite enough when you've gone through a loss like your family has," the funeral director said, looking back and forth from Holly to her father. "We do offer counselling services as part of our package, if it's something you think you need."

"I've got a counsellor, thanks," her father said.

"I think mine's in that room over there," Holly said, pointing her lips in the direction she was certain her moshom was in—that small, sterile room. She almost laughed at the lip pointing, which was incidental but very Cree. She thought that her moshom would've been proud of the gesture. Next thing you knew, she'd be telling a joke and sticking her tongue out while laughing. Or saying *deadly* all the time. "He's kind of irreplaceable, though."

There was nothing quite like silence at a funeral home. The dead were so quiet. The staff were so quiet, as though the dead could be woken.

The funeral director pushed the binder to the side and smiled robotically, as though she had been programmed to show empathy but couldn't feel it. Holly had seen better smiles at 7-Eleven, but still appreciated the effort. She appreciated the funeral director's 7-Eleven smile, which somehow, by some miracle, didn't seem disingenuous, just practised. Holly supposed that there was a requirement for that kind of distance in her line of work, seeing dead bodies and grieving family members daily.

"Would you like to see your lost one?" the funeral director said.

Lost one, Holly repeated in her mind. It was a poor choice of words. Why did people say that about the dead? Why did people say, *I'm sorry for your loss*? What exactly had been lost? It was as though her moshom was the television remote, stuck somewhere between cushions. It was as though her moshom could be found, if he were only lost. *The departed* was better. *Would you like to see the departed?* He was most certainly that. Departed to where, she didn't have the faintest idea. And she didn't think her father did, either. Her moshom had been a minister but had never pressed his beliefs on the family. Holly liked to think of herself as practical. If she were able to see evidence of the afterlife, fine. Until then, her moshom had taken a one-way trip to the great void. Maybe, she thought, that's what *loss* meant. The departed were lost in the void of nothingness. *Fuck, you're so depressing.*

"Hallelujah?" her father said.

"Huh?" Holly's mind stopped wandering, and she came back to reality.

"Did you want to see your moshom?"

"Do *you* want to see him?"

"No," her father said. "I don't think I will, but if you'd like to . . ."

"I wouldn't fucking *like to*, Dad," she said. "I wouldn't *like to* see my grandfather's body."

"I know, I'm sorry," her father said gently, as though she were brittle. On the subject of her moshom being dead, that wasn't an inaccurate description. But she was more than brittle; she was already broken, just like her father, just like her kōkom, and the one person she would have turned to with something like this was her moshom. Where the fuck was he now? She didn't even think she could speak to Rebecca, the Elder, about it, because that would just remind Holly of how she wished that Rebecca was her moshom.

"What I meant," her father said, "what I was trying to say, is that you haven't seen a body before, and if you want to see him, that's obviously your choice, but wherever his body is right now, wherever you're going to see it, your moshom is somewhere else."

"Do you really believe that?" she said.

It was as though her words were knives. Her father placed his hand over his chest as though he'd been stabbed through the heart. But then he deflated, as though her words weren't knives at all, just pins. She'd let the air out of her father. He went from looking taken aback to exhausted.

"That's not him in there," her father said.

Holly felt outside of her body and unable to control her actions or words the longer she stayed in the sales room. That's what she'd decided to call it, the *sales room*. Her heart was beating rapidly. She felt hot, and not from the fireplace, though she wanted to throw the funeral director's stupid fucking binder into it, along with all the brochures. Her fingers were shaking, and she was doing her best to keep them hidden from view so that she wouldn't appear as vulnerable as she felt.

As brittle.

"It's okay if you don't want this to be your last memory of him, the last time you see his face," her father said. "It's okay if you want to keep it a good memory."

"Don't put your own shit on me, Dad. I'll go see him, even if you can't."

Holly got up from the table. It didn't matter whether she wanted to see her moshom or just to get out of the room before she lost her cool more than she had already. It didn't matter whether he was gone, lost, or departed. It didn't matter if the body wasn't really him. Maybe it was and maybe it wasn't.

"You know I don't even remember the last time I saw him. I told you that."

Holly figured that any last memory was better than none.

Holly left her father behind in the sales room and followed the funeral director past the front entrance, past the staircase and then around it, toward the back room. They stopped a few feet before the doorway. From where she was, if she looked, Holly could have seen her moshom lying in a plain wood casket, opened and ready for viewing, but instead, she looked at her shoes, of all things, the Converse sneakers she'd thrown on before leaving the house, the ones her mother told her not to wear because it was too cold out for them. The laces on her right shoe were untied. She bent over and tied them methodically. She tied them too tight, like basketball players did when they sprained an ankle, to keep the swelling down. She didn't loosen them, hoping to trade one pain for another.

The funeral director was waiting patiently, and gone was the fake, plastic smile. She knew when and where to pull out the 7-Eleven smile. In its place were more genuine, sympathetic eyes.

"Take your time," she said.

"I'm ready," Holly said.

The funeral director, whose hands were folded together in front of her stomach, stretched out one arm, palm up, to usher her inside the room. Holly hesitated after taking a step. She was still looking at her shoes, refusing to look at the casket.

"Do you want me to come in with you?"

"No." Holly shook her head. "That's okay. You don't need to."

She took another step. Then she glanced back at the woman. "But could you wait right there?"

"Of course I can," she said. "I'll be here."

Holly watched her feet inch forward as she took another step, then another, drawing closer and closer to her moshom's body. When she stopped at the casket, her knees felt weak, and they began to shake. She put her hands on the edge of the casket to steady herself. She was worried that she might pass out. The room was bright with fluorescent lighting, but it felt as though it had dimmed.

The other night, she'd gotten lost in the abyss of YouTube, and she'd wound up watching a video of a soldier who was suffering from post-traumatic stress disorder and travelled to the world's quietest room in search of peace. The room she was in felt like that sort of quiet, a pervasive silence that she could feel in her bones, in her veins. When she swallowed, it sounded like ocean waves crashing against the shore. When she blinked, it felt like a crow erupting into flight.

How odd.

The body was her moshom's, clearly, but at the same time, her father had been right: it wasn't him at all. It was a puzzling dichotomy. When her kōkom had found him, she thought he was asleep. It wasn't until she had walked to his bedside and nudged him, to try to stir him, that she realized he was gone. An hour earlier than that, she'd peeked into the room, seen him, and thought nothing of it; she'd decided to let him sleep a little while longer. By then, according to when they'd estimated his time of death was, he'd been dead for hours already.

Holly's moshom looked moulded, like a figure at Madame Tussauds. She reached forward and touched his cheek, and it was hard and cold, and felt precisely and appropriately like wax. She removed her hand as though she'd held it to a fire.

"Moshom," she said. "Tansi, Moshom. Kisakīhitin."

He was wearing his favourite outfit: navy slacks, a cloud-white Oxford shirt, a simple black tie. He wasn't wearing any shoes, though. Holly wondered about that. Why hadn't they dressed him in shoes? It wasn't his favourite outfit without his Hush Puppies.

"I'm sorry I didn't come to see you," she said. "I called you, you know. I called you that day. I was having this dream." She moved strands of hair that had fallen on either side of her face behind her ears, but she did not wipe away the tears that had fallen, that were streaking down her face. "It was about me and Dad. It was so fucked up, Moshom. I was so confused, and I just needed you to tell me what it meant. I called you, and you were probably . . ."

She bent down until her forehead was pressed against his shoulder. She sobbed into his Oxford shirt. Her tears dampened the shirt until parts of it were see-through. When she lifted her head, she could see that his skin there was pale. His face wasn't. His hands weren't.

"They put some kind of bronzer on you? Really? Like you're a settler actor playing an Indian on television?"

She ran her fingers across his hair, just so the strands tickled her skin. His hair felt like straw.

"Holly?" The funeral director poked her head in. "I really hate to make you feel rushed, but—"

"It's fine," she said. "It's okay. Can you just give me one more minute?"

"Of course."

Holly took that minute to stand beside her moshom and take in every detail of him, not worrying about what was real and what was not. It wasn't him. It was him. It was what it needed to be for her to have a moment. Not good. Not bad. A moment, and one that she would remember. When the minute was over, Holly bent over and kissed her moshom's cold forehead, and then walked out of the room.

The funeral director led her back to the sales room, where her father was waiting, and they stayed for at least another hour while the lady finally got her sales pitch in. She toured them through another area of the funeral home to look at different urns, guest books for the funeral, pretty caskets he would burn to dust in, mugs they could have his face on, and holy god, the price of it all.

Her father had more peppermint tea and several cookies that the funeral director set out for them. He whispered to Holly that for the price they were paying, they might as well get as much free stuff as they could. Holly had more coffee with sugar and cream but couldn't stomach a cookie.

By the time they left, they had been there for more than two hours, and neither her father nor the funeral director had noticed that she had no shoes on her feet, even when Holly scurried across the parking lot as if she were walking on hot coals.

Memories break down like your body does, as though it's not just your life that is slowly falling away, but whatever came before you. It makes life seem shorter, because there's less behind you. It's like dreams upon waking. But some memories are stubborn. Some memories mean too much to become insignificant.

That's you.

It was a week before Christmas. Your mother was two weeks late, so she had to be induced. She liked to think that you just didn't want to leave her. I like to think that, too. We had three midwives at our house. Kind of odd that there were no alarms and no surprises, that we knew you were going to come that day.

I'd been waiting for you to arrive for a month. Every time your mother came into the room, I imagined that she was going to say her water had broken, and then we'd frantically get everything together and rush to the hospital. Your mother would be in the back seat, yelling at me to hurry up, that you were coming, and we'd get there just in time.

I watch too many movies.

It didn't change anything, that there was no rush. It helped us savour your arrival even more. Such a contrast, that everything was calm. We were calm. And so were you.

They broke your mother's water and then we waited for the contractions to start. The first thing your mother wanted to do was walk, so we bundled up and went to the end of the block, just to the stop sign and back. We held hands. The contractions started halfway through the walk.

"She's coming," your mother said.

We hadn't thought of your name yet. We'd thrown around a ton of options. Your mother thought that when she looked at you, she'd know what to call you. You know how sometimes people just look like their name. She wanted people to look at you and say, "Yeah, that's the perfect name for her."

It didn't happen that way. Life never happens the way you expect, or the way you want. It has its own plan.

Between the first contraction and the second, your mother ran into a yard we happened to be walking by and lay down in the middle of it. There'd been a fresh snowfall that morning. She started to make a snow angel. She was laughing so hard. She was crying from laughing, and, I think, from relief. We never thought we'd have a baby. We'd tried so many times before. You were our miracle.

The stars were brighter than they should have been, seeing as how we were in the middle of the city. They'd no business being that bright. I'd only ever seen them that bright in Norway House, where there were no city lights. It was as though they burned brighter to welcome your arrival. I know how cheesy that is. I know it's impossible, and maybe it was me seeing the sky so bright because I wanted to remember it that way, but that's how it was. Sometimes the meaning we put on something matters more than the truth of it. Sometimes the meaning of it becomes the truth, and I don't see anything wrong with that. I remember it that way, so that's how it was. Remember that game you had as a kid, Lite-Brite or something? All those holes of bright white. That's what the sky was like.

I watched the sky and the stars, watched your mother, watched her flap her arms and legs back and forth, listened to her laugh with such joy because of the miracle of you, and because of all of that, I called out to her, "I know her name."

She stopped making her snow angel. She sat up and held her arm out for me to help her up. She took my hand and got up carefully, so her angel wouldn't get ruined. We looked at the snow angel and I told your mother your name.

"It's perfect," she said. "Holly for short. We'll have to call her Holly, you know, when she's older."

"Halls," I said.

"She's not a throat lozenge, Matt."

Once we got back from our walk, it happened quickly. The contractions were a minute or so apart, and then it was time to push, just like that. You were born in our bedroom. I managed to hold her hand and watch you come into the world. I remember thinking, Oh my god, that's a human being and we made her. I know it's biology, but if you think about it, you started out smaller than nothing, grew in your mother's stomach, and came out a perfect human being. I'm not a God kind of guy—you know that—but that was probably the only moment in my life that seemed supernatural to me.

You didn't nurse properly. You weren't gaining weight the way you should have, and we didn't know why. That first month, we didn't get much sleep. Especially your mother. She couldn't have slept more than a couple of hours that whole month. I'd take you from time to time and walk around so she could nap, but convincing her to let go of you was almost impossible. She'd nurse you, but you wouldn't latch right, so she'd supplement your feeding with milk that she'd pumped, and then she'd pump more when you were done, and, well, it just never seemed to end. I've no idea how she kept going.

It won't surprise you to know that it was your mother who figured out what was wrong. The doctor wanted you to go on formula. He said that some babies were just formula babies. Your mother was having none of that. She thought you had a tongue-tie, which kept your tongue from doing what it had to do to nurse properly. She fought to get your procedure done. The doctor cut a little piece of flesh that connected your tongue to the bottom of your mouth, and when we got home, you were nursing perfectly. That night, your mother slept well for the first time in a month. No more supplementing. No more pumping all the time. You gained weight like normal, and I think that was a miracle, too.

Hallelujah. Hallelujah.

I also think that being tongue-tied, well . . . isn't that just a perfect fucking metaphor, Holly? Getting that little piece of flesh cut. You've never been at a loss for words. That's why when you said you didn't want to talk to me, it hurt so much more. You always said what was on your mind, and whatever I'd done, you had no words left for me. After your moshom died, when we talked, it felt like you were just being kind or something, like you knew I was hurting and so you made sure I wasn't hurting more than I had to. Like you didn't want to give me more than I could take—my grief, yours. I should've been the one protecting you. Point is, I knew things weren't fixed between us, because I hadn't fixed myself.

According to your moshom, there was only one place where I could do that.

15

Matthew was in the basement of his parents' home, his father's favourite hiding spot, the place where he preferred to go when he wanted to be alone—especially in the last couple of years, when walking long distances was too much for him. Before that, when he wasn't with Matthew or Holly, his father would walk a little more than six city blocks to a place called Omand's Creek. Matthew knew the place well; in high school, that's where most of the bush parties happened. That's where he'd kissed a girl for the first time, in grade ten. His father would walk from Wellington Crescent to a foot bridge that led over the Assiniboine River, follow a path along the river, and then head down to the riverbank. There was a felled tree near the riverbank. He would sit on that tree for as long as he liked, watching the river, listening to it, feeling it, as though it were part of him. He used to say that it was. He used to say that water is life.

The basement was no river. You couldn't listen to the sound of water, except when somebody flushed the toilet. It was, however, something of a sanctuary. There was a television set that his father used to watch sports or his favourite shows, like *NCIS*.

There were two dumbbells on the floor by the couch, light ones, ten pounds each, and he'd intermittently do a few biceps curls, usually during commercials. There were bookshelves that took up an entire wall, full of an overwhelming number of books that he'd read over the years, and games that he used to make Matthew play, like Pente, which nobody in Matthew's class had heard of, or cribbage, which was his father's preferred game. As with golf, Matthew had never beaten his father at cribbage. Matthew did even worse at cribbage than at golf, more often than not getting skunked. His father had a Rubbermaid container full of tobacco that he'd been given over the years as an Elder, for doing opening prayers and giving workshops. When Matthew had discovered the container filled to the brim with the sacred medicine, his father had told him that when offered tobacco, you should offer it to Mother Earth with a prayer, and then bury the tie.

"Why do you have so many ties, then?" Matthew said.

"You can only pray so much," his father said.

Made sense.

One shelf had a collection of at least a hundred notebooks, all filled by his father throughout his adult life with musings on the state of Indigenous education, workforce development, land protection, language revitalization, reconciliation, and more. There were quotations, too.

I am only one,
But I am one.
I cannot do everything,
But I can do something.
What I can do, I ought to do;
And, what I ought to do,

By the grace of God,
I will do.

"That's pretty vague, Dad," Matthew had said once. "Do what?"

"Do what you can."

His father had summed up the quotation that easily. He had a way of doing that, of making hard things seem . . . not so hard. Not easy, but not impossible, either.

On the floor, underneath the shelves, were prizes he'd won at charity golf tournaments but had never opened: a putting mat, a Dustbuster, a set of beer glasses, a bunch of shirts and hats with logos of Indigenous organizations, a disposable camera, an empty photo album.

There was a display cabinet near the stairs with a bunch of Indigenous artifacts that he'd been gifted or had collected over the years: a stone he'd dug up by the riverbank that was shaped like an arrowhead; an inukshuk; a wood carving of an eagle; a bigger inukshuk (people loved giving out inukshuks); a braid of sweetgrass; a smudge bowl with a bundle of sage in it; a carving of a wolf that looked like it had come from a Haida community; birchbark biting; a talking stick; a miniature canoe; and a framed poem that Holly had written when she was thirteen.

There was a TV tray in front of his father's spot on the couch, where a thick blanket he used to sit on still held the imprint of his body. Atop the TV tray was a disposable plate that had a blue floral design all around the edge. On the plate was a mouldy piece of toast, hardly eaten, slathered in peanut butter and strawberry jam, two slices of an apple that had browned and dried, and medication that he had never taken. He often said that he preferred traditional medicine over Western. When he could get away with it, he avoided taking it.

"The land has everything you need, including medicine to make you well," he'd said.

Beside the plate was a cup of cold herbal tea. Lemon ginger. His mother must not have had the heart to take any of these things away, nor to move the blanket and disturb the imprint, as though his father might still come and finish his toast and apple slices, drink the rest of the tea, and maybe even take his medication.

Matthew stared at the bite in the toast, and a drop of peanut butter that had spilled over the edge, collecting on the plate in a mound that looked like a miniature pile of shit. He had always used too much peanut butter. He had always spooned a big mound of jam in the middle of his toast and let it spread to the edges on its own.

"It's a science," his father had said, "knowing how much jam to put on the toast."

"Fascinating," Matthew had said.

His mother bought sugar-free jam, in consideration of the helpings he used. She bought natural peanut butter for the same reason. She'd always taken such care of his father. She'd fed him healthy food or, at least, mitigated the unhealthy food he snuck when she wasn't looking. And what had it mattered?

There was his bite mark. On the day he died, or the night before, he'd started to eat the toast, had eaten a mouthful of natural peanut butter and sugar-free jam, then stopped for some reason. He would not take one more bite of that toast. He would not take one more sip of herbal tea.

That's what was on Matthew's mind when he heard his

name, then felt Claire nudge his hip with her elbow to draw his attention.

He looked away from the toast.

"What was that?" he said. "What's the plan?"

Matthew assumed they were still on the subject of where his father's final resting place would be. His parents had never discussed it. As a matter of fact, they'd made no plans at all. That's why they'd planned the funeral according to what his father had liked and what his father had not liked. For instance, he did not like attention, and so it had been a small affair, with just family and close friends. His favourite song was "Amazing Grace," so the sparse crowd had sung the hymn. His best friend, a fellow Elder, had sung a travelling song. Matthew had given most of the eulogy, but when he broke down, Claire finished reading it for him. At the reception, there was bannock, butter, peanut butter, jam, Klik, herbal tea, and apple juice. The cremation had occurred beforehand. A framed picture of him was placed beside the urn at the front of the church, along with his medicine bundle, rather than flowers. That was the only picture. He hated pictures of himself. There was no slideshow. There was no poster with photographs glued to it at the front of the church near the guest book. There was no guest book.

"Do you think we should bury your father in Norway House or in the city?" his mother said. Winnipeg was an option because, she reasoned, "We spent half of our lives here," even though they'd both been born and raised on the rez, and had met there while working at the Northern store together, stocking shelves.

"Mom, this isn't a family discussion, is it? He was your husband."

"And he was your father."

179

"Yeah, but . . ."

Matthew sunk into the couch. He looked to Claire, sitting on a chaise, for help, but she shook her head apologetically. If it wasn't his decision, it wasn't hers, either. He closed his eyes and pressed his palms against his face, and kept them like that for a few seconds, breathing deeply, trying to maintain calm. He moved his palms away, opened his eyes, and settled his gaze on the toast, the shape of his father's mouth. He'd been eating it without his dentures in; Matthew could tell by the texture. A fucking piece of toast. He hadn't cried since the night he found out his father had passed away, and that's what was going to do it? He took another deep breath and tried to find something in the room that didn't remind him of his father. He ended up looking into the laundry room. The light was off and it was pitch black in there. It was a good place to look.

"It's not my call. You've got to bury him where you think he should be, and where you think you should be, when . . ."

The black, the endless black.

"Like, a long time from now."

"I just want us . . . him . . . to be somewhere you can visit without making a big deal of it," his mother said. "If he got buried on the rez, in the new cemetery, I mean, first off, it's not the prettiest spot."

"The old cemetery's way nicer," Matthew said. "Right by the lake there."

"They don't manage it, though, my son. How many unmarked graves are there? And the ones that aren't, the grass has grown over them."

"What else? You said, 'first off,' so what's second?"

"It's just so far."

It was far. Depending on who was driving and how many cars were at the ferry, it could take as long as eight hours to get to the community. If his father was buried there, they'd have to make a trip of it. As soon as Matthew had the thought, he liked the idea.

"It'll give me an excuse to get up there more often," he said. "It's kind of my home, too, right?"

"It's absolutely your home," she said.

There was regret in her voice when discussing the possibility of burying his father in Norway House. He could tell, just by her tone, that she didn't want him to be there, and that she didn't want to be there either. Matthew knew that she loved it up there, so that wasn't it. They hadn't raised their family there; they'd raised it here, in the city. His father had worked here, and so had his mother. They'd lived in the same house for years. They had just as many relatives here as they did up north, and more friends.

"Look," he said, "just bury him here. He should be here. You were looking at that spot . . ." Matthew snapped his fingers several times, trying to remember.

"The one by the college," his mother said, nodding to the northwest as though it were visible from the basement.

"Yeah, that one," he said. "By the college, close to the airport."

"It's nice there," Claire said, quiet and careful. "His mother's there, isn't she?"

"She is," Matthew's mother said.

Matthew reached over and put his hand on his mother's hand, assuring her that it was the correct choice. "That's where you want him to be, so that's where he should be."

His mother nodded, then, after a pause, said, "You'll still visit the rez, won't you?"

"Yeah," he said. "Yeah, of course. You know, I want to bring

Claire up there, and Hallelujah, too. She should see where you guys grew up, one day."

"If you want her to see where we grew up, you'd have to take her out onto the land," his mother said. "That's where we really grew up."

"Right, the land. Dad liked to talk about that."

"I know." She chuckled softly. "I lived with him, remember?"

As quickly as she chuckled, she turned serious and got up from the couch, which Matthew took to mean that he and Claire should stand as well.

"So that's settled, then."

His mother turned toward the stairs. Matthew and Claire followed her, and with each step, he noticed again that nothing of his father's had been moved or even touched. If somebody were to visit the house and didn't know better, they would think that he'd just stepped out, that he'd be right back. His galoshes were placed neatly on the boot tray by the back door. His coat was hanging on one of the hooks. His tartan flat cap, which paid homage to the very little Scottish blood in his body, was hanging beside his coat. He paused, while following Claire and his mother, to check the pockets of his father's coat—quickly, so that nobody would see. There was a gas receipt from two days before he'd died, and a candy bar wrapper. He wasn't allowed to eat candy bars, but snuck one every once in a while. His father didn't do much he wasn't supposed to do, but candy bars and Klik were two of his indulgences. Snickers. He must have bought it when he filled up the car.

Matthew couldn't reconcile it, that forty-eight hours before his death, he was getting gas, eating a chocolate bar; that the day of his death, his father had sat down with a piece of toast, apples, and some tea. Why hadn't he finished the toast? Why had he taken only one bite, then left it? He'd not touched his tea. He always let it cool until it was lukewarm. Then it hit Matthew: his father had put his breakfast in front of him on the TV tray, had taken a bite of his toast, and then he, Matthew, had called in a panic.

As Matthew, his mother, and Claire walked through the kitchen, he saw that the chair his father had always sat on was pulled out from the table. The kettle was out and there were two cups of water left in it, beads of condensation clinging to the water window. Beside the kettle was a bowl of white sugar, a tiny spoon sticking out of it. There was a package of herbal tea. By the toaster, there was an opened bag of whole wheat bread. The bread tag had been taken off and left flat on the counter. The bread would be stale by now. There were crumbs in front of the toaster. There were dirty dishes in the sink.

In the living room, while his mother and Claire veered off toward the front door, Matthew walked to the middle of the room and stood on the throw rug, looking for more relics. He could see why his mother had not touched any of his father's things. He found himself almost able to fool himself, in passing moments, that his father might walk into the room. Like he had just gone to the bathroom and would appear any second now, finish the crossword puzzle that was resting on the arm of the couch, figure out a four-letter word for "Lost no time."

His mother and Claire were talking by the front door as Claire got her coat and boots on.

"What's a four-letter word for 'Lost no time,' Claire?" Matthew said.

Claire was good at crossword puzzles. She and his father

would often call each other to brainstorm answers. It was how they connected. She thought about a possible answer to the clue while tying her boots on the bench in the entryway.

"Any letters?"

Matthew put his finger just below 50 down, and then ran it up across all four blocks. Three of them were empty, one was not.

"*P*," Matthew said. "The second letter is *p*."

"*Sped*." Claire pulled her toque over her ears. "It has to be *sped*."

Matthew picked up the pen that had been placed there, almost certainly the day his father had gone to sleep and not woken up. He held the newspaper steady with one hand and, with his dominant one, wrote *s*, then *e*, then finally *d*. When he finished, he placed the pen exactly where he'd found it. His mother and Claire were looking at him as though he'd broken an artifact at the museum.

"Lost no time," Matthew said.

His mother gave him a look that was hard for him to decipher, before saying, "Sped."

"It fits," Claire said.

It fell quiet. Matthew put on his coat and toque, then sat on the bench and slipped his feet into his boots before tying them. He opened the front door and was about to turn to his mother to say goodbye, when he stopped at the screen door.

It was another cold day. It had been a cold winter. The cold brought with it a clear, perfect blue sky. The sun was shining. Matthew couldn't look at the snow for too long, so bright was its reflection. Just looking at it for a few seconds caused his eyes to tear. He recalled a novel he'd read when he was younger, *Lost in the Barrens* by Farley Mowat, and how near the end of the book, the two boys, Jamie and Awasin, became snow-blind.

"*Awasin* doesn't mean anything in Cree," his father had pointed out when Matthew asked him what the name meant.

Cree names always meant something, except when a white writer made one up, Matthew supposed.

"*Awas* means 'go away,' though," his father had said.

He pictured his father sitting at the edge of his bed, the book on the nightstand spotlighted by the reading light. He'd turned off the light, and for a moment, everything had gone black.

Matthew pictured his father walking with him on the sidewalk on that last day, the blustery wind trying to push them back the way they had come, as though it knew something they did not. The cold, the deep snow from the snowfall—it had been too much for his father.

Matthew thought he knew then what the look his mother had given him meant.

"You don't blame me for Dad, do you?" he said while staring out the screen door, at the memory of their short, difficult walk.

Lost no time.

"No," his mother said. "No, of course not."

She'd paused. What did that mean?

The silence.

Of course not.

Matthew wasn't sure if he'd said the words or thought them.

He heard his father's voice, raised over the howling wind. "The land has all the answers," he'd said. "When it's summer, we'll go. I haven't been for so long. You can take me before I can't go any longer. We'll find my trapline . . ."

Summer would never come for his father. His father couldn't go anymore, and was that because of Matthew? If they hadn't gone for a walk, would his father still be with them? Would he

185

have finished the toast, the apple slices, the cup of tea? Would he have slid the chair back into place at the kitchen table, the chair legs scratching against the floor? Would he have finished the crossword puzzle? Lost no time. Sped. Would they have gone to his father's trapline together?

"Your father wanted to go for a walk," his mother said regretfully, as though she wished that she could take back how she'd looked, that she could have assured Matthew, that she wouldn't have paused. "It was his choice."

"It might have just been his time," Claire said.

She put her hand on Matthew's shoulder. It was the first time she'd touched him with care, really, since she'd checked his phone. He put his hand over hers before she moved it away. He turned around, and his mother was there with her arms out. He hugged her and said, "He wanted me to take him onto the land this summer. He wanted me to take him to his trapline."

"He didn't even know where it is anymore," his mother said.

"We were going to find it," he said. "We were going to find it together."

Their embrace ended, but his mother kept her hands on his arms before placing them against his cheeks.

"What are you getting at, my son?"

"Do you think . . ." Matthew thought about leaving it be, then realized he couldn't. It was a last wish that he needed to make happen. "Can I bring some of his ashes up north with me? If I can find it, I think he'd like it if I brought him there. Just, you know . . ."

Her eyes welled up with tears.

There was another pause. What did that mean? The silence.

"Okay," his mother said. "Take him."

"Really?" Matthew said. "If you don't want me to, I don't—"

She shushed him like she had when he was a child, when he felt lost and all he could do was cry. She nodded her head, and it shook her tears loose.

"I think he'd like it, too," she said.

16

Holly was in the kitchen, making herself a snack before bed, when she heard a light knock on the front door. She ignored it and kept constructing a miniature version of a charcuterie board, something her mother made on a larger scale from time to time. She'd pulled out a small, rectangular plate from the cupboard and was halfway done covering the dish with almonds, raspberries, a chocolate chip banana muffin from the freezer, blackberries, and pecans. She was about to add grapes, red and green, and some crackers and hummus when there was another knock, this time a bit louder, as though whoever was on the other side of the door realized that their first knock had been too soft. That, or they were getting cold. It had been a clear, sunny day, and clear, sunny days in the winter usually meant frigid temperatures. Holly finished spooning hummus into a small dish, placed it on the plate, clapped the cracker crumbs off her hands, and went to answer the door.

Normally, she left the task of answering the door to her parents except when she knew it was one of her friends, Char or Christian. Lately, just Char. Tonight, Holly knew that her parents were not likely to answer the door. Since coming home from her kōkom's house, they'd been in their bedroom talking—about what, she didn't know. But the fact that they were exchanging words at all felt like a good sign.

They'd not spoken this much in a long time.

When Holly arrived at the front door, she saw a black silhouette through the frosted glass that provided no clues as to the identity of the visitor. She flicked on the porch light and the figure remained black, only surrounded by bright white light now. Her father had installed a halogen bulb for this very reason. The entire porch was illuminated. If anybody came to the door with bad intentions, they'd be scared off. The dark stranger on the porch did not leave, just shuffled around a bit in anticipation of being welcomed out of the chill. Holly tried to guess who it was by the shape and height of the person, and it wasn't long before she figured it out.

She rolled her eyes, though nobody was around to see it, sighed deeply, briefly considered turning off the light and finishing her snack preparation, then opened the door a crack.

"Hey." Christian was noticeably shivering. "Can I come in?"

Holly stood in the doorway, guarding the entrance. "You can't just show up like this anymore, Chris."

"What else can I do? You haven't been answering my texts or my calls," he said, then blew warm air into his hands.

"I'm aware of that," Holly said. "That was deliberate. I clearly saw that you were calling and texting. Actually, it was fucking annoying, to be honest. Like, did you not get the message?"

"I just told you that you didn't *send* any messages back."

Christian had a smirk on his face. He thought he was being funny. Holly wanted to punch him in the teeth.

"A dad joke? Really?"

"It was more like a *bad* joke."

"Holy fuck, if I let you inside, will you stop?"

Holly went from wanting to punch Christian to wanting to pull her hair out. She stepped aside, backed up, and sat on the bench. He came inside, shut the door, and leaned against the opposite wall. He was still shivering and kept breathing into his hands.

"Do you want some hot water?" she said.

He took his hands away from his mouth. "Nah, I'm good."

"I'd make you tea, but I don't want to."

"I don't like tea."

"Coffee, either."

"Now that hurts."

"Well, you deserve it."

Holly crossed her arms and leaned back herself. She did her best not to make eye contact or to seem interested in him. It was hard, because even though she was monumentally pissed off at him, she still liked him. He was her first serious boyfriend, and he had to go and fuck it up by being an asshole. It only made it worse that he'd been an asshole on the day her moshom had died. She'd found a way to blame her pain on him, so that losing her moshom wouldn't hurt as much. It was easier to be mad at him than it was to miss her moshom.

"I get to say things about my father; you don't. Got it? You just have to . . ." She sighed again. "Just listen, Chris. You know? He's been fucked up, and so I've been fucked up, and you're not supposed to fuck it up more. You were supposed to un-fuck things."

"I know, Hall. I'm sorry, okay? I get it. I really get it."

Christian pushed off from the wall and took a step toward Holly. She uncrossed her arms. She glanced at him, then looked away.

"Do you know what happened that day?"

Christian stuffed his hands into his pockets. "Yeah, I know. Char told me."

"Right, so, I'm dealing with that." Holly put her hands on her knees and pushed herself off the bench. She and Christian were standing only a few feet away from each other. She started to cry. He stepped toward her. She shook her head and moved away. "I needed you that night, when I heard. I needed you the next day. I needed you all fucking week. I needed you, but you were a jerk and so you weren't there."

"I would've been, if you'd have called me," he said.

She recrossed her arms. "No, you see, I needed you, I *would've* needed you, but then you became more. Just, fucking *more*. Like, my moshom died and then what? I'm supposed to make up with you so that you can comfort me, Chris? I don't need *that*."

"What are you saying? Can't I make it right? I don't . . . Are we breaking up?"

His voice was quivering as though the cold had moved from his body to his words. He was crying, too. He didn't get to cry. He didn't get it. Nobody did. What was it with boys? Holly didn't have the energy to make him understand. She'd said all she had to say. She'd let him in the house, but the only thing she wanted to do was finish her charcuterie board, sit on her bed, cry, and listen to records.

Alone.

"No, Chris," she said, "we're not breaking up. We broke up."

"Hall . . ."

Holly guided him to the door, and he followed her as though hypnotized. He stopped on the porch and turned around. She had her hand on the door, ready to close it.

"Maybe we can be friends," she said.

"Yeah," he said, sounding totally defeated. "Maybe."

He looked like he wanted to say something else. He even opened his mouth. Then he blinked, and his eyelashes stuck together for a moment before coming apart. His tears were freezing quicker than they could fall. She shut the door, and if he said anything, she didn't hear it. She watched his silhouette linger on the porch for a moment longer, then she flicked off the porch light and he was gone.

Holly filled up the remainder of her board without much attention to detail, feeling uninspired now. Before, she'd been rather proud of what she was creating, trying to make the snack look as good as something her mother would've put together. Now, she cut up some cheddar cheese and placed the pieces on the board like fallen dominoes, poured walnuts on haphazardly, and finished it off with a handful of olives. She brought the board with her to the family room, placed it at her side, and turned on a show. She watched the TV insofar as her eyes were on it, but her mind was elsewhere. She blindly ate her snack, caring as much about what she put into her mouth—a cracker with hummus, a grape, an olive that she thought was a grape by the shape of it, an almond—as what was happening on the screen.

How audacious to waltz right up to her front porch at night after she'd ignored his texts and calls for well over a week. Some other time, she might have thought it was sweet, but tonight, she decided it was creepy, a bit stalker-ish. If he was trying to win her favour, he'd done a piss-poor job of it. Of course, he hadn't known that her moshom was going to die that day—her moshom was alive when they'd fought in the hallway of the school—but he'd still talked smack about her father.

Her thoughts moved to her father. They'd drifted apart like ice floes, and he hadn't noticed because he was too busy worrying about himself. After his dad died, she'd been sure that he'd only get worse, that he would implode, that he would disappear completely. She wouldn't have blamed him, either, despite everything, despite how insignificant he'd made her feel. Because people fell apart when their parents died. Parents were supposed to be invincible. Immortal. Holly had once yelled at her father that she wished he were dead to get a reaction out of him, but she couldn't imagine him dying. She would've been devastated, and so she knew that he was devastated now. But oddly, at least where she and her mother were concerned, he'd changed.

After the funeral, late in the night, he'd come into her room and asked if she was okay.

"I know you loved him as much as he loved you."

He'd sat on her bed, but didn't say another word. Neither did she. But he put his hand on her foot, which was covered by her bedding. They listened to a song together, just a random song, whatever record was spinning at the time. Holly didn't remember. The only thing she cared about was feeling his hand on her foot, and how they watched the black circle turn together. When the song finished, he squeezed her toes, smiled at her, warm and apologetic at once, then left. It had been a little thing, but little things were really the big things in the end.

Now, her parents were in their bedroom talking, actually talking. She could hear their voices rise above the television. It made her feel nearly as good as having her father's attention, but she was curious too—what were they talking about?

Her show was only halfway through, her snack half-finished, when she got up, causing olives and grapes to roll off the board and onto the couch. She walked stealthily down the hallway toward her parents' bedroom, stopped outside the door, and pressed her ear against it. She listened intently. Every sound was crisp and clear through the plywood and hollow core, each movement they made and, most importantly, each word they said.

"You could come, you know," her father said.

The light was off in the hallway. The light was on in the bedroom. It snuck out of the room through the crack between the door and the floor, and covered Holly's toes. She remembered walking along beams of light when she was a kid, pretending they were pathways to the most beautiful places. Her parents thought it was cute. They'd follow her as though she were the Pied Piper. They went to those beautiful places together, back then.

"I'd like to go up there with you," her mother said, "but I think for this, it's something you need to do without me. Plus, you're bad with directions."

"And he kind of gave me bad directions," her father said.

"Maybe when you get there, they won't seem so bad," her mother said. "Maybe they'll be totally clear, like you've plugged them into Google Maps or something."

"Follow the river northeast until you hit Hairy Lake, then, *also* northeast, find the narrowest river, and somewhere along the shore, I might find a dilapidated old cabin?"

"If there's a cabin, that's kind of hard to miss, isn't it?"

"After, what, decades? How many decades?"

"Several decades."

"After several decades, who says it'll even be standing? Dad wasn't sure it would be standing, but if he were . . ." There was a break in the conversation. "If he were here . . ." Another break, and this time, Holly heard her father trying to catch his breath. "If he were still here, he would know where to go. He waited so long to take me, and now I have to go alone."

He was speaking through tears. Shadows moved across Holly's toes. Footsteps led from one side of the bed, all the way around it, to the other. The mattress compressed. Her mother had gone to sit with her father. She heard rustling—sheets or clothing. His sobbing became muffled. He'd buried his face into her shoulder.

"You won't be alone," her mother said quietly. "He'll be with you."

"Do you really think that?" her father said, sounding, for a moment, like a child desperate for hope.

"I do," her mother said. "He'll show you where you need to go. I really think that."

There was a long silence. Holly noticed that she'd been crying, too. She moved the side of her face away from the door, wiped tears away with her sleeve, then pressed her ear against the door again.

"He didn't even know where to go," her father said, "not a hundred percent." He laughed, then sighed. "We were going to have an adventure."

"See? And that's exactly why I can't go," her mother said. "If we both went and got lost, Holly would be orphaned. We can't do that to her."

"Very funny," her father said. "But I guess you're right, and there's no way our daughter is going into the foster care system."

"That's why our will says she'll stay with your mom, Matt."

"Yeah, I know." There was more rustling. Somebody stood up. The mattress creaked. "She'd take good care of her."

"She would," her mother said, "but I think I'd like to keep her for myself for a little while longer."

"All right, good," he said. "As soon as the ice breaks up, I'll go. Just me and Dad."

"He would've liked that," she said.

"He would've liked that," he agreed.

Holly continued to listen, but the conversation had ended. She took her ear away from the door and stood in place in the hallway, in the dark, facing her parents' bedroom, feeling a strange compulsion.

When she was thirteen, she and her parents had gone on a road trip. Her thirteenth year had been the worst year of her life; she didn't understand anything, the world or herself. It had been a year of sad music, dark poetry, blue jeans and black shirts, true crime podcasts, crossed arms, sketches of demons and eyes and literally bleeding hearts in the margins of her scribblers, muted emotions, and thunderous outbursts.

"We should get away for a while," her mother had said, and so they did.

They went as far away as they could without driving right into the Pacific Ocean.

The first half of the trip was a disaster, and Holly was well aware that she had been the reason. Something was wrong with everything. Her father chose to play a song she didn't like, and when he said he had picked it for her, she felt as though he didn't know her at all. Her mother had filled a binder—a literal binder—with their entire trip planned out to the letter, booking the prettiest campsites months ahead of time according to the schedule and deciding all the places they'd eat. When they stopped at one restaurant and Holly saw nothing vegan on the menu short of fries and a bun with lettuce, she blew up at them, even though she'd just decided that summer to be a vegan and hadn't told them.

"Do you want me to starve?"

Her mother had forgotten to pack her favourite pair of sweat shorts. Nobody had bothered to pack nail clippers.

"I swear to god I'm going to claw my eyes out before this is over."

She got her period for the first time soon after they'd reached the mountains. She'd emerged from the tent with a towel wrapped around her waist and flushed with embarrassment, shouting at her mother to take her to the nearest store for a pad. She got even angrier that her mother had come prepared and packed some for Holly. "Oh, I've been that awful that you figured I was going to get it?" She couldn't wear her second-favourite pair of shorts until they stopped at a laundromat in a blink-and-you'll-miss-it nothing town, in the middle of nowhere. How did anybody come to live there? Half the houses and businesses were boarded up. Holly mumbled that it was a ghost town, and her father quipped that ghosts must've had to do laundry.

"All those sheets," he said.

"What the hell, Dad."

The shower was out of order at one of the campsites. She didn't want to go on any of the hikes her mother had planned out in her stupid binder. The only footwear Holly had wanted to bring were her Converse, and she broke a lace while tying them aggressively after her father said that she had to go on the hikes, that she didn't have a choice. So then she had to hike with one loose shoe, and it was all his fault. She screamed at her mother.

She made her mother scream back at her. They almost turned around before boarding the ferry to Haida Gwaii.

Something changed on the ferry ride, even though it should have been the worst part of the entire trip—being stuck on a boat with her parents, who were irritating the hell out of her, and feeling seasick within minutes of climbing up from the parking deck to the passenger deck. She left the space her parents had found to settle in for a long trip. They were reading and didn't notice when she wandered off. She went outside to get some fresh air, starboard side. To her right, she could see the coast, which quickly became a stain on the horizon. In front of her and to her left, she could see only ocean. She leaned against the railing, closed her eyes, and breathed deeply. She had never before taken clean air like that into her lungs. She could hear the ferry's motor, and the water churning directly underneath her. Then a voice cut in over the intercom and announced that a pod of whales had been spotted by some fishermen, starboard side. Before long, most of the people on the ferry were crowded around her. It felt like a mosh pit. *This is how people die at rock concerts*, she thought, and started to panic. A man to her right shouldered his way to the front to get the best view. A mother to her left tried to stop her kids from climbing up on the railing. And behind her, holy god, behind her. She'd gone outside to get air, and now it felt as though there was none left for her.

Holly was shooting her best pissed-off looks at the people around her and elbowing everybody but kids to try to create some space, until there was a collective gasp, and each person gazed in the same direction. A tail that had broken the surface disappeared back into the ocean. There was another gasp moments later when a shiny black body appeared and water spurted out of its blow hole like a geyser. And then the full body of an orca burst out of the ocean, flying through the air, and time froze.

Everybody on the deck was gone.

The sound of the motor was silenced.

The churning water stilled.

It was Holly and the whale. Just the two of them in the entire universe. She had never seen a whale in real life before. It was beautiful and enormous, but as big as it was, she didn't feel overwhelmed by its size; she didn't feel small in comparison; she didn't feel inconsequential. She had never felt so important. It was as though the whale had jumped only for her. She reached out her hand as if she could touch it. Time started again. The whale landed. The biggest cannonball in the history of the world. It had been close, not close enough to touch, but close nonetheless, and it sent water spraying onto the deck, over the crowd. Across Holly's face. It blended with her tears. She smiled.

Holly's euphoric state didn't last, but according to her parents, the remainder of the trip was far more pleasant. Her mother and father had not seen the whale—they'd gotten there too late—but Holly gave them the play-by-play. Her excitement made them happy; they didn't care much about the whale. All she could remember about the second half of the trip was the whale breaking through the water, hanging in the air like an ornament, and then splashing back into the ocean. That one moment took up all the space in her memory, living rent-free in her mind, and pushed out everything else. She had an image of herself standing on the shore at the northern edge of Haida Gwaii, the tide in, watching the gently rolling waves distort her feet, but that one thing, that single moment, was all she needed. And when her parents recalled the trip, she thought it was all they needed, too. They never talked about the time leading up to the ferry ride, only the whale, and how her eyes were as wide as the ocean itself while recounting the story to them.

The impulse Holly felt, standing outside her parents' bedroom, was born from that moment. It was what made her raise her fist and knock on the door, and then open it before her parents asked her to come in. It was what made her walk to the foot of her parents' bed and stand there, looking back and forth from her father to her mother, from her mother to her father. It was the need to seek out another memory, another moment, no matter how small, for her and for him. To push out everything bad that had happened, and replace it with something better. Something new. Something good. Her parents were looking at her, waiting for her to speak.

"Why've you guys never taken me to Norway House?" she said.

"I don't know," Matthew said through a sigh. "I wish I had a good reason, Hallelujah. I always meant to. I just . . ."

"Same old, same old, I guess," she said. "Right, Dad?"

"I guess," he said.

A silence followed, but Holly interrupted it before it pushed the air out of the room.

"I want to come with you," she said.

Her father exchanged a look with her mother, seeking approval, which was given without hesitation. He didn't ask why, nor comment on the fact that she had been eavesdropping on them.

"Okay," he said. "I'd like that."

After you asked to go up north with me, winter slowed to a crawl. I didn't think it would ever end. The one good thing about it was that I had time to think, and I ended up thinking a lot about the last time we'd gone on the road together, that first year we didn't go up to the lake. I know I've told you that I was upset you didn't want to go, but the trip was a good thing. There were times that sucked—nobody would argue with that—but there were times that didn't, even during the first half of the trip.

I remember staying at a campsite outside of Canmore, in Bow Valley Provincial Park, right beside Kananaskis River—your mother picked the best spots to camp. At night, you could hear the river and it was like a lullaby. I slept better than I'd ever slept before. It was like listening to a never-ending rainstorm. One morning, I got up and you weren't in the tent. I panicked a bit, because the day before, we'd gotten into a fight. I rushed all over the place trying to find you. You were sitting on a log by the riverbank, watching the water, and you looked peaceful. You were watching the water, I was watching you, and I felt peaceful, too.

A night or two before we got onto the ferry to Haida Gwaii, we stayed at a campsite in Ucluelet. When we were driving in, we thought there was a statue of a black bear, a baby, sitting on a log at the entrance, but right after we stopped to take a picture, it darted into the woods. A mother bear had been spotted in the campground the same day, and so all the campers were warned to be extra diligent. Your mother had booked a site at the edge of the trees, pretty much on the beach, a few yards away from the ocean. I sat outside on the picnic table at night because the ocean was calmest and clearest then. Like a sheet of glass. The moon hovered above it, and it cast a path of white light from the shore to the horizon.

On the second night, you came outside. I thought you were going to sit with me, but you had to go to the bathroom, and you wanted me to walk you there because of the bear sightings. It was a pretty good walk to the outhouses, and halfway there, you screamed that you saw a bear. We ran to our campsite. I looked back while we were running, and I swear you mistook a bush for a bear, but walking with you and running with you was like, "Okay, things can be normal. Things aren't so bad."

On the ferry ride, you saw a whale. I was jealous that you saw one, but you describing the whale was about as good as seeing one. The next best thing.

After that, it was like a whole new road trip. On Haida Gwaii, we stayed in that cottage on the beach on the northern tip of the island. There was no running water and no electricity. During those four days without television and without cell service, the world could have been ending and we never would have known. I remember thinking that that was how my father used to live, and it was the first time I got why he loved it so much. I liked being away from the rest of the world. We played board games and read by candlelight when the sun went down. We walked to a house in the middle of nowhere that people flocked to in the morning from all over the island, a bakery with cinnamon buns that dissolved on your tongue. We hiked to the top of Tow Hill, and you said that you could see Alaska. We cooked hot dogs on the beach and made bannock on sticks. I burned mine and it ended up looking like a cattail.

"What kind of Cree am I?"

On the morning of our departure, I saw you standing at the water's edge. The tide was out. Your mother and I finished packing up the car, and then she waited on the porch, reading a book, while I went to get you. You had your shoes in one hand and your feet were in the water. I took my socks and shoes off and stood beside you. You reached out and took my hand.

"Remember that bet we made when you were nine?" I said.

"Yeah," you said. "I already lost. I owe you a hundred bucks."

A big wave hit our legs. It got you wet up to your thighs, me wet up to my knees. It pushed us back, but we held each other steady.

"Want a do-over?" I said.

"Nah," you said. "I like this moment too much to make it about money."

"Me, too," I said. "The only thing better would be if a whale swam right by us, right now."

"Maybe on the way back," you said.

"Yeah," I said, "maybe then."

You squeezed my hand. That moment was my whale. It's crazy, right? We stayed out there for maybe half an hour. You squeezed my hand for maybe a second. The average lifespan is about 700,000 hours—700,000 hours, Hallelujah. Don't ask me how I know that. When you put it like that, doesn't it seem like we live forever? We fit so much into those 700,000 hours, but that half-hour is one of the things I remember more than most. Thirty minutes. And that second, that's as clear as anything else in my life. My calculator says that 700,000 hours is 2.5 billion seconds. How can one second out of 2.5 billion be so clear? A moment in time. Razor thin. It makes you think. It really makes you think.

17

Matthew's mother gave him a portion of his father's remains.
That's what she'd said, that she was giving him a portion of his
father's remains, as though he were part of a recipe. His mother
kept his ashes in a simple wooden urn in his old study over the
winter, one that would, once put in the ground, disintegrate over
time. It was environmentally friendly, though she'd opted not to
go with the kind that a tree grew out of, because "What if a dog
comes around and pees on the trunk? I don't want a dog peeing
on your father."

For the first couple of months, she didn't go into the study.
She couldn't bring herself to do it, just like she couldn't bring
herself to take away the toast in the basement. But eventually,
she began to spend more and more time in there. She'd sit in his
recliner. She'd listen to classical music with his earphones.

They had decided to wait until the fall to bury him, because
that was his favourite time of year, when he used to go onto the
land. That was looking unlikely now. His mother had admitted
as much.

"We'll bury him when it's time to bury me *with* him," she said.

She'd used a one-third measuring cup to pour some of his

father into a mini urn Claire had purchased on Etsy. It fit in Matthew's pocket. It was slightly bigger than a bottle of pills.

Matthew had walked down to the river every morning as spring approached, to watch the ice melt. He'd take a cup of tea with him and sit on a park bench halfway down the riverbank. Sometimes, Claire would sit with him. Sometimes, Hallelujah would. Often, he would go alone. By early May, the last of the ice was gone, and Matthew and Hallelujah hit the road with two backpacks, a tent, a cooler, and his father's canoe strapped to the top of the car. He and Claire had arranged for Holly to take a week off school. Bookended by weekends, this gave them nine days to complete their journey.

The eight-hour drive had always been peaceful and, at a certain point, scenic, especially in the autumn, when the leaves looked like flames. Matthew liked the trip up to Norway House almost as much as he liked being in the community. He had only ever gone with his father, and on the way there, his father used to point out landmarks—the same landmarks no matter how many times they travelled the same route. As a boy, Matthew liked hearing about them, like picture books you could listen to over and over again. As he got older, the stories grew repetitive, and Matthew simply tolerated them.

After passing by the first few sights, he thought that he would give anything to hear his father talk about the same things one more time. Just once. He wanted his father to tell him about the people he knew from St. Laurent, a Métis community about forty minutes outside the city. He wanted his father to tell him about Manipogo, a Loch Ness monster–like creature from Métis folklore that supposedly lives in Lake Manitoba.

"It's like Mistapew, Big Foot, for us Cree," he could hear his father say. "People think creatures like that are make-believe, but they aren't. I know you don't believe it, but they aren't. I've seen them."

Matthew and Holly took turns playing songs, but they needn't have. Every song Holly picked, Matthew would've picked himself. They communicated for the first two hours through music. They sang along to every selection. They both cried when they sang "Times of Trouble" by Temple of the Dog; they always had. They tried to stump each other with music trivia.

"Did you know that 'Times of Trouble' is pretty much 'Footsteps' by Pearl Jam? It has the same guitar chords or whatever, just with different lyrics," Matthew said.

"Yep," Holly said. "I know."

Matthew realized that he, too, had been telling Holly the same things ever since she was a little girl. And now she simply tolerated them.

"Speaking of one song that sounds like another, what unreleased song by Justin Vernon is super similar to 'Holocene'?" Holly said.

"Oh, I know this one," Matthew said. He sang the first few lines of "Holocene." "'Hazelton.'"

"Correct." She played air guitar with her eyes closed. "I like it almost as much."

"Me, too."

She searched for it on YouTube and played it. Matthew took the mini urn out of his pocket and put it on the dashboard underneath the rear-view mirror, like a dashboard bobble-head. They passed by a community on the right.

"That's Fairford," Matthew said. "It's a reserve like Norway House. That's its English name, anyway. It's really called

Pinaymootang. That's its Indigenous name. A lot of communities use their Indigenous names now."

"What does Pinaymootang mean?" Holly said.

Matthew shrugged. They were both better at music trivia.

"Does Norway House have a different name?" she said.

"Kinosao Sipi, I think." He pre-emptively told her that he didn't know what that meant, either. She asked him why, and he told her that his father hadn't taught him Cree.

"Because of those schools," she said.

"Right," he said. "My grandparents went, my parents went, and that was that. If they spoke Cree, they'd get their mouths washed out with a bar of soap, like they'd swore or something. And that's if they were lucky, Hallelujah. Your kōkom lost the language, your moshom managed to keep it. Your kōkom under- stands words, but, you know."

"Yeah," she said. "I know."

"That goddamn school burned down twice, and I wish it was still burning. But, you know, it's my fault now. I could've learned on my own. I always meant to ask your moshom to teach me, but . . . well. It's too late now, I guess."

"I guess it is," she said. "Too late to learn from Moshom, any- way."

They were six hours away now. Holly picked another song. Her words repeated in Matthew's mind. *Too late to learn from Moshom, anyway.* He knew what she'd meant, that even though his father couldn't teach him Cree, it didn't mean that he couldn't still learn the language. His father had said once that not teach- ing him Cree was one of the things he regretted most. He said that the world made more sense in Cree.

It was what Matthew regretted most now, too.

They stopped for gas at the next reserve, Grand Rapids. Matthew didn't like to use his status card that much. He always said that he knew it was a right, but other people actually needed the benefits and he didn't. It was satisfying to pay less for gas, though, even if it was only twelve cents off per litre. With a full tank, they found a parking spot and got a bite to eat in the restaurant, a greasy spoon that had the best burgers and fries between Winnipeg and Thompson. Holly agreed non-verbally by quickly devouring her food.

"A lot of people think we get gas for free," Matthew said. "That whole free-ride stereotype."

Holly finished chewing. She wiped her mouth while nodding. "That's where the whole lazy Indian thing comes from, hey?"

"That's one of the places where it comes from, for sure," Matthew said. "One celebrity says they think they're part Indigenous so they'll get free gas, and before you know it, everybody's talking about how the natives don't pay for gas."

"Who said that?"

"Justin Bieber."

"He's native?"

"Everybody's native, haven't you heard?"

Matthew and his father used to stop here on each trip up north, and back down to the city. They'd fill up on gas, then eat at the restaurant for burgers and fries. Matthew could never finish the whole plate when he was a kid; his father finished it for him. When his father got older, the roles reversed, and he'd finish his father's food.

Holly pushed her plate away and tried to burp quietly.

"You can have the rest," she said.

Matthew was almost done his plate. He just had the coleslaw

left, which nobody ever ate. He moved his plate to the side and pulled Holly's plate toward him, took a bunch of fries and stuffed them in his mouth.

"Gross," she said. "Take a breath."

After Fairford, he'd pointed out a few more sites to her, and everything he told her was what his father had told him. And there they were, eating the same food he'd eaten with his father, and more than that, he noticed that he'd chosen the same table, the one in the back corner, by the window, which his father had liked because he could look out for people he knew. He liked to see people he knew. Holly had said it was too late to learn from Moshom, but was it? If Holly learned from Matthew what Matthew had learned from his father, wasn't Holly, in some way, learning from her moshom?

"Maybe I'll learn Cree," Matthew said.

Traffic thinned out considerably after Grand Rapids. There were stretches where they didn't see a car for half an hour. This was where his father used to make up a lot of time, driving at least seventy-five miles per hour until they hit the end of Highway 6, but Matthew slowed down instead. They looked for wildlife. Matthew saw a few deer. Holly thought she saw a bear. A fox trotted on the side of the road. They saw two eagles.

"That's a good sign," Matthew said after he pointed out the first one soaring overhead, with a wingspan that made it look like a plane. "It means good travels."

"What does it mean when you see two?" Holly said when they spotted the second one, minutes later.

"That's a *really* good sign," Matthew said.

They came to the T intersection at the end of Highway 6 and turned right. In less than two hours, they'd be in Norway

House. Holly said that Matthew could choose an entire album if he wanted, so they listened to *I Am Easy to Find* by the National until they reached the turnoff to Cross Lake First Nation.

"We've got some relatives over there." Matthew lip-pointed in the direction of the community because both his hands were on the steering wheel. "Cousins."

"That feels like a stereotype," Holly said, "that we're all cousins."

"We do have a lot of cousins, though."

Holly checked the display on the dashboard underneath the mini urn, where it showed the temperature outside, the distance they could travel with the amount of fuel they had in the tank, and the direction they were headed in.

"We're going south," she said.

"I call the route from Winnipeg to Norway House 'Candy Cane Lane,'" he said. "You drive north for a long time, then you turn right to go east for a little bit, and then you go right again and drive south for an hour or so until you hit Norway House. The route looks like a candy cane, if you look at the directions on your phone."

Holly did just that and, moments later, looked impressed. She showed him her phone.

"It totally does look like a candy cane, if a kid made one out of a pipe cleaner or something."

"Candy Cane Lane," he said.

That was not something his father had told him. It didn't matter that it was likely not something Holly would pass down to her own children, if she ended up having any.

"Sounds like one of those drives you go on in the city during Christmas," Holly said. "Remember we used to go on those? All the houses on the block, like every single one, would have polar bears or something like that? And at the end of the street, there was that house where the lights went on and off in time with music?"

"I remember," he said. "I think there was a Candy Cane Lane, actually. That's probably where I got it from."

"You're probably right," she said.

18

Norway House was the first reserve that Holly had been to. She'd seen a lot of news stories that showed reserves, but she knew all of that was surface-level. You can't know what a book is about by looking at its cover. Some terrible books have great covers, some great books have terrible covers, and everything between. To Holly, it seemed as though reserves, for the most part, were books that had been given awful covers. She wasn't naive—she knew there were struggles in First Nations communities, some that she was aware of, some that she couldn't understand—but in driving through Norway House to get to the cabin she and her father had rented, she knew there was more. She knew there were good things.

There were kids bouncing up and down on a trampoline outside of a house, under the watchful eye of their mother, who was sitting on the porch with a Tim Hortons coffee cup in hand. An old lady with a cane walking on the road was picked up by a young couple in their truck. Fans were cheering in the stands at a baseball game. A large group of community members were congregating outside the mall entrance, eating food and drinking coffee and feeding dogs and laughing like they were all in on the joke. And almost everybody who passed them, whether they were driving or walking, waved at them.

"It's like a small town here," her father said. "It's got a small-town vibe. Strong community."

Holly rolled her window down, put her hand outside the car, and felt the wind rush through her fingers like cold water. She breathed in, and the air was fresh.

It took them less than twenty minutes to get to their cabin, which was on the West Island, overlooking the Nelson River. Her father told her that she had some Scottish in her blood because of the river; years ago, it was a trading route.

The cabin was relatively new. It had a full kitchen, two bedrooms, a bathroom, and a big couch in the living room that faced a television with a satellite connection. Her father made spaghetti with meat sauce. They ate it on the couch while flipping through channels, but they never settled on a program.

After supper, her father asked if she wanted to drive around the community with him, to see where her moshom used to live. They'd had a surprisingly civil—Holly was tempted to even say enjoyable—ride up to the community, and she didn't want to push it, so she declined his invitation. Her father looked disappointed, but to his credit, he stopped short of verbalizing that, and just promised not to be too long.

"Doesn't matter," Holly said, gathering the dinner plates and bringing them to the kitchen. "I'll do some writing or put on a movie or something."

Her father went to the door, stepped outside, then leaned back inside, swaying like a wind chime. Good god, was he ever trying. Holly didn't know whether to appreciate the effort or be annoyed.

"There's not much to do anyway. I don't gamble or anything," he said, referring to the casino attached to the reserve's hotel. "Your moshom loved to play the slots. He'd play the smallest amount of money so he could play for as long as possible. Nickels. He didn't care if he won or not."

"I didn't know that," she said. "That's funny."

"Yeah," he said, lingering there a moment longer. Then he shut the door.

Holly listened to his footsteps head down the stairs from the front porch, toward the car. She heard the door open, then close, and the engine start. She heard crunching gravel. She looked out the window and watched as her father drove away. When the tail lights disappeared around the bend, it looked completely black outside. Her moshom used to tell her that you'd never find a darker night than you would in the north. She turned away from the window, did the dishes while listening to music, and then sat down at the kitchen table with her notepad and wrote poetry while the dishes dried in the rack.

> *You are alone tonight and*
> *Your heart misses blood like*
> *Your veins miss the rushing crimson*
> *You miss the nightmares but*
> *You never dreamed of black*

"So, Holly," she said, "you had spaghetti for supper and then a big fucking dish of teenage angst for dessert. How original."

She closed the notepad and pushed it across the table, like it was a plate of food she didn't want. Teenage angst. The music continued to play.

Before I let go
Before I turn around
And turn my back on you
Before I leave
We are both alone

"Oh my fucking god, if you're not writing it, you're listening to it."

She turned the music off and tossed her phone onto the couch. By then, the dishes had dried, so she put them away. Washing the dishes and putting them away weren't chores she'd have done in the city. They weren't chores any teenager would have done unless under threat, like having their screen time taken away. But something about being up here made her want to have everything in its right place, everything just so, like that would help her to feel the same way. She wiped the countertop, wrung out the cloth, and hung it neatly over the faucet. She swept the floor, moved the perishables they'd brought from the cooler to the fridge, then paced back and forth from the kitchen to the living room. She alternatively looked out the living room window and kitchen window, hoping to see headlights and wishing, despite her reservations, that she'd gone with her father. Her heart started to pound and she broke into a cold sweat. She sat on the couch and took her pulse; it was hard and quick.

"Not again," she said.

She tried to distract herself by turning on the television and finding a movie. *Ghostbusters.* That didn't help. She turned the television off, dropped the remote beside her phone, then got up and went into her father's room. His backpack was on top of the bed, untouched since he'd thrown it there after letting Holly pick which room she wanted to sleep in. She'd chosen the one with the window facing the forest, not the owners' house.

"I know I'm going to look out the window in the middle of the night and see a silhouette in their attic window, Norman Bates style," she'd said.

Holly rummaged through her father's backpack until she heard a familiar rattling. She took two Xanax without any water, just chewed them up and swallowed. She put the pill bottle back where she'd found it, along with everything else she'd removed from the pack, then went outside to the porch for some air and to wait for her nerves to settle. It was a clear night. The temperature had dropped. It was one or two degrees from her being able to see her breath. There was one cloud overhead. It looked like a spider's web. It looked as though stars were caught within its netting. There were houses on the other side of the river; their lights reflected off the water. She walked down to the shore, stepped onto the dock, and lay down on a beach towel somebody had left behind. The mini urn was in her hand; she'd not noticed picking it up before leaving the cabin. She held it tight. She put her hand over her heart.

"Tell me about the stars, Moshom," she said.

"Which stars, my girl?" he said.

"You always knew the ones I needed to hear about."

He pointed to one star that burned brighter than all the others, that brought light into the darkness, like a beacon.

"That's Keewatin, the Going Home Star," he said. "If you look long enough at the sky in the night, the stars will appear to move, but it's really the earth that's moving. One star, just one, the Going Home Star, will never move. It will stay right there, always. When First Nations people realized that it was stationary, they used it as a guide. We were nomadic, a long time ago. Kayas. If we kept the star on our right shoulder, we knew that we would head west, but it worked for all directions. Whatever direction we wanted to go. It worked when we wanted to go home, too, of course."

"The Going Home Star," she said.

"Ehe," he said. "Yes, Keewatin stands still while all the other stars dance around it. It watches them dance."

Holly felt a tear fall from the corner of her eye. It slid across her temple and disappeared into her hair. She wiped at the line of salt water it left behind.

"Why doesn't it dance, too?" she said.

"Because it has a job to do," he said. "The other stars are dancing in celebration, because we were never lost. But if Keewatin began to dance, where would we be?"

"Where would we be?" she said. "Wherever you went, Moshom. That's where they would have gone." She turned away from the stars and looked at her moshom. "Are you lost?"

"Mwach," he said. "No, I'm not lost. There's the star. The star is right overhead. It always will be."

"Am I?" she said. "Lost?"

"Keep it on your shoulder," he said, "and find your way."

"I miss you," she said.

He didn't respond. There was no memory left.

Holly remembered spending time with him in the backyard of his house, while her kōkom was inside visiting with her parents. He had a zero-gravity lawn chair that, in the last year or so, he needed help getting out of, and into. He used to sit in the middle of the yard, between the garage and a large bush, and lean back all the way so that he was facing the sky. Holly would lie down on an air mattress that her kōkom kept in the garage, or better yet, at the suggestion of her moshom, directly on the grass,

217

so she could be closer to Mother Earth. She liked feeling the grass tickle her exposed skin. How soft the ground was, especially when her grandparents hadn't mowed it for a couple of weeks.

Her moshom would tell her stories of the sky, and how they were blessed to live under a blanket of stars. He used to tell her that they would never run out of stories, because there was one for each star, each constellation, so there would always be stories for him to tell, and stories for her to hear, and he was right. They had never run out of stories.

She sat up on the dock and stared out over the water, wondering how many more stories there were that she'd not been told yet, that she would never know now.

"At least you told me the stories you did," she said to the mini urn, which she had set down on the towel in front of her.

The pills were working. Her heartbeat had slowed. She felt calm. The breeze was cool against her skin. The lights went off in one of the houses across the river. Holly moved the urn out of the way, slid the towel out from under her bum, and wrapped it around her shoulders. She picked the urn up and unconsciously started to rotate it with her fingertips—her moshom had become a fidget spinner.

When she noticed what she was doing, she stopped, and placed the urn back on the dock. She heard a car approaching behind her. It sounded like rushing water. Headlights cut through the darkness, gravel crunched underneath rubber tires. Her father pulled up in front of their cabin, got out of the car, and walked over to her. No greeting. She moved over to give him room, and he sat down beside her. She offered him half of the towel she'd been keeping herself warm with. It was a big towel. He refused.

"How was the drive?" Holly said.

Her father shrugged. "Bittersweet." He breathed in deeply. She heard his breath quiver when he exhaled. "It's weird, Hallelujah. You pass by where he used to live when he was a child, when he wasn't on the trapline, in the summer; you remember when he took you there, when you walked with him to the lake, when he showed you where he used to stand by the shore and look at the freighters, where he used to swim and jump from rock to rock; and he's just . . . gone."

"It doesn't seem real," Holly said.

Her father buried his face in his hands. He gasped for air. She reached toward him, to put her hand on his shoulder, but pulled her hand away without him seeing.

"My dad died, Hallelujah."

"I know," she said. "You can cry. You should cry."

He picked up a pebble from beside the dock and tossed it into the river; the reflection from a house's lights flickered from the ripples.

"I want you to have memories of me like I have of my dad," he said. "Have I fucked that all up?"

Holly hugged the towel around her body. She remembered going to the beach with her father when she was a toddler. They were images more than memories, really. Like pictures in a photograph album. She was shivering from the cold water. He picked her up and swaddled her with a towel. He hugged the towel around her body. He hugged her. There were things like that. Tiny moments. And there was now. She would remember sitting on the dock with her father tonight, in her moshom's home, more than the time he'd not been himself. But she didn't want to give him that. He hadn't earned that. Not yet.

"I want to have memories like that, too," she said.

Your mother and I broke up after we'd been dating for about a year. She came over and I thought somebody had died, but she was mourning the death of our relationship before it had ended. She knew what she was going to do. She told me, a few weeks later, that she'd been thinking about it for at least a month. A month doesn't seem that long, I know, but when you've only been dating for twelve months, that's about ten percent of the time. We were sitting on my bed. I was trying to make eye contact with her, but she wouldn't look at me. She was holding my hand, and it was the strangest thing to be that close to somebody but for them to feel so far away.

She hadn't taken off her jacket. I should've known that was not a good sign. She kept running her fingers through her hair. She looked so pretty when she did that. She kept rubbing her thumb against my palm. I put on a CD to fill the silence. When "One" started, your mother started bawling. I'd played a breakup song without knowing that she was breaking up with me.

She reached into her pocket and took out one of those miniature packs of tissues. She pulled out half of them and wiped her cheeks and left the rest of the pack on the bed. I guess she thought that I'd need them, too.

"I love you," she said.

"I love you," I said.

"You can't love me."

"Of course I do."

"How can you love me if you don't even love yourself?"

"I do, though."

She shook her head. She moved her thumb toward my wrist. I was wearing a long-sleeved shirt. She pulled it up. There was a bandage on my wrist. She peeled it away and there were all these thin red lines that had started to scab over. She touched them with her fingertips.

"You love yourself, or you love me?" she said.

"I love you," I said.

"No," she said.

I moved her hand away and replaced the bandage. I covered the bandage with my sleeve.

"I told you what happened," I said. "I told you why I did that."

"I'm not judging you. You know I'm not judging you. But as long as you need to do stuff like that, as long as you need to drink for the same reason, I can't be with you. If I stay with you, I feel like I'm . . . I'm not going to be your razor blade, and I'm not going to be your bottle."

"I'll stop," I said. "If I stop, will you stay?"

"I don't want you to stop for me. I want you to stop for you. Do you understand?"

I turned away from her. I curled my knees into my chest. I pressed my forehead against my knees. I hid my face. I made myself into a ball. I was waiting for her to get up from the bed, but she didn't right away. She stayed, and I didn't know what that meant. Looking back on it now, I don't think at all that she was reconsidering her decision. You know your mother. You're like your mother. When you make up your mind, that's it. There's no stopping you. There's no stopping either of you. Looking back on it now, I think she was worried about me, and she didn't leave because she wanted to make sure that I was going to be okay.

You would've liked my room back then. You would've liked the '90s. I had a ghetto blaster that played CDs and tapes. Pearl Jam. Radiohead. Beastie Boys. Rage Against the Machine. The Smashing Pumpkins. R.E.M. U2, of course. Achtung Baby. *I had movie posters on my bedside wall—*Rushmore *and* Pump Up the Volume. *I had a closet full of plaid shirts and Doc Martens. I had a chain wallet attached to my jeans, which were on the floor with all my other clothes. I had a see-through phone. I had a Firefly skateboard. There was a floating shelf over my desk. It was full of Douglas Coupland books, comics, textbooks, and at the very end, closest to my bed, there was my father's old Bible. Hidden in the bindings of the Bible, there was a razor blade. One edge of it was stained with blood. She didn't know it was there. Nobody did. She didn't know I kept it so close. All she knew was that I was trading one sort of pain for another.*

"I understand," I said, but I don't think that I did. I understood it conceptually, but not really. Not the way that she meant.

"I'll wait for you," she said. "I'll wait for you as long as I have to."

"You don't have to," I said.

"I know," she said, "but I will."

She did wait for me, but not that night. She sat with me for a little while, until I'd unfolded myself and lay down in my bed, until the last song had played. "Love Is Blindness." You cannot make that up, Hallelujah.

We didn't talk for a few weeks, and then on the weekend, on a Saturday, we went to the bar together with a bunch of people. I guess it was an attempt to see if we could be friends. There was a bar down

Portage Avenue where outside, beside the parking lot, over a hill, was a stream that fed into the river. I thought the night went well. For the most part, she stuck with her crew and I stuck with mine. We met up on the dance floor for fast songs, and tried not to make eye contact when slow songs came on. It was like we were in middle school again, like we had crushes on each other but were too shy to do anything about it. I'd be looking at her, and when she looked at me, I'd turn away. I caught her looking at me a few times, too, with sad eyes. Neither of us wanted to be apart.

After midnight, our favourite song came on. "Crazy Mary." I asked her to dance. She said yes. And there we were, in the middle of the dance floor, her head against my chest, rotating in circles. Near the end of the song, she looked up at me with these big, glittery eyes. They looked like mirror balls. They were apologetic and pleading and conflicted and sad all at once, and I didn't know what to do, so I didn't do anything. When the song was over, we let go of each other, backed away from each other, and she just . . . left.

I found her sitting by the stream after I'd circled the parking lot a few times. I sat down beside her.

"You know," I said, "I don't . . . do that because I'm, like, already hurting or something."

"Why do you do it, then?" she said.

"I think I do it to try to feel something at all," I said. "My whole life, I've felt numb. I don't even think I hate myself. Not really. You have to feel something to feel hate."

"You don't feel anything at all," she stated.

"Fear, maybe," I said.

"Fear of what?" she said.

"Of nothing," I said. "Of nothingness. That everything we do means nothing in the grand scheme of things."

"It doesn't matter if what we do means nothing to the universe, Matt. It matters if what we do means something to you, or to me. No matter what anybody does, the world's still going to stop spinning one day, and everybody on this earth is going to end up in the same place."

"Wow," I said, "you really know how to make a guy feel better."

"I'm not trying to make you feel better," she said. "That's just the way it is."

"What place is that?" I said. "Where are we all going to end up?"

"No idea," she said. "It might be nothing, or it might be something. You know what, though?" She didn't wait for me to respond. "How we get there, that's the thing, and who we get there with."

"Is this your way of un-breaking up with me?" I said.

"Depends on what you say next," she said.

"I love you. I really do."

She kissed me. You probably don't want to hear that, so that's all I'll say.

She kissed me, and then she said, "Doesn't that feel like something?"

19

The next morning, Matthew and Holly got up early and packed. They put their meals—peanut butter sandwiches, Mr. Noodles (which Matthew insisted were amazing raw if they couldn't boil them), and packets of instant oatmeal he'd found in the cupboards of the cabin—in his backpack, and snacks—energy bars, nuts, bananas, a couple of muffins, and apples—and tablets for water in Holly's. Their other source of food would be delivered courtesy of two fishing rods stored in the canoe.

"And you've fished before," Holly said.

"Do you know how much time I spent here with my dad when I was your age?" Matthew said.

"That's conspicuously not an actual answer," she said.

They had various other items, including a Thermos, a map of the area, the tent, sleeping bags, and warmer clothes for when it was colder at night and first thing in the morning, before the sun rose. Matthew thought they were prepared. They had bacon and eggs with toast and peanut butter, got dressed, and left the cabin.

They portaged the canoe across the parking lot and the owner's front yard, to the dock. They pushed off from there, starting their journey on the Nelson River. Matthew had never seen Norway House from this perspective, from the water on the west side of the community. They could've left from the ferry crossing, several miles north of where they were now, and closer to their destination—starting this far south meant they had a long way to go just to catch up to where they could have been—but Matthew wanted to launch from West Island. He wanted to canoe down the same river that his Scottish ancestors would have used, to drift past where his father used to swim when he was a kid, to cross the lake where his grandfather would have hauled sand on a barge when he helped build the hospital, to pass by the church where his father used to preach when he first became a minister.

Along the way, he told Holly everything he knew about the community. All the history, all the stories.

"Your moshom used to say that when the ice broke, everybody who had spent the winter on the trapline would come home together in a huge parade of canoes. They'd have all the fish and meat they'd stored to give out to families in the community." He pointed to a clearing on the shore on the other side of the river. "People would wait for the trappers right there, with bannock and stew and open arms, and they'd have a feast."

"That's cool," Holly said.

They were against the current to start, because the river flowed into Little Playgreen Lake, north to south, and they paddled hard toward the ferry crossing. Sometimes it felt like they weren't moving at all, and it was late in the morning before they reached the crossing and the boat launch for the community. They decided to stop there for a break, pulling the canoe onto the shore amidst a fleet of aluminum boats. They sat together on a large rock and ate an energy bar each. Matthew's shirt was soaked from sweat and water, and so was Holly's. They put on something dry when nobody else was at the launch and the ferry was on the other side of the river. They didn't stay long. Blackflies were swarming around them; Holly said they were as bad as mosquitoes in the city.

The river opened up on the other side of the ferry's cable, and the current wasn't as bad as a result. Matthew pointed out a spot on the west shore that looked kind of like a marsh.

"People from the community have seen Big Foot right around there a bunch of times," he said.

"Yeah, right," Holly said.

"That's what I think, too, but they swear by it," he said, "and what gets me is that the people here, they're the salt of the earth. I think about that. They're honest people. They have no reason to lie, especially about mythical creatures. So why would they say they saw Big Foot, unless they saw Big Foot?"

"You sound like you're trying to convince yourself," she said.

"Maybe I am," he said.

"You know what's ironic? Moshom used to say that Big Foot represents honesty, in the seven sacred laws. So Big Foot represents honesty, and if they're lying about it? That's real, honest-to-god irony."

"Or they're telling the truth," he said.

"Or that," she said. "That'd be wild."

"But honesty," he said, "the kind of honesty you're talking about, in those laws, that doesn't mean being honest in what you say. Like, telling the truth when you, you know . . ."

"When you text another woman who's not your wife?"

They'd been speaking without making eye contact, Matthew in the stern and Holly in the bow, both of them facing north. She

227

glanced back at him, and in that brief moment, her eyes burned into him.

"Right," he said, keeping his breath even, "so that didn't take long. Parental evisceration within the first four hours."

"Is that what I just did to you, Dad?"

"No," he said. "No, that's not what you did. It was a shitty attempt at humour."

"Sorry," she said, and half sounded as though she meant it. "Speaking of being shitty."

"Don't be sorry," he said. "I deserve it."

She started to paddle again.

"It's just that, I don't know, I've been, like, pushing it all down into my stomach," she said, her voice quivering. "I've been keeping it to myself because of Moshom, and—"

"You granted me a reprieve."

Holly swivelled around on her seat and kept paddling, pushing instead of pulling now. "That's pretty dramatic," she said.

"I know."

Their conversation abruptly came to a halt, and for the next while, as they headed farther north, they paddled through a gentler current but a strong silence. Behind them, the ferry and the dock and all its boats had vanished in the distance, and with them any semblance of civilization. The cabins that dotted each side of the river fell away as the day wore on. Finding one became like spotting a rare wild animal. Or Big Foot. By late in the afternoon, after they had canoed over fifteen miles from the community, it felt as though they were the last two people on earth, with nothing to say to one another. The river had continued to expand, welcoming islands within its arms. The first of those islands was directly ahead of them. They'd kept looking at each other, then looking away, and Matthew felt a need to break the quiet that had fallen between them.

"I always make things about me," he said, continuing their conversation as though the long pause had never happened. "Your mother tells me that. She says that it's 'poor Matt' all the time, and she's right. She's usually right. I don't know why I do that."

"People are generally narcissistic, Dad." Holly sighed, then shook her head and started to paddle harder, still pushing, and Matthew tried to keep pace. The canoe cut through the water. "It's really none of my business, anyway. You didn't do anything behind *my* back."

"I did, though," he said. "We're a family. I hurt your mom, and so I hurt you. I know that. I know it now. I should've known it from the start. I never would've . . ." He sighed. "I wouldn't have been such an asshole."

"So why did you, then?" she said. "You must have had some self-awareness that, you know, texting another woman, flirting like that, was fucked up."

They passed the island on the left, and the river spread out wide again. Matthew looked ahead. There were more islands in the distance. They'd get there in a few minutes. He slowed the pace, and Holly did as well. They were both sweating. Matthew had warded off a panic attack during the lull and was still having trouble catching his breath. He breathed through his nose, held his breath, then breathed out through his mouth.

"Do you ever feel just empty, like there's a piece missing from you?" he said.

"Oh my god, are you about to quote a Shel Silverstein poem? Tell me you're not," she said.

"No," he said. "No, I'm not. What I'm trying to say is that I felt empty, for a long time. I think it was always kind of there. The emptiness, I mean. And I tried to fill it the wrong way."

"Well, fuck," she said.

"Yeah," he said.

"You didn't . . ."

"No, I didn't."

The islands drew closer. Matthew tried to remember which way they had to go, left or right. Around one of these islands, according to his father, was a waterfall. Depending on which way they went, they would either ease their way downstream to a lake that branched off into another river, or they'd encounter the waterfall and drop ten feet before they knew what had hit them. A slight breeze danced through the forest, rustling leaves. It sounded as if they were being applauded. Their paddles broke the surface of the river, urged the canoe forward, then came up for air. They'd found a rhythm. The vessel lunged forward, paused, lunged forward, paused.

"You were saying," she said, "about honesty."

"Right," he said, "honesty. It's not the kind of honesty where you don't lie . . ." He paused, as though Holly might throw another dagger, but none came. "Honesty means being true to who you are, how Creator made you, if you believe in that kind of stuff."

"What if you're lost?" she said. "How can you be true to who you are if you're lost?"

"I guess you have to find your way," he said.

20

Holly's hands were blistered and her shoulders had never been this sore. Water polo had nothing on canoeing. The closest they'd come to being this sore was when she helped move her bedroom to the basement. It took the better part of the day, and when she was done, she felt like Atlas must've felt holding up the heavens. She got her mother to bring her ice packs, and she lay on her bed with one pack under each shoulder. Her father gave her ibuprofen unprompted, because he'd heard her moaning all the way from the main floor. That soreness was nothing compared to what she felt now, paddling the canoe with her father north up the river toward a trapline they weren't even sure they'd be able to find.

"When are we going to stop for supper?" Holly said. "It's pretty much suppertime."

"Soon," her father said. "After we make it past this island."

She rotated in the bow seat to face north. They were getting closer to another island with each passing second, albeit slowly. He seemed hesitant to her, beginning to steer the canoe right one moment, and the next moment, drifting left.

"Do we plan on going through it or around it?" she said.

"Around it," he said, but there was a pause before he spoke.

Of course they'd go around it, but Holly began to realize that the direction mattered.

"Which way?" she said.

"Uhh, right," he said. "We're going right."

"You sure about that?" she said.

"Yeah," he said, "totally."

"Oh god."

Honesty.

Holly thought of the conversation they'd had while passing by the spot where, supposedly, Big Foot had been seen by locals. According to her father, Big Foot didn't represent the sort of honesty that required somebody not to lie. It wasn't cut and dry like a commandment. *Thou shalt not . . . bear false witness?* she thought. She should've known that, her moshom having been a minister and all. She was pretty sure that's what it was, as sure as she was that her father had just broken that commandment.

"Don't worry about it," he said, and he began to guide the canoe to the right.

"What's the worst that's going to happen if you're wrong?" she said, and when he didn't answer her immediately, she turned her head to face him and shouted, "Hey! Matt!"

"Hallelujah, don't call me Matt. Please?"

"I won't call you Matt if you answer the question, and also if you stop calling me Hallelujah, because you know that I hate it, *Dad.*"

"What's the worst that can happen?" he said.

"That was the question," she said.

"Do you remember when we went to the West Edmonton Mall? When you were like, I don't know, seven or eight?"

The island was almost upon them, and whatever he was going

to tell her about the worst-case scenario, it was too late anyway. She knew they'd gone to Edmonton when she was younger, but the trip was a blur. There were pictures. She'd seen the pictures.

"Kinda?"

"Well, you wanted to go on the roller coaster all by yourself, the Dragon Wagon, because you said that you were a big girl. But you were too short to go on your own, so I went with you. Your mother was freaking out because some of the bumps were really big, and she was worried you might fly out of your seat. I told her that I'd put my arm around you to hold you down if the metal bar across your lap failed. For a little roller coaster inside a mall, that thing was deadly. After ten seconds flat, you were hanging on to me even when there weren't any bumps. And when there *were* bumps . . ." He laughed. "You screamed so loud I thought you were going to bust my eardrums."

"What's your point?" she said.

"Oh," he said, as if she should have gleaned what his point was, like he'd just given her enough warning for what was about to happen. "The worst that's going to happen is no worse than the roller coaster ride at West Edmonton Mall."

The current picked up, but it wasn't something that they were paddling against; it was pulling them forward. They picked up more speed with each passing second. It began to feel as though they were caught in some rapids.

"What the hell is going on?" she said. "Tell me we're not about to go whitewater rafting with a fucking canoe, Dad."

She spun around to face him in time to see him securing his paddle in the canoe, underneath the thwart. Holly did the same, eyes wide.

"I may have guessed the wrong way," he said.

They were shouting over the sound of the rushing river. The waters had been so peaceful, but now, within seconds, they were roaring like a Thunderbird.

"I knew you were guessing!" she said. "You're a horrible liar. No wonder Mom—"

"Can we not talk about that right now? If we survive, you can take shots at me all day!"

"*If* we survive!"

"*When* we survive."

Holly swivelled one last time and saw it up ahead: the drop-off, the waterfall. There was no avoiding it. She thought of jumping out of the canoe and trying to swim to the shore, but as quick as the thought came, she knew that she'd never make it. They were racing toward the edge. The river below looked so far down. She turned to her father and met eyes with him.

"Dad?"

"It'll be okay!" he said. "I promise."

The canoe tumbled over the waterfall. Holly closed her eyes and screamed. She and her father were thrown out of the canoe before it struck the water below, and this was a blessing. The vessel crashed as though the river was cement. It was the last thing Holly saw before she plunged underwater.

It was dark, as though she'd fallen into night, and unbearably cold. She could feel her body, her quickly numbing skin, being pulled in two different directions, farther underneath by the current, which was stronger at the base of the waterfall, and back toward the surface, thanks to her life jacket. She'd taken enough swimming lessons to know that if she panicked, it wouldn't help, so she kicked her legs as though she were swimming at Pan Am Pool, and tried to ignore the burn of the icy water. She pretended that she was a kid again, that she'd dove to the bottom of the pool to retrieve her bright-orange locker key, and now that she had it, she was on her way back to the surface. Eventually, her head popped out of the river, and she gasped for air. She saw the canoe drifting north, both of their backpacks in the water near it, too far for her to reach.

She didn't see her father.

Holly frantically looked around for him. She tried to stay in place even as the current worked to pull her away, egg-beater kicking like she did while playing water polo and using her arms to slowly rotate her body in a full circle, searching for her father in all directions. Her body was already stiffening from the river's frigid temperature, making it harder for her to stay afloat. And if it was hard for her, a girl who'd been swimming all her life, she didn't want to imagine how her father would cope.

"Dad!" she said. "Dad, where are you?"

Holly turned herself around once more and, this time, thought she caught a glimpse of something near the riverbank. Navy blue. Brown. Orange. It was drifting away from her like the canoe, bobbing up and down, below the surface and then above. She pictured him first thing that morning, walking from the cabin toward the dock. He'd been wearing a navy-blue windbreaker with a sweatshirt underneath it, and brown cargo pants.

"Dad, nobody wears cargo pants anymore," she'd said.

"I do," he'd said.

He'd given her a yellow life jacket with blue straps. He'd taken the traditional orange life jacket with black stripes.

"I kind of look like a bee, right?" he'd said.

"The life jacket is orange, not yellow," she'd said.

"Imagine if your life jacket had black stripes, though," he'd said.

"Stop talking to me like I'm ten," she'd said.

It was him. He was face down and motionless.

"Hang on!" she said.

Holly transitioned into a front crawl and took off down-stream as though she were in a race, willing her joints into movement against the freezing water. If her father wasn't breathing, it meant that every second counted. She kicked as hard as her legs would allow, reached as far as she could with each stroke of her arm, and pulled at the water with her hands. Even weighed down by her soaking wet clothing, even shaking from the frigid waters, she'd never swum faster. Within seconds, she caught her father by his ankle, used both hands to haul him toward her, and when he was close enough, threw an arm around him. She turned around so that her back was facing north, made sure his head was resting against her chest with his face out of the water, and reached out with her free arm to try to grab something, anything, to help get her father to shore. She almost got hold of some thin branches from a dead tree hanging over the water, but missed because her fingers weren't functioning. It was as if she were outside in a blizzard without gloves on. She managed to grab a fistful of long grass, and it stopped their momentum, but then the grass came out of the ground and they kept floating north.

"Come on!" she said. "Please!"

That was the closest Holly had ever come to praying. She dug her fingers into the mud under the water and blindly gripped a tree root. She fought to hang on, willing her hand to find the strength, no matter how numb it was, but there was nothing else she could do without letting her father go. She screamed like she was on the roller coaster, the Dragon Wagon, right into his ear, but he didn't stir. She craned her neck and glanced over her shoulder. Her vision was going blurry, her head was pounding. The riverbank wasn't too steep where they were, but still, to get her father safely ashore, she'd have to flip him over to her left side without losing hold of him, and she knew she wasn't strong enough.

She glanced again.

Farther north down the river, along the shore, was a beaver dam. On the drive to Norway House, her father had told her that on the land, there were more beaver dams than there were McDonald's in the city. Before all hell broke loose, they'd seen a number of them; now here was another, and it was their only chance.

She let go of the root.

Holly and her father drifted north along the riverbank for several agonizing seconds before striking the beaver dam. Some twigs and branches shifted within the intricate structure, but it held them in place. She propped her father's head against the dam so that his face was out of the water, slipped her arm out from underneath his neck, and put both of her hands firmly around his wrist. From there, she climbed onto the shore and, with all of her strength, pulled him out of the water. It felt as though he were twice as heavy because of the wet clothing, because of her failing limbs, because of her own exhaustion, but she managed to drag him up the riverbank to a relatively flat patch of land in a clearing. She unhooked his life jacket and threw it to the side.

"Dad! Wake up!"

He was still unconscious. She picked up his arm, let it go, and it slammed against the earth. She slapped him across his cheek and his head fell to the side. She straightened his head so that he was facing the sky. She held her hand just above his mouth and

237

waited to see if she could feel a breath, but she felt nothing. She leaned in closer and saw that his lips were blue.

"Dad!"

She interlocked her fingers and slammed down on his chest with both of her hands, then felt for a breath again.

Nothing.

"Think, Holly," she said, her words shuddering. "You took CPR. You know what to do."

When she'd slapped him, his head had turned to the side, and she remembered that that was exactly where it needed to be before she did anything else. She put her hand against his cheek and, gently this time, turned his head, but no water drained out of his nose or his mouth.

"Fuck."

She repositioned his head, tilted it back, pinched his nose, put two fingers under his chin, and breathed into his mouth, slowly, two times. After the breaths, she put her ear near his mouth and watched his chest for any sign that he was breathing again. She checked his pulse but couldn't find it.

"Come on, Dad!"

Holly did everything over again. She tilted his head back to open the airway, pinched his nose, and breathed into his mouth to push the air past any water blockage that was in his throat. She breathed again, and again, and again. She put her ear close to his mouth and listened for a breath. She stared at his chest, watching for the slightest movement.

Still nothing.

"Open your fucking eyes!"

Holly repeated the cycle a third time, and then a fourth. She thought back to the medical shows she'd watched. She pictured that moment, the one that every medical drama had, when one doctor kept doing chest compressions, or kept shocking the patient when they were coding—"Clear!"—and refused to quit until another doctor put their hand on the desperate doctor's shoulder and made them stop.

"They're gone," the doctor would say.

They're gone. Was her father gone? She struck his chest with both her fists again. His head jerked up. Had he done that? Had she? There was a stream of blood coming from a wound on his temple that she'd just noticed, and it gave her an idea of what had happened. When they crashed into the river, he must have hit his head on something. The canoe. Some rocks. It had knocked him out, and he'd drowned as a result.

She tore off her life jacket, then moved to real compressions, pushing down on his chest as hard as she could thirty times. She performed mouth-to-mouth for a fifth time. Listened for a breath, watched for movement. She sat up.

"Don't leave me!" she said. "Please don't leave me!"

Holly clasped her hands together, raised them high above her head, and smashed them against his torso between his chest and stomach. She bent down, tilted his head back, pinched his nose, two fingers under his chin, and gave him her breath. River water spurted out of his mouth, into hers. She fell back onto her ass. He coughed. More water shot out as though he were a statue in the middle of a fountain. He gasped for air and then coughed violently. She threw her arms around him and sobbed.

"You're back," she said, her voice weak and hoarse from yelling. "You're back."

Her father winced in pain, then dabbed his fingers, trembling like hers, at the welt on his temple. He held the fingers, the bloody fingertips, above his face, as if to look at them, but his eyelids fluttered and refused to open. His arm fell to his side. He went limp.

"Dad!" Holly said.

She pressed her ear against his chest, listened intently, and heard a faint heartbeat. She rolled over onto her back and rested her head against his stomach, hands over her chest. The light was dying, and with it, the warmth of the day. She remembered the chilly air from last night. What good would it do to have saved her father's life only for him to get hypothermia? His clothing, soaked with cold river water, and the dropping temperature, almost guaranteed it. She could feel his body shivering against the back of her head even now. Something needed to be done. Gathering whatever strength she had left, she got to her feet.

"Okay," she said, fighting off panic and tears with breaths as deep as she could manage, though they were still shallow, still quick. "Okay."

The smartest thing to do was to get herself and her father out of their wet clothing, and so Holly pulled off her boots and socks, then stripped down to her underwear. She hung her sweater, pants, shirt, and socks on branches at the edge of the trees, then put her boots out in the dwindling sunlight. Getting her father undressed was a bigger chore; he was far heavier than her, and being unconscious seemed to double his weight. She got his hiking shoes off, and his socks, took off his cargo pants, rolled him from one side to the other to get his windbreaker off, then pulled his sweatshirt and shirt over his head and arms, leaving him in his boxer shorts. She hung her father's clothing with hers.

Holly paced back and forth in the clearing after that, not

sure what to do next. Getting rid of the wet clothing was obvious; what to do next was a mystery. Eventually, she sat beside her father, who was still shaking uncontrollably, and made herself into a ball, pulling her knees into her chest, wrapping her arms around her shins. Shivering herself, she watched the river flow by, envious of its relaxed pace, of its deliberateness.

"What now, huh?" she said to her father, and tried to imagine what he would say, but no words came to her.

There was dirt all over her feet, from walking around the clearing. She brushed the dirt away thoroughly, just to occupy the time, and then looked at her father, who was dead to the world. She wondered what he was dreaming, if he was dreaming at all.

"Do you remember that time we were driving on Moray, on, like, the coldest night of the year?" she said. "January or something." Her teeth chattered.

She imagined that he nodded his head. It was easy to imagine him nodding his head.

"We were stopped at the red light at the intersection of Moray and Roblin, and the car just fucking died. The van. The Sienna. Worst. Car. Ever. You loved it, of course. It had a tape deck. You bought tapes at the flea market, and we used to drive around listening to them." She laughed and rubbed her legs for warmth. "I didn't even know how to put them into the deck to play them. I'd never seen a tape before.

"The light turned green and we didn't move. You turned the key and nothing happened. We'd been cranking the heat and it got cold so fast. I started to freak out; I thought we were going to freeze to death. You got on your cellphone and called roadside assistance. Mom had a blanket in the car, and we kept warm under it until the tow truck came."

Holly pulled at the grass with her toes, and then even though she'd cleaned off the dirt, pulled more grass out with her hands and sprinkled the blades over her feet.

"You figured out what to do, you know?" she said.

She kicked the blades off, then stared at her father for a minute, took in every detail of his face. His beard. Some stray hairs on his cheek. His once-olive skin, now pale. She looked away, reluctantly, to the river.

That's when she saw it. Her backpack, caught on some branches on the shore of another island. She remembered that her moshom's ashes were in it. Her father had let her carry the urn to start the day. She knew she didn't have a choice.

She got up, put her life jacket on over her bra, and walked to the river's edge. She dipped her toes in the water, as if she thought it might have warmed since she'd pulled her father to safety. If anything, it had gotten colder. The longer she waited, the colder it would get. She tied her hair back into a ponytail, took a deep breath, and then waded into the water. She eased forward, step by step, trying to get used to the cold water like she did at the beach, in the lake, as a child. She shuddered violently but kept going until the water was up to her waist, swallowing her into the chill. With one last deep breath, she lunged into a front crawl. She swam as hard and as fast as she could, racing against the cold as it swept across her body.

Either the current had gotten stronger as the day wore on or she was exhausted, or it was both, but by the time she made it to the other side and grabbed onto the same branches that had caught her backpack, she wasn't sure she could get back to her father. He wasn't that far away from where she was, no more than fifty yards, but it might as well have been a mile. She could see him lying there in the clearing, his skin the colour of the rising moon.

She could see him.

She could see him walking away from her.

She needed to reach him before he was gone.

"Also," she said in response to the million thoughts running through her brain, "I'm not dying in my fucking underwear." She slid the straps of her backpack through each arm.

Holly closed her eyes, let go of the branches, and drifted away from the riverbank. She allowed herself to float for a moment, to feel weightless, to forget about the cold, to feel deliberate, to feel relaxed. Then with everything she had left, she kicked furiously and charged to the other side of the river. She pulled herself out of the water and onto the shoreline.

She passed out there.

When she opened her eyes, it was night, although she wasn't sure how late. It was night, but it wasn't dark. The sky was clear, and the moon was high overhead, casting soft white onto the land. The stars were countless pinholes of light. She was desperately cold. She'd slept long enough to dry off, but every inch of her body was quavering, screaming at her not to move. She hooked her fingers around a root near her hip, pulled herself off the ground, and then got to her feet. With her life jacket in hand, she slung her backpack over one shoulder, and it weighed far more than it should have, soaked with water as it was. She stumbled through the long grass and underbrush and, minutes later, came to where she'd left her father.

Holly dropped the backpack and the life jacket on the ground and checked on her father. Relieved that he was okay, or as okay as one could expect, she sat down beside him. She took inventory of what they had, fumbling through item after item with clumsy fingers that felt frostbitten. Each of them had packed a book of matches, and thankfully she had placed it in a Ziploc bag that had kept the river water at bay. It was one of the only items that hadn't been soaked, along with, miraculously, her moshom's ashes. She arranged almost everything on the ground and put their snacks into a plastic bag, which she hung on a large burl, high enough so that bears couldn't get at them.

After emptying the backpack entirely so it, too, could dry out, Holly wrapped her father in a mylar blanket, then gathered kindling—dried leaves, dead twigs and branches—and constructed them into what resembled a tiny log cabin. The fire started easily, and she kept it burning with thick branches and driftwood she pinched from the beaver dam. She'd made the fire near her father, and once the flames were high and hot, she shuffled him even closer to it. She sat with him for a good while, gathering in the heat herself.

The fire gave her a second wind. Before that, she'd been doing everything despite feeling like she might collapse at any moment. She cut off a long section of twine from the roll she'd set on the ground, and tied each end to a tree, stretching the line over the fire. She moved their clothing from the branches at the edge of the forest to the line and hung up the wet clothes that had been in the backpack, too. She put on her driest shirt to keep herself warm, then lay down beside him.

"Please be okay," she said, and tried to imagine that he was, and that he said something in return.

Good night, Hallelujah.

She did her best to imagine it hadn't all gone wrong.

But she had nothing left. Not tonight. Facing her father, her arms tightly around him, the flames at her back, their heat making her skin feel as though it had been sunburned, she closed her eyes.

21

When Holly opened her eyes, it was light out. The fire had long since died, leaving in its wake a pile of blackened wood, grey wood ash, and smouldering embers. She wasn't shaking any longer; the flames, her shirt, and the blanket had helped ward off the cold. Her phone had been in her backpack, but even though she had kept it in a bag like the matches, water had seeped through the plastic, irreparably damaging it. There was no service out on the land, but it could have, at least, told her the time. Now she was left to guess, and with the sun directly overhead, she thought it was around noon. She'd slept a long time, had needed it, and was glad that her father was still sleeping. He needed rest more than she did.

She slid out from under the edge of the blanket and tucked her father in, as he had done for her when she was a child, making sure that he was completely covered. He had his colour back, a shade of dark olive, and his lips weren't blue. He wasn't shaking anymore, either, but he was still unconscious. She got up and pulled her clothes off the line. They were still damp, but dry enough. She put on her pants, exchanged her shirt for a different one, pulled on a fleece hooded sweatshirt and wool socks, and put on her wet boots.

She walked to the water's edge, took more wood from the beaver dam, and made the pieces she'd taken into a teepee over the remnants of last night's fire. After tossing dried leaves and grass and birchbark over the embers, she blew on the kindling until a tiny flame erupted that, within minutes, rose into a generous fire.

She gathered water from the river in a stainless steel water bottle she'd secured in her backpack's sleeve, added a purification tablet, then ate an apple and an energy bar while waiting for the water to become drinkable. She tossed her waste into the fire, watching the wrapper melt and curl around a twig before burning into ash. As she sat near her father, she warmed her hands over the flames, slowly rotating them as though they were on a rotisserie.

She wondered how far they'd gone, and how far they had left to go.

With the immediate danger out of the way, her mind wandered into deep concern, and it made her wish for her father's Xanax, but the pills, along with everything else in his backpack, had been taken by the river. That included the map he'd printed out of the path from Norway House to where he believed the trapline was. He'd drawn a crude line from the community to an area past a body of water called Hairy Lake, and an X, as though it were a treasure map. So there was no map, no sandwiches, dried noodles, or oatmeal packets, and no extra clothing for her father. They'd lost the tent and sleeping bags, and the fishing rods were gone along with the canoe.

* * *

It was early evening when Holly heard rustling behind her, and then a moan. She turned quickly from the fire to see her father rubbing his chest, his face contorted from the pain.

"Dad!"

He moaned again, writhed around under the blanket, and then his eyes fluttered open. They looked at each other.

"Are you okay?" she said. "Can you talk?"

"I—I think so."

His voice was faint. He tried to sit up, but Holly eased him back down. She'd prepared more drinkable water, and poured some into his mouth.

"Chill, Dad," she said while he drank. "You literally have been unconscious for, like, an entire day. *And* you almost died."

"What . . . what happened?"

He put his hands back on his chest, feeling around one particular area, the spot where she'd punched him out of desperation.

"The waterfall," she said.

He just nodded at that.

"We should've gone left," she said.

"I'll know for next time," he said. "Did you . . ." They locked eyes again. "Did you save my life?"

Holly put her hand on her father's forehead and ran it back through his hair. He reached for her hand, but when he did, she moved it away. She put it on her thigh.

"It doesn't matter," she said.

He craned his neck up and looked around, then rested his head back against the land. He winced and grunted.

"Why is my chest so goddamn sore?" he said.

"Chest compressions," she said. "I probably broke a rib. Or two."

"That explains it."

Her father tried to sit up on his own again, but stopped half-way. This time, Holly took his arm and helped him. "And you say that I'm stubborn."

He stayed upright, leaning back on his hands for support. She gave him the rest of the water, and then he waited while she refilled the bottle and added another tablet.

"So you did save my life," he said, as she walked back from the river.

"I guess so," she said. "But I think it was more the resuscitating and less the chest compressions. I'm not sure you needed the chest compressions—I was just freaking out." She shrugged. "I was trying not to, but, you know, when your father's lips are blue and he's not breathing, it's hard to keep your head on straight."

"I'm here, aren't I?" he said.

"Yeah," she said. "You're here. Wherever the fuck here is."

Holly took a deep breath to keep herself calm, and from crying. She undid her ponytail, and then redid it so that it was tight.

"Thank you," he said.

"Sure," she said. "You're welcome."

"She's all casual about it," he said, and then chuckled, but instantly stopped. He put his hand on his chest, breathed in through clenched teeth.

"Sorry," she said. "That must suck."

"Don't be sorry," he said, "but, holy god, who knew getting your life saved hurt so much."

"Hey," she said, "you think *you* have it bad? You threw up into my mouth, Dad. Like . . ." She pretended to vomit. "That's fucking gross."

He looked mortified. "I did not."

"You did," she said. "I'm not sure I'll ever get rid of the taste."

"Maybe in a few years, we'll be able to laugh at it," he said. "Now that I'm alive and all."

"Try in a few decades," she said. "That is, if we ever get home. We've got pretty much nothing with us now. We lost it all."

"Everything?" he said.

"Almost." She picked a Ziploc bag off the ground and handed it to her father. It was filled with what looked like diarrhea. "Care for a muffin?"

He tossed it back onto the ground. "Pass."

Holly stood up and looked out over the river, from south to north, her eyes carried that way by the current.

"How far are we?" she said.

"How far are we from where?" he said. "From home or from the trapline?"

"Either," she said, then turned around and looked down at him. "If you had to guess."

"Maybe . . ." Her father still sounded out of it, quiet and raspy. "I don't know. The map . . ."

"Is gone, yeah."

He tried to stand up but didn't get further than a sitting position. At that point, he cried out in pain.

"Dad, sit the fuck down," she snapped. "Honestly."

"Sorry." He rested his elbows on his knees, facing the river. He looked northward. "I think we're almost at Carpenters Lake. That's got to be twenty miles from Norway House."

"How many miles from the trapline?" she said, walking over to him. She sat down beside him. "Again, if you had to guess. Especially since it's a guess even where the trapline is."

"Fifteen miles?" he said. "We're closer to the trapline than we are to the community—I know that. We have to be."

"We have to be, or you want to be?" she said.

"Do you?" he said. "Want to be?"

"I don't know what I want," she said. "Yesterday, I wanted you to be alive, not dead, and now that you're alive, I don't know what I want. Okay?"

"Okay," he said. "Okay."

She took a deep breath. She looked him over carefully. He was still unclothed. The blanket was wrapped over his legs. He was holding his rib cage. She could tell that he was trying not to look in pain for her benefit. She tried to assess his condition, and what that meant for them. "Can you even walk, Dad? I mean . . . Jesus. You should be one day in the fucking ground."

"The walking dead."

"Shut up."

They were quiet for a while. The fire spit out embers. It cracked and snapped. The river rushed by, heading somewhere, leaving them behind. What if they couldn't go any direction at all? What if her father was unable to walk the distance? She picked up her moshom's ashes and held them in both of her hands as though warming them with a hot coffee cup. She wondered, if they spread the ashes here, whether they would find their way to his trapline. Would they know the way? She liked the thought of that but, at the same time, acknowledged that it was a fantasy, nothing more. Her moshom wasn't in the ashes. The ashes weren't sentient. They were just ashes. If they were spread here, they would become absorbed by the river and eventually feed into Lake Winnipeg.

"So Moshom never took you up here," Holly said. She didn't ask, because she knew that he hadn't. Her father had told her as much. "That would have been helpful."

"No, he never took me up here," her father said, his tone

suddenly jagged. "He was supposed to. He would've been with us now if he hadn't . . . you know. If he hadn't . . ."

"Yeah," she said, not wanting to make him finish the sentence. "I guess we're on our own."

"I guess we are."

Her father hugged the blanket around his body.

"You hungry?" she said.

Before he could answer, she handed him a banana, then opened a bag of nuts and placed it between them. She put one in her mouth.

"You better eat something."

He took a bite of the banana.

"Just don't puke it up on me."

"I'm never going to live that down, am I?"

"Likely not." She sighed. She glanced at him, reached over and pulled a small piece of the banana off, then ate it. "We don't have to go anywhere right now. We can just stay here, decide what we're going to do in the morning. Just figure it out tomorrow, you know?"

"See how I feel."

"Yeah," she said. "See how you feel."

The sun was starting to set. The forest was painted in warm colours. In reds and oranges and yellows. If she didn't know any better, she would have thought it was autumn.

"I'm supposed to save *you*, you know?" her father said. "You're not supposed to have to save me. It's not supposed to be the other way around."

Holly folded and stacked some clothes on the ground beside her father. She eased him onto his side and rested his head on the makeshift pillow.

"You should get some rest."

She sat by the fire while her father drifted to sleep. She'd brought a notebook. It was wet, too. She hung it on the line with all the clothes, so that by morning, the pages would be dry enough to write on. She'd planned to keep a journal of their expedition. The pen she'd brought was ruined, but she had a small pencil that would do fine. In fact, it was the perfect thing to write with, given where they were. Her moshom had kept a shoebox full of miniature pencils in his study. He'd liked to steal pencils from golf courses. There were hundreds of them in that shoebox. The last time Holly was over at her kōkom's place, she'd taken a handful. She'd brought one of them with her on the trip. It was dull, but that only meant her letters would be fat. The notebook had had poems in it that she'd written in ink. Now they were all distorted by the river and illegible. Only one stanza had survived. One stanza out of the hundreds she'd written.

We are too cautious
We are losing time
And hope
And forking paths.

I still don't know how it happened. The last thing I remember is falling. I don't remember hitting my head. I was falling and then, next thing I knew, images were hurtling toward me, one after another, split seconds of my life in chronological order, from being bathed in a sink by my mother, all the way up to paddling with you on the river, in my father's canoe. I guess what they say is true, that when you die, your whole life flashes before you, and it's strange because the images are coming at you so fast, at warp speed, and you've got no business seeing what each one is, but you do. There were the images, then everything turned yellow, then everything went black.

That was the second time I'd almost died in less than a year. Granted, drowning in the river was much closer to dying than almost driving off an overpass. It was different the second time. The first time, I wasn't scared. Living was worse. But that second time, I was so glad when I woke up, and I couldn't figure out why at the time. Part of it was that I knew how it felt to lose my father, and you didn't have to feel that way. Part of it, I think, was that I've started to care again.

After your moshom died, I went off the Xanax. I'd been taking it for years. It started out that I took it on an "as needed" basis. That's what the prescription said: as needed basis. Turns out that I needed it *a lot, so the prescription changed. I took them twice a day. Two pills in the morning, two in the early afternoon. Sometimes, I took them more than that. I took them twice a day, and "as needed." My body was so haywire, my mind was so fucked, that I didn't want to deal with it in a good way; I just wanted it to stop. And everything stopped. I got lost in this fog. Lost myself.*

I went cold turkey at first. It didn't go well. I had the worst rebound anxiety you could imagine. I'd been taking Xanax for years, it had built up in my system, and it was in my blood, running through my veins. I couldn't just stop taking it. I learned that the hard way, but I'd wanted to feel something. I tapered down after that. I went from four pills a day, two in the morning and two in the afternoon, to three and a half, two in the morning and one and a half in the afternoon, and every two weeks, I stopped taking another half. That's how I got off of them. I still carry them with me. I still need them sometimes. Sometimes, I don't want to feel. Mostly I do, though. But I don't know the last time I took one. It's almost like it's good enough now to know that I have them. Your moshom used to help me breathe normally when I was panicking. He'd put his hand on my stomach and make me breathe deep and slow. I don't have that anymore. I wish I had that.

I didn't know why I started writing these letters in the first place. You're the writer. You always have been. I put down whatever I couldn't say to your face. I know why I'm doing it now. Your moshom said a lot of smart things in his life, and a lot of smart things to me. Sometimes I listened to him, and sometimes I didn't.

One of the things he said often, I suppose so he could drill it into my brain, was that we can't know where we're going unless we know where we've been. We can't be whole until we know wholly who we are. That was one of the rare cheesy things he said, but he wasn't wrong, either. Like I wrote before, your mother broke up with me because I wasn't whole. That's what I think now, anyway. You can't love yourself if you aren't sure who you are in the first place. Anyway, I know that I've been a complete asshole the last while, and this isn't me trying to make excuses; it's me stating a fact. I'm not trying to make excuses, but I am trying to help you understand, and I think there's a meaningful difference there. I'm trying to help you understand why I was the way I was, the way I've been, and at the same time, I want you to know where we've been, not only since I tore us apart, but all the time before that, when things weren't so bad. I want you to know that things weren't always that way, that they were okay, even if they could have been better. That you were okay.

That it was never you; it was me.

I was so wrapped up in myself that I never thought about what it was doing to you. Then I saw it. This shit was always there, since I was a kid, just festering, and then it was too much, and it exploded. I think I saw that in you, when you were drinking. I'm sorry I made you feel like you weren't good enough, and that it made you feel like you needed to numb it out. I never wanted you to inherit that from me. Now I've got to figure out how to put myself back together. For you and for me and for us. I feel clearer out on the land than I ever have, and not only because I almost died.

Your moshom used to say that the land is medicine. Maybe it is.

Maybe that's why.

22

Matthew woke up intermittently as the sun died, and into the night, but still felt too weak to move, so he lay where he was, the space blanket wrapped around his body. Every time his eyes blinked open, Holly was sitting by the fire, wide awake. She would be taking inventory of the items they had brought, even though she'd done so several times, tending to the fire, or watching him. They made eye contact once or twice. She shushed him to sleep when this happened, put her hand on his leg and rubbed it gently, as one might pat the back of a fussing baby. He would close his eyes and drift back into a dreamless sleep.

At one point in the night, Matthew slept for a longer stretch, and when he opened his eyes, he found Holly sleeping on the ground, on the other side of the fire. He had no idea what time it was. His father used to be able to look at the night sky and guess, with startling accuracy, the time. Matthew had no such skill. The fire was dwindling. He pushed himself to his feet, which ushered a surge of pain into his head and chest, but he managed to stay upright (he was glad Holly was asleep, or she would've been pissed to see him standing). With the blanket around his shoulders, he navigated the riverbank to gather some wood from the beaver dam. On the way back to the fire, he wondered if he needed to lay tobacco down for the beaver dam because they'd taken a bunch of wood from the structure. You put tobacco down when you killed an animal, so why not when you took pieces of their house? He had a tobacco tie in his pants pocket, had brought it in a Ziploc along with a stack of papers, folded to fit. But he decided against it, mostly because he couldn't see somebody laying tobacco for a bank if they robbed it.

The flames swelled, and the land and trees around them lit up as though it were a miniature sunset. Matthew pulled his clothing off the line and got dressed. The clothes were warm from the fire, which was soothing, especially in the chilly air of the northern spring. Holly was shivering in her sleep, despite being fully clothed, and so he covered her with the space blanket. With the fire getting higher and hotter, he was satisfied that it would keep her warm. He intended to stay up and make sure the fire didn't go out so Holly wouldn't get cold. He'd slept long enough, and it was the least he could do after she'd spent the rest of the evening and a good chunk of the night looking after him.

The sky was clear and bright, the stars crisp and immeasurable, and each constellation presented itself like a book on a bookshelf, stories waiting to be told and retold. There was a notebook hanging on the line along with Holly's extra clothes, and out of curiosity, Matthew reached up and grabbed it. It was a yellow Hilroy, and Holly's name was written in longhand on the front. He opened it to find blue ink running off fuzzy letters like tear streaks. He hadn't read much of his daughter's poetry—she'd not shared it with him for years—but once in a while, she'd leave it out, maybe purposefully, he thought, and so he would read it.

One stanza had survived the ordeal. He noticed it while flipping through the warped, dried pages.

We are too cautious
We are losing time
And hope
And forking paths.

Forking paths. He understood that, at least. It evoked a recent memory, of the choice he had made of whether to go right or left around the island. He'd fucked up royally, and look where it had gotten them. They were near a riverbank, at the edge of a forest, somewhere between Norway House and his father's trapline, in a precarious situation. Worse. Not up the creek without a paddle. Up the river without a fucking canoe.

Forking paths. The choice he had made that led him to a bathroom, in the middle of the night, to cut his arm like he'd done when he was younger, just to see if he could feel something. The choice he had made to embrace misery over his own daughter, his own wife. To blind him from the fact that they could have filled him with better stuff, but he'd chosen to text Jesse instead, and how fucked up was that? How fucked up had that made everything?

Forking paths. Life was a series of choices, split-second decisions that changed everything, every time.

The smallest moments.

Matthew, as carefully as he could, tore out a number of pages from the notebook, then hung it back on the line where he'd taken it from. He patted each pocket on his cargo pants until he found the one with the Ziploc bag, slipped it out, and inspected the

259

contents to make sure they'd not gotten wet. The seal had held. In the bag, he'd carried the tobacco tie, a pen, and the folded-up paper, which he now unfolded to reveal a number of letters he'd been writing to Holly. He put them down on the ground, close enough to the fire that he could see what he was doing, and then flattened the papers he'd taken from Holly's notebook and put them on top of the pile. He started to write a new letter to Holly.

Matthew had not written more than a few words when he heard rustling in the trees, not far from where they were, maybe twenty feet off. A breeze swept through the makeshift camping spot. The flames flapped and flickered like a flag in a strong wind. The leaves sounded like sheets of rain. He closed his eyes and listened to the sounds. The flickering flames. The raindrop leaves. The rustling. Unexpectedly, he felt close to his father, closer than he had since he'd passed away. Up until that moment, he'd felt removed from his father; he'd not felt his presence.

Days after his father died, Claire had come across a dime on the floor in their bedroom, near Matthew's side of the bed. She told him it was a sign that his father was close by. She wasn't sure where she'd heard that from but said, "It's a thing." She placed the dime in Matthew's palm, and he felt nothing. Dimes kept presenting themselves after that, but each time, he shrugged it off, reasoning that it was like cars. If you bought a red Honda Civic, all of a sudden you'd notice red Honda Civics all over the city. It wasn't that they weren't there before, it was just that you'd become hyper-aware of them.

The dimes had always been there.

Matthew opened his eyes and looked out over the water, which, in the night, looked like black tar flowing by. He imagined his father as a boy, sailing past the riverbank, the beaver dam, in a boat with his own father, his mother, his siblings. At some point, maybe his father and his family had stopped where Matthew was now, for a rest while on their way to the trapline. It was a good place to rest. If they'd gone to the left, the arms of the river met back up again in time to find your way here.

Another sound came from the forest, and it was closer. A bush shook, as though trembling in the cold. A twig snapped. Dried grass compressed under the weight of footsteps. The rustling had not been the breeze. The sound was fifteen feet away. Ten. Something was coming toward them. Matthew placed the pen on the papers and crept over to the other side of the fire, beside Holly, putting himself between her and the forest. Whatever was coming would have to go through him to get to her. All manner of predators lived in the forest. Worst-case scenario, it could be a wolf or a coyote. He hoped for a deer or a moose. Holly had only just saved his life, and he didn't want to die. He wanted more time. With Claire. With Holly. He wanted to make up for the time he had lost with them when he'd been so obsessed with his own problems that he'd forgotten to be a good husband, a good father. Death wasn't the thing anymore. It was life.

Whatever it was, it was at the edge of the trees. Matthew heard a low grumbling, a moan. He put his hand on Holly's shoulder protectively and stared into the darkness. A silhouette emerged from the woods. A thick, moving shadow no more than four feet in height. Even when the low flame of the fire washed over the thing, it remained a shadow, as though immune to the light.

Matthew took a thick branch from the fire and used it as a torch, standing and holding it toward the figure. He almost fell backwards over Holly and into the fire when he saw that it was a black bear, but he steadied himself even as his heart beat faster and harder, his breath coming quicker and more shallow, his hands shaking. He nearly dropped the torch because his fingers felt like they couldn't grip it. He put both hands around it and held it like a sword, ready to swing at the bear if it attacked him or his daughter.

The black bear kept coming, its movements slow and calm, like it was out for a stroll and nothing more. In fact, there was nothing threatening about it, but Matthew knew it could turn on a dime if he surprised it, so he stood in place. The closer it came, the smaller he felt. It was a large animal, bigger than any black bear he'd seen before, as wide as it was tall. Its brown eyes glistened in the light. They looked almost human. It had a light-brown snout and sniffed the ground here and there as it walked. It looked at Matthew when it was a step away from him, paused briefly, then strolled through the clearing toward the riverbank.

Matthew watched, dumbfounded, as the black bear lumbered down to the river, then sat by the water like a person would, upright and on its behind. He lowered the torch and returned it to the fire. An image flashed in his mind, of him as a child, playing on the rocks on the shore at Clear Lake in Wasagaming. He'd stopped playing to see where his father was; he always wanted to make sure his father was close by. He saw his father sitting on a bench at the end of the pier, looking out over the water.

Matthew walked around the fire, toward the riverbank. He sat down there, watched the bear looking out over the river, looking north, and one word came to him.

"Dad?"

23

It was daylight when Holly woke, now two days since embarking on their journey. Her father was at her side, tending to the fire. He'd just finished eating a snack from their meagre supplies. She opened her eyes in time to see him toss a wrapper into the fire, along with an apple core. She saw that he'd gotten out the same meal for her. They'd not had supper last night—the banana and nuts didn't count—and she was having hunger pangs. Her stomach growled and it sounded like a wild animal had found its way into their camp.

"Morning," she said.

"Morning," he said, handing her the apple.

She accepted it and took a bite. When she finished chewing, she said, "Guess you're feeling better."

"Compared to yesterday? Yeah." He rubbed his chest. "Still sore, but, you know . . ."

"Better to feel anything than feel nothing?"

"Something like that." They shared a bottle of purified water. He tossed a branch onto the fire. He'd collected a stack of wood while Holly was sleeping. "I wish my backpack hadn't gotten lost. There was a Thermos with coffee. Coffee tastes way better than this shit."

He tossed the water bottle onto the ground, then wiped his mouth with his forearm.

"Even decaf coffee?" Holly said.

"Even decaf," he said. "Plus there was a change of clothing for me."

"You never really change your clothes anyway," she said.

"Good point." Matthew, especially recently, had made a habit of wearing blue jeans and a black long-sleeved T-shirt. He'd accessorized with sweaters and dress shirts that he wore over the shirt to make it look like he had some variety in his wardrobe, but Holly saw through the illusion. "Most importantly, I had ibuprofen."

"Now that would've been useful. That and the food you were carrying. We're going to be tapped out by the end of the day."

"You know what your moshom would say?"

"What's that?"

"The land will provide for us."

"Yeah, but Dad, the land isn't going to just spit out a fucking, you know, rabbit or deer or whatever people eat out here. And we lost the fishing rods, by the way."

"I figured, since they were in the canoe," he said.

"Yep."

"Well, look," he said. "We'll figure something out."

"That's not a plan."

"Your moshom used to talk about blood memory. Ever hear about that? From him?"

"No, I must've missed that teaching."

"It's like, your ancestors, their lives and experiences, living in you," he said. "Embedded into your DNA."

"Your point being?"

"Like I said, we'll figure something out."

"Jesus Christ." Holly had been rolling a smooth rock around in her palm, tossing it back and forth from one hand to the other. Now she tossed it into the fire, got up, and walked toward the river. It wasn't long before Matthew followed her and stood at her side. She glanced at him, then returned her attention to the swift water.

"At least you're mobile," she said.

"Good to go." He tried to hide a sharp pain from her, turning his face away long enough to flinch, but she noticed out of the corner of her eye. "For the most part."

Her father looked off in the direction of a beaver dam a bit farther north. Holly thought that if he couldn't do a hike, at least they had a ton of wood for fires. Apparently, besides that, they'd just . . . figure it out.

"So, were you up all night?" she said, trying to hide her annoyance at her father's naïveté. Or hubris. Or both. Both seemed like a bad combination. Both led to accidents on waterfalls.

He nodded. "After I woke up and saw that you were asleep, I couldn't get back to sleep myself. I wanted to make sure you were safe and warm and all that."

"Trying to make up for lost time?" she said.

"I've got a lot to make up for," he said.

"Well, thanks," she said. "You're a good dude."

"A good dude." He chuckled. "Turns out it was a good thing I stayed up. There was a bear here last night."

"A bear?" she said. "What?"

He pointed to a spot at the edge of the trees. "Came right out of there."

"No way," she said, but when she looked closer, the long grass around where her father had indicated was flattened or bent. "That's crazy. Didn't I hang the food up?"

"You did." He gazed into the fire, lost in thought. "It was weird. Usually bears, black bears—that's what it was—avoid humans. But this one"—he grinned—"this one just sauntered right into the camp, didn't bother with us, and sat down over there by the water." This time, he pointed to a spot on the river-bank. "Right there."

"It just sat and what? Hung out?" she said.

"Pretty much," he said. "It sat like you or I would, on its behind. It may as well have pulled up a lawn chair. It was so weird."

"What was it doing?" she said.

"It looked like it was, I don't know, watching the river in the moonlight," he said. "And I felt like . . . It was almost as if . . ."

He kept stopping because he couldn't find the right words, and then he buried his head and seemed to be wiping at his eyes.

"It was almost as if . . ." Holly prompted.

"It's stupid," he said. "It's beyond stupid."

He glanced at Holly. He looked conflicted.

"But at the same time," he said, "it was right there in front of me, and I thought . . ."

He sighed. His head emerged from between his knees. His eyes were shimmering in the morning light. He'd been crying.

"I thought, *Man, that's my dad.*"

He wiped at his eyes again.

"Just for a second, I had this feeling come over me that it was my dad coming to check on us because we're stuck out here and everything."

Holly tried to picture it. She tried to picture a black bear walking out of the woods, past her and her father, and then sit-

ting at the river's edge. She knew that her father didn't believe
in the supernatural. He never had. But she knew, as well, that
the supernatural was something he was curious about, because
he wanted there to be something beyond the natural world, to
fill the emptiness. As for Holly, she fell somewhere near the middle, stuck between belief and disbelief. Was confusion better than
curiosity? Were the two mutually exclusive?

"I don't think that's stupid at all," she said. "Isn't it kind of
awesome to think that Moshom is watching over us?"

He threw his arms up and then motioned toward the river,
as though the black bear was still sitting where it had been last
night.

"It's . . . awesome . . . to think about, but do you think your
moshom would really possess a black bear so that he could keep
tabs on us? I mean, why not appear to us like a Force ghost or
something?"

"Maybe because bears are more significant than *Star Wars*,
Dad. Moshom used to always say that—"

"Bears are our relatives, I know." He shrugged. "Maybe they
are."

"Can I tell you something that happened? I don't know if I
thought it was stupid or anything, but I thought it was kind of
crazy. Like, 'no fucking way' kind of crazy."

"Sure."

Holly told him about an experience she'd had a few days after
her moshom died. She was alone in her room; both her father and
her mother were asleep. She knew they were because she'd gone
to check on them. She wanted to talk to them about her moshom,
because that night was one of the nights when she was just so
sad. Losing somebody was like that, she found. She'd never really

lost anybody close to her before. There were some nights when she thought, *Okay, I'll be okay, I'll get through this*, and then there were some nights when she thought, *This pain will never go away, this pain will always hurt*. But when she found her father sleeping on the floor in the living room, headphones over his ears playing the saddest music (*Carrie & Lowell* by Sufjan Stevens, as she recalled), she let him be, and when she found her mother sleeping in bed with a book on her lap, a rare moment of peace, Holly took off her mother's reading glasses, placed them on the nightstand, and didn't bother her, either. She went downstairs, returned to her bedroom, and decided that her father had the right idea, that she was going to listen to some sad fucking music and cry herself to sleep. *Carrie & Lowell* was a good choice. Despite all the things that set her apart from her father, and the space that had been between them, there had always been music. They shared that. They would always have that.

She opened the drawer of her bedside table to get her AirPods, but found that the case was empty. This was not the first time she'd lost her AirPods somewhere in the house, but the timing sucked. She tore her bedroom apart, searching every inch of it—under her bed, in her jewellery box, in her backpack, in her drawers, behind her collection of snow globes, in the kangaroo pouch of her hooded sweatshirt that she'd put in the laundry basket earlier in the day. She searched in places that they would never be—inside her pillowcases, rolled up with a pair of socks, trapped between her fitted sheet and mattress, in one of her shoes. It was as if they'd disappeared. She looked through the rest of the basement as well, and all she came away with was a few quarters and an earring she'd lost a few months prior.

By then, her sadness had turned to anger, and she didn't listen to anything at all, didn't bother to compromise and put on a record. She curled up on her bare mattress (she'd thrown all her bedding on the floor) and fell asleep like that.

Sometime in the night, bathed in darkness, Holly opened her eyes. She felt something in her hand, which was closed in a fist. She opened her hand and stroked her fingertips over the small objects resting on her palm, and then she rolled them around as though they were dice. Finally, she reached for the reading lamp on her bedside table and flicked on the light. There, securely in her hand, were her AirPods. Her bedroom door was locked, so neither her mother nor her father had come into her room and placed them in her hand. There was no way they could have known that she'd been looking for them, anyway. She had never sleepwalked in her life, and even if she had, she wouldn't have been able to find them in a state of semi-consciousness when she hadn't been able to find them while wide awake. There was no logical explanation as to why her AirPods, which had seemingly fallen off the face of the earth, would be trapped within her balled-up hand. She lay there in bed, the AirPods resting on her palm, and one word came to her.

"Moshom?"

She put them in her ears. She jiggled them around until they were snug. She picked up her iPhone and connected it with her AirPods, then played the album that she'd wanted to play. She fell asleep with no explanation, but for one night at least, she had been saved from her anger, saved from her sorrow.

"That's pretty crazy," her father said, once she finished telling the story.

Holly was staring at her palm, as though the AirPods were still there. She closed her hand into a fist and held it to her chest.

"But you don't really think that your moshom, as a ghost, found your earbuds, carried them to you, and placed them into your hand," he said.

"Do you have a better explanation than that? What else could have happened?" she said.

"I know you said that you've never sleepwalked, and I can't remember you ever doing it, but that seems way more plausible than a ghost finding earbuds and giving them to you." He picked up a stone and tossed it into the water, hardly able to hide his annoyance. "Next time I lose the remote, I'm going to ask my dad to find it for me."

"You're patronizing me." She felt her chest start to burn, like an ember had been spit out by the fire and landed on her sweatshirt.

"No, I'm not."

"Moshom believed in Creator and the afterlife."

"I know he did." Her father stared into the forest. "And maybe he was right. Nobody'll ever know. But that doesn't mean he'd care about your AirPods. Why would he care about a pair of AirPods?"

"Why would he not care?" she snapped. "He'd care about my fucking AirPods because *I* cared about my fucking AirPods. Because I was sad and I missed my grandpa, and he wanted to let me know that he was still there. How is that any different from your goddamn bear?"

Her father put his head down and nodded, then met eyes with her again.

"You're right." His tone softened. "I just . . . I don't want to have false hope that he's here, when he's not. At least, not in a tangible way. Like, looking for earbuds and possessing black bears. He'll always be with you."

"What, in my heart?" she said.

"Is there something wrong with somebody being with you in your heart?" he said. "If that's all we've got . . . I don't know. Maybe it's not as bad as I thought it was. Maybe it's enough that people will miss us just like we miss your moshom."

"You think way too much," she said.

"I know," he said.

"Like, can't you just let me believe that Moshom gave me the AirPods? Why can't you let me have that?" Her chest, which had been burning, felt like a wildfire now. "False hope is still hope, and isn't that enough?"

She stormed off from where they'd been standing, back to the camp. With shaking hands, not from the cold but from anger, she filled her backpack with her clothes, half of the snacks, her notebook, and some matches. She was about to put the urn with her moshom's ashes into the side pocket, but stopped. She stared at it for a long time, because the longer she looked at it, the calmer she felt. When she glanced up, her father was looking at her with pleading eyes.

"I'm an asshole," he said.

"I don't know which way to go," she said.

"I know," he said.

"Which way should we go?" she said.

"Maybe you're right about the AirPods," he said. "Maybe I'm just mad it wasn't me that he found something for. He found your AirPods, but he left me out here, searching for a place I might never even find. You know?"

"I'm out here, too," she said.

"That bear," he said. "When it sat down, when it looked at the river, it spent most of its time looking north. Do you think that's a sign, Holly? Could it have been a sign?"

"Maybe," she said. "I mean, it wasn't looking south, right?"

"Which way do you want to go?" he said.

"I'll go where you go," she said.

Her father turned around and walked to the spot where the bear had sat. He looked north, too, at first. Then he looked south. When he did, her heart sank. She knew which way she wanted to go, but didn't say anything to him. It was his choice. Her moshom was his father. Sometimes she forgot that. It hurt so much to lose him. It must have hurt so much for her father to lose him.

He turned to her, walked to her.

"I think we've come so far," he said. "We shouldn't turn around now. I know what's there, if we go back. I've been there."

"How far did you say it was? Fifteen miles?" she said.

"Give or take," he said. "We have to follow the water on the right. If we follow the water, we shouldn't get lost."

"Is your chest okay?" she said.

"It'll be fine," he said.

"It's hard to stay mad at you when I'm appreciating the fact that you're not dead, you know."

"That's a conundrum."

"As problems go, it's a good one to have," she said. "I mean, at least you're around to get mad at."

"You could be mad at me posthumously."

"Let's quit while we're ahead."

Her father took the lead on their hike northward, entering the brush west of the treeline, the path of least resistance. Holly followed close behind, taking advantage of the path her father was carving out. Still, the going was difficult. At times, the brush and long grass were so thick that she wished they'd brought a machete, as if they were in a jungle and not in a northern terrain. Other times, she thought they would have done well if they had climbing gear, so drastic were the land's undulations, the large, rolling hills, the low valleys, the steep inclines that led to cliffs. They stopped at one of the overhangs and had a late-morning snack. Holly hung her legs off the edge and kicked them back and forth like a child would. They ate the last of the nuts and each had a banana, which left only enough food for supper, and a small one at that. When she wondered aloud what they'd eat the next day, her father said, "We'll cross that bridge when we come to it."

Climbing down from the cliff using roots and bush like jugs on a climbing wall, Holly said, "Shouldn't we deal with it today?" She lowered herself carefully; she was above her father and didn't want to fall on top of him. He was already partially broken. "At least figure out a plan so we don't starve?"

"Your moshom used to say that when he wanted to eat, he caught something. So, when we run out of food, we'll catch something."

"You've pretty much said that before, and the concept is nice, but it's not an actual solution."

"Okay, we'll pick something. We'll pick berries."

"Yeah, but we can't just eat berries the whole time," she said, "and that's even if we can find berries."

"There's berries all around." He stepped onto level ground, then turned to help Holly if she needed it, holding his hands close to her waist like a spotter at the gym. "Your moshom taught me which ones are good for you and which ones are not."

"Right, okay." She got down without assistance. "And we *can't just eat berries the whole time.*"

"Then we'll catch a fish," he said. But she caught his tone: he was unconvinced. Worse, he sounded nonplussed. She began to realize that he was acting composed about the whole food situation so that she wouldn't worry, but somebody with anxiety can always spot somebody with anxiety.

"If there's more gravity to this problem, you might as well say it," she said. "A little urgency wouldn't hurt, rather than just fucking waiting until tomorrow and hoping for divine intervention."

"A couple of times when I fished with my dad, we caught a boatload. Your moshom tied them together, and they looked like a hand of bananas," he said. "There are lots of fish out here."

"First of all, how do you know what a bunch of bananas together is called?" she said. "That's so random."

They started up a less intimidating hill.

"Probably *Jeopardy!* or something," he said.

Holly thought that made sense, because it wasn't uncommon to find her father on the couch late at night, watching reruns of game shows.

"All those bananas clustered together look kind of like fingers."

"That's true," she admitted. "But, second of all, we don't have any fishing rods, remember? What are you going to do? MacGyver us a fishing rod? Use some twine and find a paper clip?"

At the top of the hill, they stopped, and Holly observed her father looking out over the land in a full circle before they met eyes.

"I love that you know about MacGyver," he said.

"One of your parenting wins," she said. "That and liking Pearl Jam and vinyl and *The Fugitive*, right?"

"It makes me feel like I'm not such a fuck-up," he said. "And it also means that when I ask, 'Do you recall what Tom Hanks did in *Cast Away?*' you'll know what I'm saying."

Holly punched her father on the arm. She made sure not to punch him anywhere near his fractured ribs, or his temple, where a pretty impressive goose egg had formed.

"We're not going to throw spears into the water and catch fish!" she said. "Are you fucking kidding me? It was four years before he could do that, and regardless, it was a fucking movie, Dad. This is real life."

"Hallelujah, I know this is real life, and there's truth in fiction. People actually have caught fish that way."

"You're right, there's truth in fiction, and that's why he caught fish that way *after four years*," she said. "It takes practice."

"We could get lucky," he said.

"You're trying to convince yourself more than me," she said.

He looked around again, 360 degrees, taking in every detail of the land that surrounded them, that embraced them in its arms. The river, where it forked off into two paths, left and right, like a wishbone. The land and its bush and lush forest and rolling hills and cliffs where people, over generations, had painted pictures, written in syllabics, left initials with dates, longing to be remembered.

You could be forgotten out here, even if the land did not forget you.

The beaver dams, the eagles' nests bulging at the top of thin, dead trees, the muskrats sliding through the water like eels, their fur slick and shimmering, the waterfalls and their dangerous beauty.

"If not, maybe *they'll* have a fishing rod we could borrow," he said, pointing.

Holly peered into the distance. To the north, on a hill alongside the right river branch, was a cabin that looked like a smaller version of the prefab houses that populated the reserve.

"Oh my god! That's what I'm talking about!" Holly raised her arms triumphantly, and then embraced her father, who immediately doubled over. "Oh fuck, I'm sorry!"

He leaned forward, facing the ground, his hands on his knees, for a few seconds.

"I'm okay."

He straightened and put his hand on her shoulder, smiled reassuringly. Tried to smile reassuringly, anyway. He looked constipated.

The cabin stood on an elevated tract of land, at the end of a manmade path that had been worn into the bush. The path started at a rickety old dock that was slanted to one side and presently unoccupied; there was no boat to speak of. Out front of the cabin and surrounded by logs of various shapes, cut clean and turned upright to act as seats, was a firepit with no smoke rising from it. Another indication that nobody was home. The cabin itself was painted green, and the roof was covered in camping tarps to keep the rain out. Whatever the roof was made of, it had likely sprung a leak at some point. The cabin had at least one window on the side facing them, but Holly could not see inside it from the distance they were at. To the west was a small construction that was shaped like a phone booth, maybe slightly bigger, and she figured it was an outhouse. Behind the cabin, to the east, was a shed. According to her father, that was likely where the owners of the cabin kept their fishing rods.

"How do you know there'll be fishing rods?" she said.

"Because everybody out here fishes," he said. "Where do you think I got mine? Your moshom."

Holly pictured the owners coming home, going into the shed to get their gear so they could catch some dinner, and discovering that they'd been robbed.

"We can't just steal their stuff, though," she said. "Can we?"

"Hall," he said, "they'll have more than one rod, and if they don't, we'll bring it back. People share stuff around here all the time. We don't look at possessions the same way."

"Example."

"Okay," he said. "When somebody catches a moose, they don't keep it for themselves. It becomes a community event where they prepare the meat and divvy it up between several families."

"Fair enough," she said. "But usually when you borrow something, you let the other person know you're borrowing from them."

"Fine, we'll leave a note." He readjusted his backpack and started walking toward the cabin. "Now come on. We better keep moving if we want to get there by dark."

Holly's knee-jerk thought was that her dad was aiming low to think they'd arrive at the cabin by dark. It didn't look far off, considering the ground they'd covered on their hike and the natural impediments they'd negotiated. But it wasn't long before she understood the goal her father had set. Between them and the cabin, there was a large body of water that they would have to go around. Holly's heart sank for a moment at how much work they had in front of them, but she knew there was no other choice, so she decided to suck it up and carry on. She was bolstered by an idea that came to her as she thought about the cabin and what might be inside it, what she hadn't been able to see through the window, as well as how they'd spent last night, with their unexpected visitor.

"Maybe we could sleep inside tonight," she said, "if it's open."

Her father chuckled. "Let me get this straight, Hallelujah. You didn't want to borrow a fishing rod, but you've got no problem breaking into somebody's house?"

"I was convinced by your argument," she said. "You're very persuasive."

"In that case, I don't see any reason why we can't check to see if the cabin's open," he said. "If they happen to come by and find us in their beds, well . . ."

"As long as it's not a bear," she said.

"Can you imagine?" her father said. "I'd never stop calling you Goldilocks."

"I'd almost prefer that over Hallelujah, you know."

"Goldilocks?" her father said with disbelief. "You'd rather be named after a fairy-tale character than something that honours the certifiable fact that you're a miracle?"

"I've heard the story," she said dismissively, "and you do know that I'm not a miracle, don't you? Your sperm hit Mom's egg and voila. I learned that in health class."

"Agree to disagree," he said. "And if you want me to call you Goldilocks, it'll be weird, but I'll do it. Actually, Goldie has a nice ring to it."

"No chance," she said. "But let's hope there's some porridge we can eat."

24

The sun had set by the time Matthew and Holly arrived at the cabin. It had been a long day, and he was relieved to have finally made it. He'd used the last of his energy climbing the steep path from the dock. The dilapidated steps hammered into the earth had, if anything, made the hike up harder. Matthew didn't want to worry Holly, but on top of wanting to collapse from exhaustion, his head was pounding; he was certain that he'd suffered a concussion from the accident. He wished that he'd listened to his father more when they'd gone into the bush around the community. Matthew was sure that his father had pointed out some natural medicines that helped with pain, which would be nice to have now, given his lack of Western medicine (namely, Advil).

He hoped there would be something for his head in the cabin, but to their disappointment, it was padlocked. Now they had to decide whether they would break in or sleep outside. At least there was dry, chopped wood stacked on the south side of the house, which would make it easy to start a fire.

"What do you think?" Matthew said.

They were standing side by each, staring at the padlock, weighing their options.

"We could get a big fire going," Holly said, "but I'm kind of coming around on the whole B and E thing."

Holly looked through the window, which was covered in chicken wire. The inside was sparsely furnished. "Literally anything at this point is better than dirt or grass." There was a table, two cots, a couple of lawn chairs, and a camping stove. There were some snowshoes hanging on one of several hooks, along with pots and pans, a coat, a Chicago Blackhawks baseball cap, and a couple of fly swatters.

Matthew wasn't about to argue with her. "Maybe we could screw off the handle so we don't have to do the breaking part of breaking and entering."

The door and the exterior wall each had a pull handle, and the padlock's shackle had been looped through both to secure the cabin. It was a sound plan, but one that would require tools. The shed was a place where tools might be kept, but its door was locked by pull handles as well. Plastic ones. They decided that if they were going to break something, it ought to be the plastic handles. Matthew fetched a log from the woodpile and hammered down on the handles until one snapped off.

The shed was packed full of supplies, including a number of fishing rods, enough of them for Holly to remark that Matthew had been right and the owners would hardly miss one. There were two rifles, more snowshoes, pails, an axe, a hacksaw, a large supply of rope, a tackle box, some extra boards that Matthew figured were for the deck, life jackets, various other items of little consequence, and not a screwdriver in sight.

"How could you have all this and no screwdriver?" Holly said.

Matthew shrugged.

"We'll have to do it the hard way," he said, and picked up the hacksaw.

"That thing?" she said. "That'll take us years!"

"An hour, maybe," he said.

"Why don't we just break the door down and apologize later?" she said.

Holly relented, and they took turns sawing at the lock, sharing a pair of fishing gloves that Matthew found in the tackle box, for some kind of protection if the blade slipped. During Holly's first turn, Matthew gathered kindling and wood and started a fire. During Matthew's first turn, at his suggestion, Holly went down to the dock to see if there were fish in the water on a line, which was how people kept their fish fresh until cleaning them. There weren't any, and they resigned themselves to eating the last of their snacks for dinner.

It was after dark when they broke through the lock. They found a battery-operated lantern inside that they turned on and placed in the middle of the room. There was a cabinet that had been out of view when Holly looked through the window, and it was full of non-perishable food items, tea bags, instant coffee, and a deck of cards and a cribbage board.

"Look," Holly said, delighted. "Porridge!"

"Oh my god," Matthew said.

There was a jug of water on the floor underneath the shelf, and they heated up a pot of water on the camping stove to make Matthew a cup of tea and Holly some coffee. They played a best-of-five tournament of cribbage while sipping their drinks, and Holly won even though she'd not played before. Then they finished their snacks with a bowl of porridge each while sitting by the fire.

"I never beat my dad at cribbage," he said.

"I know. This is not new news," she said. "Do you wish that you did?"

"Of course I do. It was so frustrating to lose every single time." He took a bite of porridge, which tasted far better than it should have, even with the copious amount of sugar he'd poured into the bowl.

"I wouldn't know the feeling," she said.

"I wish I could lose to him again," he said.

"There's a lot of things I wish I could still do with him, too," she said. "I bet when you're gone, I'll wish that I could beat you again."

Matthew finished the last of his porridge, filling his mouth as a way to avoid responding to Holly's remark.

"What? Too soon?" she said. "I was going for levity."

"You're just a sore winner," he said with a grin. "That motivates me for next time, you know."

"Bring it on, Dad."

Matthew tossed his spoon into the garbage, then threw the paper bowl into the fire and watched it burst into flames. Just as quickly as the bowl had become a fireball, it was gone.

"Ever think about anything else, or do you just want another crack at beating Moshom?" she said.

"I think about a lot of things, Hall. Memories, mostly. I play them over in my mind. Some are clearer than others. Some never fade, if they're important enough."

"I'm assuming you have an example," she said.

Matthew shifted in his chair, then leaned forward, elbows to knees.

"So, we were playing cribbage in the dining room. This story isn't about cribbage. Cribbage is just incidental. This must've been when I was a teenager. I was probably in grade ten. The room was different then. You know where that big china cabinet is now? There was a piano there. I quit taking lessons because I didn't think it was cool to play."

"Dad," Holly said, sounding genuinely taken aback, "Ben Folds."

"I know," he said, "I know. I was an idiot. Anyway, there was the piano where the china cabinet is now, and on the wall beside the piano, there was a cabinet record player. It even had an actual, real-life, working eight-track."

"Oh my god, I wish I had that fucking thing in my room," she said.

"Right? It sounded so good. Your kōkom had all this '60s music I liked to listen to. She hardly played it, though. The eight-track, I mean. She used the record player."

"A girl after my own heart."

"To a point, but she almost exclusively listened to Elvis Presley and Nana Mouskouri."

"Oh."

"I got used to Nana, to be honest. Didn't mind her. And Elvis, you know, he was the king. 'Can't Help Falling in Love'?"

"Okay, that song's awesome."

"I digress," he said. "We were actually supposed to go for a walk that night, but there was this crazy thunderstorm. It was apocalyptic. The sky was black. The rain was coming down in sheets, all that. So we decided to stay in. Your moshom was pegging a hand when there was this huge flash of lightning. The sky lit up white for a fraction of a second, and immediately after that, there was a crack of thunder. And then immediately after that, all the power went out. It was pitch black and dead silent. Your moshom reached over and took my hand. I'm still not sure if he was scared, or if he thought *I* was scared. It must've been an hour before the power came back on. It felt like an hour." Matthew shrugged. "When you're a teenager, you just don't want to hold your father's hand."

"That's a good memory," she said. "This is a good memory."

"Maybe you'll remember it," he said.

"Maybe I will," she said.

They met eyes, smiled, and then looked away from each other, as if they weren't allowed to have a moment like that yet.

Matthew cleared his throat. "And then I think about the things we never got to do."

Holly tossed her own bowl into the fire, plastic spoon included. The spoon sent out a plume of black smoke, then it melted onto a piece of charred wood.

"Like what?"

Matthew breathed deeply, as though taking in air would push the emotions down. The sadness he was feeling, the anger, the longing, the fear. Always the fear. The fear and the emptiness.

"Like, I wish he would've taken me here," he said. "Out on the land. I wish he would've taken me to his trapline. We were up here a lot, especially when I was younger." Another breath. "Why didn't he?"

"I don't know, Dad. I'm sorry." She leaned back in her chair, crossed her arms. "Maybe for the same reason you never took me to Norway House."

"Yeah, maybe." He wiped below his eyes with his sleeve. He looked at the damp spot on the fabric of his sweater. "I'll never know. That's what kills me."

"He was going to, though. I'm just, like, his proxy or whatever."

"No, I'm glad you're here," he said. "I just wish I could've done better out here for you. If he'd taken me, I would've known what I was doing. And if he were still alive, I'd like to think all three of us—"

"Don't," she said. "Don't do that. Moshom dying changed everything, Dad. You didn't ask me to go, even if you agreed to take me, and honestly, I wouldn't have wanted to go otherwise. Not with you. Not with the way things were."

"So where does that leave us?"

"It leaves us here," she said. "Because he did die."

"Things are different now. Things are better, aren't they? With us?"

"You know they are," she said. "But they're not *fixed*, Dad. That takes time."

He looked at her, but she was just staring into the fire.

"One day, if you have kids, maybe you'll play cribbage with them. People pass down traditions like that. My mother, she used to make me peanut butter sandwiches, but she'd butter the bread first, so they were really peanut butter *butter* sandwiches. That's what I called them. I made you the same kind of sandwiches. We pass down stupid things, and things that mean something. Maybe your kid will ask you about your favourite cribbage memory, and maybe you'll tell them about sitting with your dad, talking by the fire. A cribbage memory doesn't always have to be a cribbage memory."

"Fuck that," she said. "I'm going to tell them how I beat you on my first try."

25

Holly wasn't sure when she and her father went to bed, but it was late. They'd sat in front of the fire until it died out, watched the embers glow like the heart of the land, and then pointed out constellations to each other in the dark, when the stars were crisp and bright. They kept going until they'd exhausted all the ones they knew, all the constellations that her moshom had taught them, all the stories associated with them.

There was a latch on the inside of the door, a far cry from the security offered by the lock they'd cut. It wasn't about to keep bears out of the cabin, and after closer inspection, they could see that bears had tried to get in before, probably more than once. There were claw marks all over the door, which was likely why it had been built sturdier than anything else in the house, and why there was chicken wire covering the windows. They had found blankets underneath the cots that smelled like dust mites, and used them after shaking them out thoroughly by the firepit. Holly was assigned the cot in the far corner of the room, because her father insisted on sleeping between her and the door to protect her against any predators. He put the axe beside him, leaning it against the wall, before turning in.

Holly wasn't sure why the window on the cot wall had been built so close to the ceiling. It wasn't all that functional where it was, but she found her own use for it. She lay down so she could see the night sky through it. She put her hands behind her head to use them as pillows, crossed one leg over the other, and counted stars until her eyelids grew heavy and she drifted to sleep.

Holly opened her eyes to find that she was standing, and there was a large black bear between her and the door. Its eyes appeared to glow in the gathering morning light. It didn't roar when face to face with Holly; it didn't so much as growl. It had been sitting, but now it got to its feet, which made her think that it had been waiting for her. The thought should have been ridiculous, but it didn't feel that way, especially after she combed her hair behind her ears with her fingers, and the bear, in response, shook like a wet dog.

"This is a dream," she said.

"It is," the bear said.

"What are you doing here?" she said.

"Waiting," the bear said. "It shouldn't be much longer now."

"I'll wait with you," she said.

"All right," the bear said. "I'd like the company. Shall we go outside?"

The bear turned and walked out of the cabin, and she followed it. They sat by the fire, which was burning high and bright and hot, Holly on a chair, the bear on the ground, sitting like a person.

"You remind me of my moshom," she said. "You talk like him."

"According to your moshom," the bear said, "we're related. There's bound to be some resemblance."

"Yes, I guess there is," she said.

Holly contemplated whether or not this was the same bear that her father had seen the night before, if it had followed her here, and why it would have.

"What do you want?"

"Look." The bear pointed at something approaching in the distance, on the water. It had been speaking softly, as soft as a bear's voice could be, but now it sounded excited. "He's here."

"Who?" she said. "It's too dark."

The object came closer, and the moonlight seemed to shift, to spotlight whatever it was that came this way. When it did, Holly saw that it was a canoe, and inside it, there was one person. A man. He was paddling calmly, in no rush to get anywhere.

"Do you see him?" the bear said.

"I do."

Right when the bear spoke, Holly had known it was her father in the canoe. He was headed toward an island. He looked over at her, they met eyes, his glowing in the night like two little stars, and then he sailed past her and just kept on going. He didn't say anything to her, didn't wave, didn't smile, just paddled past. As he continued on his way, he gazed straight ahead, and Holly noticed that she was cold out here on the riverbank. The blanket was wrapped around him now, not her. She supposed that he needed it more than her, that it must be cold on the water. But she knew, as well, that wherever he was going, he would be waiting for her, and if she was cold, he would give the blanket back to her, so that she could be warm. She watched until he moved out of sight, and when he was gone, the bear got up and walked around to the north side of the cabin. It stopped there for a moment. She waved at it. It nodded. Then it walked away, off into the woods. Holly decided to lie down right there in the long grass on the riverbank and go back to sleep.

Holly woke up on the cot. She opened her eyes to find the stars still visible outside the window; it wasn't morning yet, though the sky had turned from black to navy blue. She looked over at her father, and saw that he was still asleep. There was a piece of paper on his chest, resting on top of a Ziploc bag full of more sheets of paper, folded to fit, and the lantern, switched off, was beside his bed. At some point in the night, he must've been writing something. Holly thought that was odd, because she'd never known her father to write anything other than a note in a birthday card. She'd always thought that writing was a skill she had not inherited from either parent. She took the sheet and brought it and the lantern back to her cot, where she sat on the edge. She flicked on the light and placed the lantern at her side. Straightening out the paper against her lap, she read.

> *Regret covers everything. It's thick like fog. It's hard to see through. Your grandfather says that he doesn't regret anything because you can't change what happened. I don't know if I believe him. I think we all wish that we could go back and do at least one thing over again. I wish I would've sent you that text, Hallelujah. I wish I would've sent you that text even though you had told me not to talk to you. Because I was a coward and you deserve better. Because I wouldn't have done*

what I did next. Because I wouldn't be blaming myself for something that may have happened anyway. I think it's my penance. How fucked up is that? We can drown in regret.

Holly set the paper down beside the lantern, and just sat there for a long while, staring at her father, who was sleeping in the cot between her and the door. She wondered what the other letters said, folded up in that Ziploc bag, but she couldn't bring herself to read them. It would feel invasive, like reading a diary, even though the words were clearly meant for her. She would read them when he gave them to her, if he did at all, and if he didn't, what she'd read was already enough. She only wished that he'd said it to her face, but, like he'd written, you can drown in regret.

"Oh, Dad," she said, and, with the lantern still on, took the paper over to her father and put it back on his chest. She looked down at him. He had one hand resting on his stomach, as though emulating the way her moshom used to calm him. His legs were sprawled out over the sides of the cot, which was too small for him. His other hand was at his side, his fingers curled around a pen. The sleeve of his sweatshirt had pulled up over his forearm, and she noticed a thin, raised area of skin. She lowered the lantern to get a better look at it and saw that it was an uneven scar. She thought back, took inventory of the clothes he typically wore, and couldn't remember him wearing short sleeves often, just that long-sleeved black T. She touched the scar with her fingertip. She moved her finger away, put it back, moved it away. Each time she moved her fingertip away from the scar, she wished it was gone, because she knew what had caused it, and she didn't want to believe it.

She pulled her father's sleeve down over his wrist, hiding the scar.

She pressed her sleeve against her eyes, hiding the tears.

We can drown in regret.

Holly made herself a cup of coffee, then unhooked the front door and went outside. She was greeted by a cool breeze, and air so crisp that it stung her nostrils, a sensation that she was quickly falling in love with. In the city, she just felt like she was taking in air when she breathed. Up here, breathing was like taking in life, and it made her feel vibrant. She hoped the same was true for her father.

She sat on the log she'd sat on the night before, facing the river below, and tried to exist in the calm. She breathed deeply, often closing her eyes when she did. There were goose pimples all over her body; it was chilly out this early in the morning. She held her cup with both hands for a little bit of warmth, and kept it close to her body so the steam kissed her cheeks. She took little sips, nursing the beverage. She thought of her dream, even as it faded, and tried to decipher its meaning. But she was at a loss without her moshom, or even Rebecca. She decided that she would see Rebecca when they were back in the city and ask her about it. To do that, she figured she ought to write down what she remembered before she lost more of it. She put her cup on the ground by her feet, pushed herself up, and turned to head back to the cabin to grab her notebook from her backpack.

But she stopped there, facing the cabin, and pictured the bear from her dream, before it had left. It had gone to the north side of the cabin. It had been on its way to the forest, but it had stopped there, and waited. She'd waved at it, and it had nodded at her. Why had it done that?

Holly walked toward where the bear had stopped, as though it were there now, and imagined that she was following the bear.

Wait, she thought. *Wait up.*

She followed it even as it disappeared into the darkness, the long, dewy grass cool against her bare feet, dampening her legs all the way up to her knees. She followed it until she came to the treeline, and then ended her pursuit.

Goodbye.

She turned away from it, away from the darkness, away from the forest, to the south, and when she did, she saw a canoe leaning against the cabin, two paddles underneath it.

"Well," she said. "Fuck me."

Holly's father woke up soon after. They brought the canoe to the dock, put the paddles and fishing rods and tackle box and backpack in it, then had some porridge and played another game of cribbage before continuing their voyage with renewed optimism.

Everything had changed now.

They went as far in one hour on the water as they would've in an entire day on foot.

This time around, encumbered by his injuries, her father sat in the bow seat, and Holly sat in the stern. She liked it back there. She could see everything. The water, the land, the sky, and her father. The letters he had written were in his back pocket; she could see them peeking out from underneath the fabric. He was always looking, his head turning to the left, then to the right, trying to remember the path that her moshom had given him, the directions to a lost trapline. From time to time, he would point something out to her, something that his father had told him, but for the most part, he was quiet, and so was she. For the most part, he kept turning his head this way and that, deliberately and fastidiously, and she found herself watching her father more than the water, the land, or the sky. His head turning, his eyes searching, the wind rippling his hair like shallow waves.

She thought of the note to the owners of the cabin they had left behind.

I wish I knew who to address this to, but I don't. If my father had been with me, he would've known who you are. Then again, if my father had been with me, we wouldn't have had to borrow your things, or break into your cabin. I'll spare you the details, because I don't want to make excuses, but we got into some trouble out here, and finding your place might have saved me and my daughter. We'll bring you back the canoe and the paddles, the fishing rods and tackle, on our way home. I hope the money I left with this note is enough to replace the lock and the handle to the shed. I don't think we would've had a chance without your help, even if it was help you didn't know you were giving. You have a beautiful place. I feel like it's just short of paradise. We were only here a night, but out of all the nights I'm going to live, this one will stick out. That might not mean anything to you, but it means a lot to me. Anyway, you probably could've just done with a simple "Sorry" and a fifty-dollar bill, so I'll stop writing. We're going northeast, up past Hairy Lake. My father had a trapline past there, somewhere, that we hope to find. I guess I'm telling you that in case anything happens to us. You probably know your way around here.

Ekosani,
Matt McIvor

26

By noon, they had reached a clearing by the water and decided to stop there, having made good time by hugging the shoreline on the east side of the river. They started a fire in a small depression in the earth, where others had built a fire before them. There was a tree that had been split, probably by a lightning strike, at the edge of the clearing, and Matthew and Holly used wood and bark from it. When the flames reached skyward, and smoke rose into the air like ghosts, they got back in the canoe and paddled out to the middle of the river, where they cast their lines.

"Live bait is way better," Matthew said, after half an hour had gone by without a bite. "You're not guaranteed to catch a fish out here."

"I like it out here either way," Holly said.

"People can go a long time without food," he said.

"Remember the hunger strike I went on a few years ago, when you took away my phone?" she said, then laughed. Her cheeks turned red.

"What did that last, a day?" he said.

"Until Mom made the greatest supper ever," she said. "On purpose."

"She's diabolical," he said.

The fish started biting not long after that, and they may as well have jumped into the boat themselves. Holly caught the first one, which she named Benny. She celebrated as though she'd won a second water polo championship, and within the hour, they'd pulled in seventeen more. Matthew tied fifteen of them together, secured the line to a tree, and submerged them in the lake, planning to retrieve them on their way back from the trapline for their unwitting benefactors. Matthew and Holly kept two for themselves, and decided to release Benny.

Matthew cleaned the fish on some rocks by the shore, clumsily, with a knife he'd found in the tackle box. He left guts and bones all over, which they cleaned up as best they could, then cooked the fillets on sticks over the fire. They ate their meal using a large, flat rock by the fire as their table.

"Oh my god," Holly said with her mouth full. "I take it back. *This* is the greatest supper ever."

"Fresh food is amazing," Matthew said, but added that he wasn't sure it was the best meal ever, seeing as how he spent as much time picking little bones out of his fish as he did eating it.

"Toothpicks," Holly said, a one-word answer meant to make him feel better about his fish-cleaning skills.

She pretended to pick at her teeth with one of the larger bones she'd found in her lunch.

It was early afternoon when they pushed off from the shore. Matthew told Holly that Hairy Lake was a ways off, but easy to find. They'd left the islands behind, and it was straight ahead from there on. You followed the Echimamish River all the way to Hairy Lake, then crossed the body of water northeast, where you had to find a tributary so thin that only a canoe could enter. That was the last place to go, the last turn to make, before, hopefully, finding an old man's childhood home.

It was a comparatively languid trip that afternoon, which both Matthew and Holly welcomed. They were with the current, which meant paddling was easy; they steered the vessel more than urged it forward.

They arrived at Hairy Lake in the early evening, with the sun hovering above the trees as though balancing on them. The lake's name, Holly remarked, was on the nose. The body of water had countless reeds protruding from the surface, as many reeds as there were stars in the sky, and they did look like strands of hair.

"That's another reason your moshom told me that we'd have to take a canoe to the trapline," Matthew said. "The reeds would get caught up in a propeller every few feet, and it'd take forever to get across, if it didn't ruin a motor entirely."

Holly searched the lake for an area without any reeds, and couldn't see anything larger than the size of her bedroom. They crossed the lake slowly. Holly said that this was the one place where they would've made better time had they been on foot, and Matthew agreed, but the pace and the calm water allowed him to safely place his father's urn on the canoe's bow deck.

"He'll take us there," Matthew said.

"I know," Holly said.

The idea that an urn filled with ashes could guide them to their destination was as believable as a ghost putting AirPods into her hand while she slept. Holly couldn't imagine that Matthew believed what he'd said, but it was a comforting thought, and wasn't that what talk of the afterlife was for?

By dusk, they had navigated through the reeds and were at the northeast end of Hairy Lake, looking for the thin river—"A stream, pretty much," is how Matthew described it—that would bring them to their journey's end. Nothing close to that description presented itself, but they went back and forth at least ten times, as close to the land as they could, as though the landscape would magically change and a secret route would open to allow them passage.

There were two rivers, both large enough to allow for a motorboat, and so neither fit the directions given by Matthew's father. Eventually, they stopped paddling and sat motionless in the canoe between the two rivers, frustrated to have wound up here after coming so far. Matthew, looking particularly dispirited, had taken his father's urn and was now holding it in his hands.

"Well," Holly said after a long silence. Matthew was staring at the urn as though it were a photograph of his father. "We can't just give up now. There's no other rivers anywhere else on this side of the lake."

Matthew looked from the entrance of one river to the other with a pained expression.

"I haven't been very good at guessing directions, Hallelujah."

"Dad," she said, "there are literally two choices. Even if we go the wrong way, we can always come back and try the other one."

"It'll be too dark by then," he said.

"You're being negative," she said. "We'll start a fire somewhere and make a torch. It'll be cinematic."

Matthew tried to collect himself.

"This wasn't my father's dying wish, you know," he said. "He never told me to do this, to bring his remains to the trapline when he was gone. He wasn't supposed to be gone."

"I know that," she said.

"We were supposed to be together, Hall. He wanted to go

to his trapline for me, for fuck's sake. Not him. I feel like it's a way to make up for going on that walk with him, the day he . . ." He swallowed down tears. "I should've known he was too weak. I keep thinking, *What if we'd just had lunch?* I keep wondering if he'd be alive if it weren't for me."

"Moshom was a grown man, Dad, and he was old. He chose to go with you, he liked going with you, and you just went to the stop sign. You've got to let that shit go. I hate that he's gone, I want him back every fucking day, but if it was his time . . ."

"It was his time," Matthew said.

"Right," Holly said. "And it wasn't *your* time a couple of days ago. Now you're here, we have Moshom's ashes, he needs to go home, so what are we going to do?"

Matthew's eyes darted back and forth, left to right, right to left. He felt his pulse quicken. He felt as though he couldn't take in a full breath. His hands tightened around the urn. He looked down at it, the small container that housed some of his father's ashes.

"Sorry, that was a little aggressive," she said.

Matthew dragged his gaze from the urn and met eyes with Holly. She was fierce. She always had been. She always would be.

"That's what I love about you," he said.

Holly tried to play it off with an aw-shucks wave of the hand, but couldn't help but smile.

"Then choose a fucking river, Dad. Let's go."

Matthew raised the urn to eye level, took in every detail of it, the wood's pattern like expression lines on a face. He imagined his father's face. This wasn't how it was supposed to be, but they were here now. They were so close.

"Which way?" Matthew asked him.

He closed his eyes. He searched his body. His jackhammering heart. His quick, shallow breaths. He placed his hand on his stomach, breathed out through his mouth, and felt his hand fall. He breathed in deeply and felt his hand rise. His heart slowed. He opened his eyes, looked one way, then another. One way, he felt a pull, like a gentle current.

"It's that one," he said, pointing to the river farther north.

"Are you sure?" Holly said. "The one on the right's a bit thinner. It's not as wide. You said a motorboat wouldn't fit where we needed to go. You said we needed to take a canoe."

"It will be, it will get narrow," he said. "There's a lake there, at the end. That's where your moshom grew up. That was his home."

"Then let's take him there," she said.

"You trust me?"

"Yeah, I do."

They entered the river from its source, at the northeast end of Hairy Lake. They hadn't gone more than 270 yards before the river narrowed enough to be considered a stream, too thin for a motorboat. Matthew glanced back hopefully at Holly, and she returned a similar expression. The river was hardly big enough to allow a canoe to pass through it. The sides of the vessel were close enough to the shore that Matthew and Holly could have used their hands to pull themselves along. The sky was midnight blue, darkening by the moment, and they were flanked by the forest and its rocky shores, both of which seemed to close in on them the farther they went. The stream became so fine that Matthew began to worry whether the canoe could take them the rest of the way. Then it opened into a lake about seventy yards wide and two hundred yards long. Almost immediately,

Holly pointed to the south side of the lake, to what looked like a structure at the back of an open area surrounded by trees and brush. They exited at the clearing, stepped onto the land, and were both struck with a sense of familiarity, as if they had been there before.

They explored the area before night fell, walking the length of the perimeter before entering the remains of the cabin. It was a one-room structure, so brittle and old from years of neglect that it looked as though it would crumble to dust if you blew on it. Two walls had already fallen at some point, and the two remaining walls were leaning perilously toward the ground. For such a small dwelling, it seemed like a lot had been stuffed inside of it, not the least of which was an entire family. There was one bed that couldn't have fit more than two people, which meant, to Matthew, that most of the family had slept on the floor, huddled around a wood stove that was intact, charred wood still inside the firebox. There was a cabinet and some shelving and a round table with four chairs. A stool beside the bed had one framed photograph behind dusty, cracked glass. Matthew picked it up and wiped the dust away, revealing a middle-aged man crouching behind a child no older than two.

"Check this out," he said to Holly, who was busy looking through cutlery and dishes that had been left behind.

Holly took the frame from her father and inspected the picture. In the gathering dark, she could hardly make it out, but saw enough of the toddler to recognize the eyes.

"Is this . . ."

"I think that's your moshom," Matthew said.

"Can I keep it?" she said.

"I don't see why not," he said.

Holly took the picture out of the frame and placed it carefully in her pocket, planning to put it in her backpack before they turned in for the night.

"Are we sleeping in here?" she said, sitting on the bed to test out its sturdiness. To her surprise, it didn't break under her weight.

"Better here than out there," Matthew said. "Maybe we can prop the other walls up somehow."

"Good idea," she said.

There was some firewood outside, against one of the cabin walls. They used it to make a fire in the middle of the clearing, where a firepit had been dug. The wood was dry and old, and it wasn't long before it erupted into flames, casting light over the area and pushing away the black. They sat on the grass by the fire and ate supper—leftover fish that they had cooked for lunch. During a prolonged, albeit comfortable, silence, Holly cleared her throat.

"You're writing letters for me, aren't you?" she said. "I mean, I know you're writing letters for me."

Matthew just nodded. "I am."

He took them out of his pocket and out of the bag, as if he was going to read them.

"Why?" she said.

Matthew shrugged. "Your moshom told me a lot of things when he was with us, and I've been able to keep most of it with me, even though he never wrote it down. Those were *his* letters, what he told me. I wanted you to have something like that."

"It's not . . ." She found it hard to say the words, so she just pulled up her sleeve to show him her wrist.

He knew what she meant. He put his hand around his own wrist.

"No, they're not that. I mean, I don't think I could do that." He looked her in the eye before looking away. "To you."

"Then why'd you do it?" she said.

Matthew looked down at his hand. He looked at the tiny hairs. He brushed his fingertips against them.

"I was fucked up," he said. "I was just fucked up."

"We're all fucked up," she said.

"I guess we are."

"But you're not anymore?"

"No, I'm not anymore," he said. "Not right now."

"So, when do I get to read them?" she said.

He handed them to her. "Whenever you want."

She accepted them, but just as she was about to slip them into her jeans, into the same pocket that she'd put the photograph, she stopped. He was here with her. She'd almost lost him, but she hadn't. She could talk to him. They could talk. There were stories to tell. There were stories for her to keep with her, and she would remember them. She held the letters over the fire. She held them firmly. The tips of her fingernails turned white. Then she let them go, and they fluttered away like autumn leaves, into the fire, erupting into flames before disappearing.

Matthew smiled and then picked up the urn.

"I think it's time to say goodbye," he said.

They went to the water's edge and took the lid off the urn. The water was calm, as if it were a sheet of black ice. It reflected the sky overhead, every single star, every single constellation, the rising moon.

"Do you want to say something?" he said.

"Just that I'm glad he's home," she said. "Kisakīhitin, Moshom."

"We made it," Matthew said to his father. "We're here, and I hope that it remembers you, as much as we will."

Matthew tipped the urn over, and his father's ashes spilled out of it, landing on the water, then sinking below the surface. When the last of it was gone, a sharp caw echoed through the clearing, and Matthew and Holly looked up in the direction of the sound, to see a crow sitting on a branch. It was soon joined by another, and another still. They flew through the clearing, like shards of night fallen to earth, then landed on trees. They kept coming until every branch on every tree that surrounded the area was occupied by a crow. Matthew walked to the centre of the clearing, and Holly followed him there.

"What's happening?" she said.

"Your moshom," he said. "He told me about this. He told me that you remembered the land even if you'd never been there before. I remembered it, when we got here, Holly."

"I did, too," she said.

"He told me that the land remembered you, just like you remembered it," he said. "And he used to tell me about the crows. He told me all about the crows. They would remember you, too, because they were the land. Everything was the land. If the land remembered you, then so did they."

All at once, the crows took off from the trees and began to fly in circles overhead. There were so many that they blotted out the sky. They flew like a tornado, and cawed, and it sounded like a song. There was a rhythm to their voices, to their flight, as they turned around and around, getting closer and closer to the land. They sang and danced, and the lower they got, the more their flapping wings sounded like the beat of a drum.

Soon, Matthew was engulfed by the flock. All he could see

was black, a void, and his heart started to pound, and his breath became short, and his feet lifted off the ground, but when he felt Holly take his hand, when he felt her hold it firmly, he wasn't afraid anymore.

You squeezed my hand.

You squeezed my hand.

I don't remember much after that. You squeezed my hand for maybe a second. The average lifespan is 700,000 hours—700,000, Hallelujah. We fit so much into those 700,000 hours, but that second, that's as clear as anything else in my life. There are 2.5 billion seconds in 700,000 hours. How can one second out of 2.5 billion be so clear? A moment in time. Razor thin.

It makes you think.

It really makes you think.

ACKNOWLEDGEMENTS

More than any other work, the act of writing this book was performed in a vacuum. Besides being with my characters, it was a solitary experience, which is appropriate. Of course, to say that I created this novel alone would be a lie. I owe a debt of gratitude to the writers who have influenced me and helped me develop a voice. O'Neill, Toews, Dey, Robinson, King, Coupland, my dear friends Niigaan and Vermette and Dimaline, and many others. *Crows* is also a love letter to the music that has been as much an inspiration to me. Vernon, Vedder, Berninger, Stevens, Finn, and Samson. Profound thanks to my friend John K. Samson for graciously allowing me to quote from "Requests," a song that helped me make it through the grief of losing my father. Deep gratitude to Lisa and Melissa for their advice on depicting CPR procedure and the injuries Matthew could've sustained from that little waterfall mishap.

There is, as always, Jill, who makes everything possible. I couldn't do any of this without her. There is, as well, Dad, forever my best friend, and my mother, who told me that I could be a writer way back when I was eight and had this crazy dream to tell stories for a living. My kids always motivate me, but in this case, Emily was walking with me every step of this novel. She's a powerhouse of a human being. A true miracle. My Hallelujah.

Thanks also to Jackie Kaiser, my agent at Westwood Creative. Writing a story, in any form, is a journey, and for that, you need a guide. I know that this is an inside joke, and nobody will get it but us, but Jennifer Lambert, you are the shit.

Ekosani,
Dave